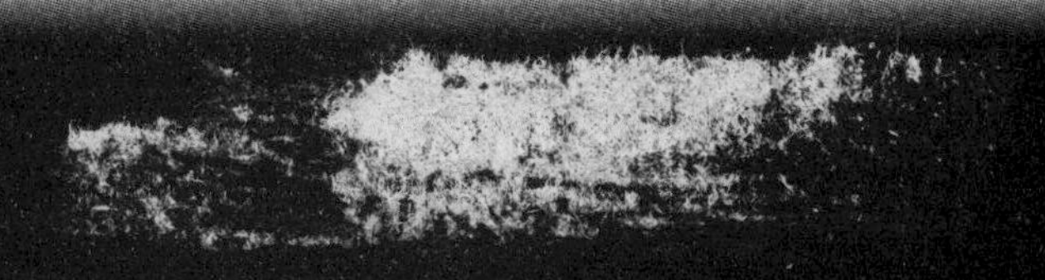

Praise for Christopher Fowler

'Fowler writes devilishly clever and mordantly funny novels that are sometimes heartbreakingly moving.'
Val McDermid, *The Times*

'Christopher Fowler is an award-winning novelist who would make a good serial killer.'
Time Out

'An imaginative fun house of a world where sage minds go to expand their vistas and sharpen their wits.'
New York Times Book Review
on the *Bryant & May* books

'Fowler repeatedly challenges the reader to redraw the boundaries between innocence and malevolence, rationality and paranoia...
He has the uncanny ability to invoke terror in broad daylight.'
The Guardian* on *Demonised

'His sentences zip along, wonderfully funny or moving – sometimes both.'
The Independent* on *Paperboy

'The climax is truly spectacular... this would make a great piece of cinema. It has everything that you could ever want from a thriller.'
The Eloquent Page* on *Roofworld

Also by Christopher Fowler

Roofworld
Rune
Red Bride
Darkest Day
Spanky
Psychoville
Disturbia
Menz Insana
Soho Black
Calabash
Breathe
Paperboy (Autobiography)
Film Freak (Autobiography)
Hell Train
Plastic

BRYANT & MAY
Full Dark House
The Water Room
Seventy Seven Clocks
Ten Second Staircase
White Corridor
The Victoria Vanishes
Bryant & May On the Loose
Bryant & May Off the Rails
The Memory of Blood

COLLECTIONS
The Bureau of Lost Souls
City Jitters
More City Jitters
Flesh Wounds
Sharper Knives
Personal Demons
Uncut
The Devil in Me
Demonised
Old Devil Moon
Red Gloves

First published 2014 by Solaris
an imprint of Rebellion Publishing Ltd,
Riverside House, Osney Mead,
Oxford, OX2 0ES, UK

www.solarisbooks.com

ISBN: 978 1 78108 210 2

A CIP catalogue record for this book is availabl
from the British Library.

Designed & typeset by Rebellion Publishing

Printed in the UK

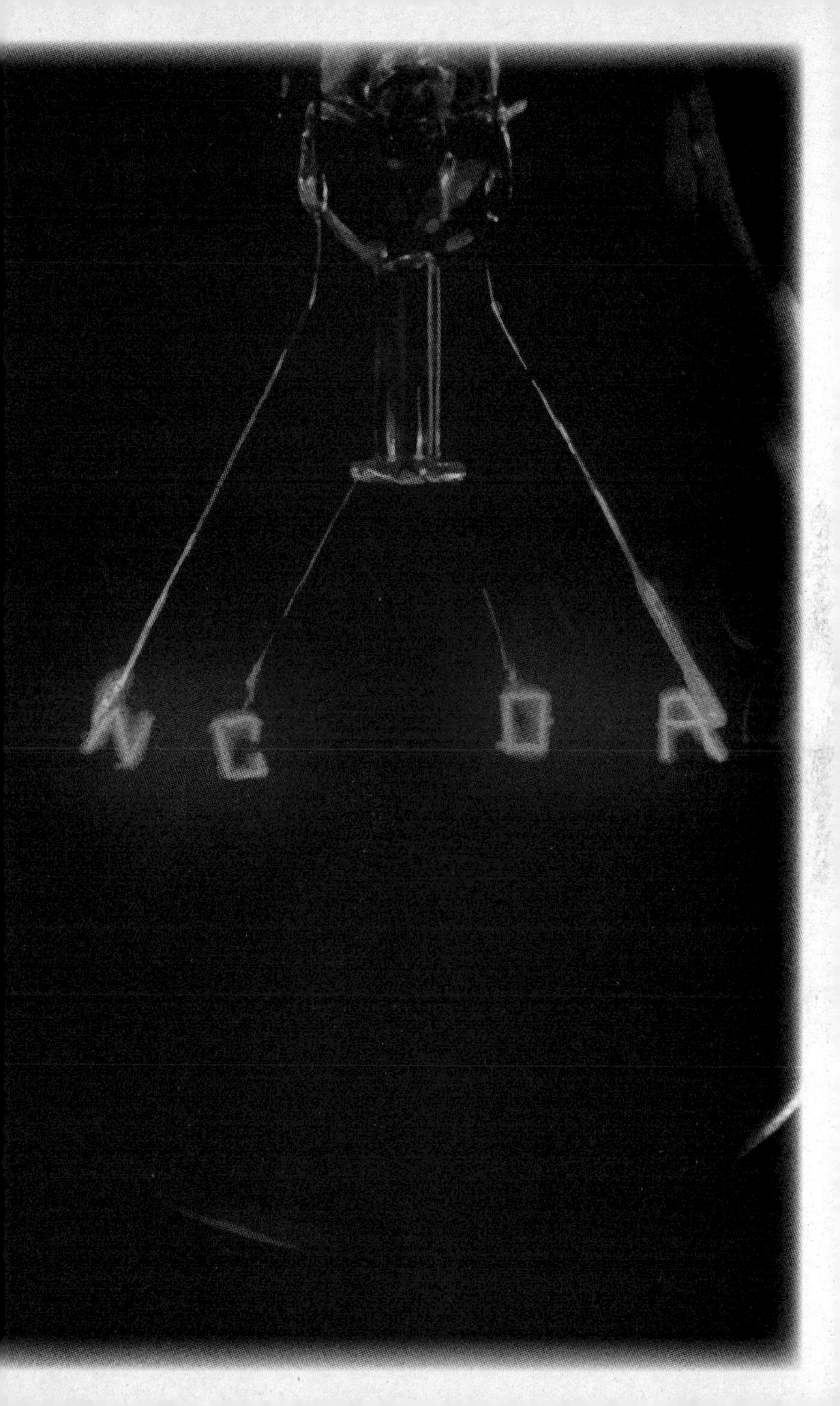

NYCTOPHOBIA

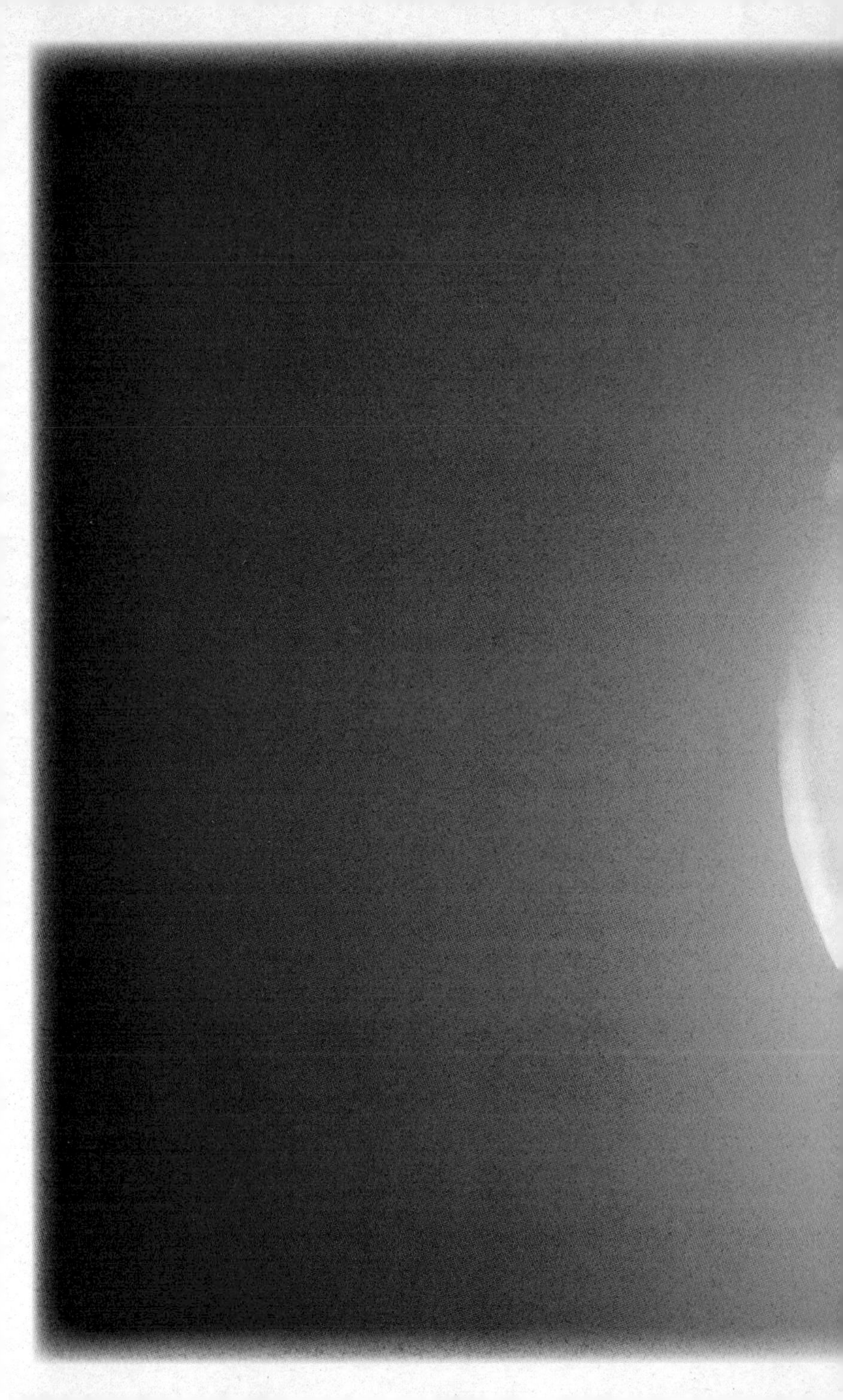

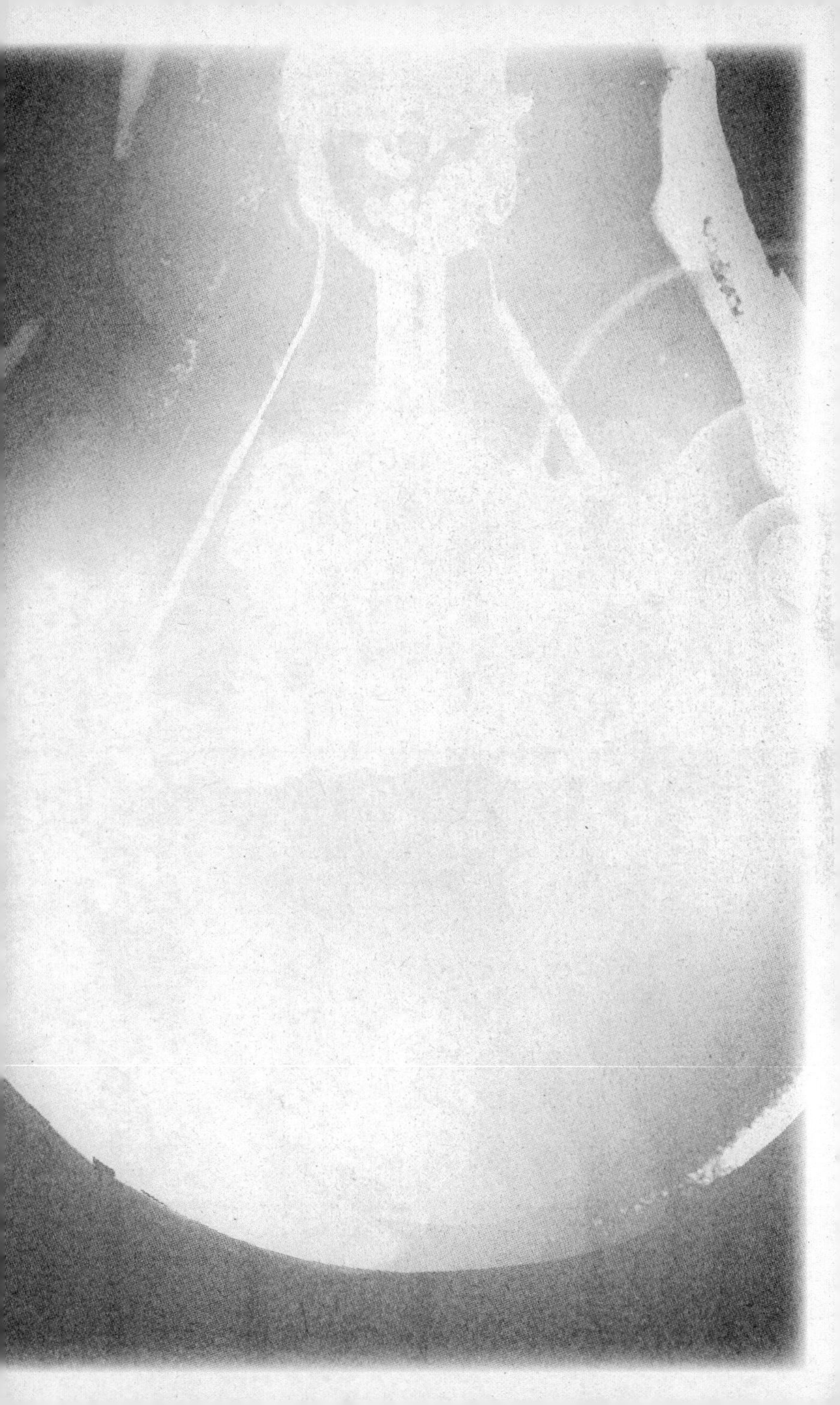

Some doors should
never be opened.

CHAPTER ONE

The Agent

THE TAXI DRIVER spoke no English, but was kind enough to be unhappy about dropping me off in the middle of nowhere. He had the most sunburned face I'd ever seen, walnut-coloured, with a cheap white sailor's cap perched on top, more like a Greek sailor than a Spaniard.

I looked out and saw the road, rocks shimmering in the heat haze, a dense dry row of gnarled olive trees. It looked like we'd driven into the middle of a spaghetti western. I half-expected to see buzzards circling the cliffs.

He turned around in his seat and raised his eyebrows again. *Are you sure this is the right place?*

I nodded. We used universally acknowledged hand signals:

(Point down) *Should I wait for you?*

(Shake of head) *No, it's okay.*

(Hand across brow, waving fingers) *It's very hot.*

(Indicate watch) *She'll be here soon.*

(Point at tree) *There's shade over there.*

I paid him and he reluctantly drove off, leaving me alone with the lizards. I sat on some dry brown grass beneath the nearest tree, pinging crickets everywhere, and waited. In my bag I had the name of Julia's agency and the card from the cab company in case she didn't show. Nothing else, not even a bottle of water. I'm from central London, we don't 'do' outdoors.

Ten minutes later, just as I was starting to get worried, an old white Mercedes SLK materialised from the burning haze. I could see a woman behind the wheel. She crunched to a stop in front of me, opened the door and climbed out, carefully uncreasing herself. Julia was wearing a pink suit jacket with huge padded shoulders and a matching skirt too short at the knee, with pink patent leather high heels and large square sunglasses. She looked like a burly flamingo.

I clambered dustily to my feet and shook her hand.

'Senora Shaw,' she cried with an alarming roll of the R, 'is a pleasure to meet ju. *Ay*.' She stopped before me and gave me the full head-to-foot stare over the top of her glasses. '*Tan bonita*.'

She rotated her left hand in a circle, rattling a gaudy charm bracelet, and pursed coral lips. She had matching coral nails and a foot of spray-stiffened hair like copper wire. Presumably she wore pink underwear. 'Ju are so young. This house, where is it –' She removed her sunglasses and gestured carelessly at the end of the tree-line. 'Ju cannot see it from the road, no? I bet ju think we are crazy or something! This house – is too big for you I think. Too nowhere. Unless there are many babies, eh?' She gave a coarse laugh. 'Get in, we go closer.'

We drove off, bumping along the unmade road, raising clouds of hot dust.

'My husband,' I began. 'He's the one who wants to live here. He likes this area. He spends most of his time in Madrid but he was born in Andalusia.'

'You marry a nice Spanish man, yes? *Muy bien*.'

'His family was from one of the towns nearby.'

'Ah,' Julia said knowingly. 'If he buys this house he must have *mucho* –' She rubbed her thumb and forefinger together and flashed a wide smile. She had huge whitened teeth. 'My husband, *ach*, he's good for nothing, a lazy fat pig. We live in a tiny flat because he spends all the money I make in the bars with his fat pig friends. One day I will kill him. Ju, ju are lucky.'

She looked around theatrically. 'Why is he not here with you, this *guapo*?'

'He's seeing another property while I'm looking at this one,' I explained. I could see some wrought-iron gates appearing between a line of fierce green conifers. 'It looks locked up. Can we get in?'

'*Si, seguro*, I have the keys here.' Julia parked and produced an immense set of keys. We got out of the car and she proceeded to attack the gate with them. 'There is a gardener, very old, and a housekeeper who has been here forever, but she is *muy loca* –' she pulled a sour-lemon face. 'I don't like her. Ju can fire them both if ju don't like. They're not here today. Is okay, we're in.'

Suddenly it was as if I'd left the set of *The Good, The Bad and the Ugly* and entered an English country garden. The change was almost unbelievable. The outer ring of cypruses and cork oaks gave way to angled barriers of what appeared to be rowans and ash trees, with wild roses in every possible colour. There were clumps of honeysuckle, campion and lavender and a dozen flowering scented plants I couldn't name. It seemed so odd to find them surviving here in the flat raw heat of Andalusia, hidden behind the walls of an estate like a private part of Kew Gardens.

'You don't need grass here, you can build a pool, a barbecue pit, whatever,' said Julia, stalking between the flowerbeds in her high heels, avoiding the immense emerald lawn, a perfect razor-cropped rectangle. 'And you can get rid of that. Maybe the old man was queer, I don't know.' There was a pockmarked statue at the centre, the figure of a naked young man holding what looked like a large plate above his head. Hooped in bronze, the disc was divided in marble halves, one black, one white.

The grass had coarser blades than the stuff you'd find in an English garden, but looked incredibly healthy. In the flowerbeds, bees and dragonflies dropped in lazy loops between clusters of petals. Beyond them, I saw Hyperion House for the first time.

It stood at the end of the driveway, backed by the great amber curtain of the mountain. It had been cut right into the cliff, so that the rock appeared to cradle it. The building was three floors high, with a cream-bricked frontage and tall, wide windows framed by green wooden shutters. At the centre was an immense double-fronted door, burnished brown wood studded with copper bolts like a castle keep. The steep red roof ended in stone statues and garlanded urns. There was something oddly shaped on the top floor, but I couldn't figure out what it was.

'Oh,' I said, taken aback. I'd seen six small photographs online which hadn't done the place justice. They really hadn't prepared me for this.

Julia's eyes flared. 'Si, *muy grande* – but wait, ju have to see inside.' Another rattle of the keys produced one that opened the main door. She creaked it back, and I realised that the walls were about two feet thick. I followed her inside, waiting for the heat to fall away and be replaced by chill air, expecting it to be like entering a Spanish church, but although the temperature was definitely lower it stayed pleasant, not cold at all. I saw the reason why; the house let in a phenomenal amount of light.

'The real name is *Hyperion House*,' said Julia, flexing her shiny pink mouth to fit each syllable as if teaching me the name, and spitting over me in the process. 'But we call it *La Casa De La Luz*. The House of Light. Ju can see why, yes?'

'Yes, I can. I've never seen so much sunlight inside a property.' We were standing in a wide blue and white Castilian-tiled hallway, with a severe stone staircase before us. Huge rooms went off to the right and left. I glimpsed a lot of very serious-looking furniture. 'They leave the curtains open?' I asked. 'Doesn't everything fade?'

'*Que*?' She pulled an uncomprehending face.

'The carpets – don't they lose their colour?'

'Ah – no, they are very old. Ju should throw those out, get some good colours in. Pink is nice. So.' She clattered across the hall. 'Big staircase, a place to meet your guests, yes? *Hello, come in, have a drink,* blah blah blah.'

Turning sharply on her heel she waved a hand at the first doorway on the right. I could just make out the corner of a blood-marble fireplace, several ugly clocks, a lot of heavy armchairs. 'Front room then *drawing* room, English word for it, yes? Then the next one after that is the music room I don't know what that is but it has a piano. All original fittings, double height, double windows, double this that blah blah. Reading room on the left. I don't know what that is for, but lots of smelly old books and again double everything. You could take out all those stupid shelves and get a big TV. You said you're an architect –'

'I trained as one, yes –'

'Then is perfect, you can rip all this old stuff out.'

'All these rooms seem to face the sun.'

'Yes, they get the sun from the dawn to the very *very* last second of the sunset. Too much sun if you ask me. I like a dark room. I don't want to see my husband sitting there all day. Is depressing. Then kitchen behind here and so on, and so on. I show ju.'

I'd never seen so many overstuffed armchairs, dressers, sideboards, striped sofas and oak tables in my life. 'I guess these rooms will look even bigger once the owner has taken all his furniture out,' I said.

'Oh no, he is not taking anything, he was in the hospital,' Julia explained.

'But surely, when he comes out –'

'He is not coming back.'

'Oh, I'm sorry to hear that. Was he elderly?'

'Very old, *si*. The furniture will stay here with the house. It comes included in the price. You can throw it out, make yourself some money.'

'Even all the statues and paintings? Surely he could sell them?'

'He doesn't want to. They were made for the house, why would he take them?' She grimaced. 'Is not my taste, is too depressing, yes?'

She walked me through the house room by room, up the staircase and through the dazzling vast bedrooms until we reached what appeared to be the back. But I knew it couldn't be. I ran the calculation and came up short. In my job you get a feel for the negative space a building creates, and we hadn't gone deep enough inside to reach the far wall.

The end of the central hallway was closed off by a narrower door, elegantly carved with entwined lilies and reeds in the art nouveau style. Julia slid the keys around, holding each to the light in turn. 'Is strange,' she said finally. 'They gave me all the keys but I can't find one for this. Wait, come with me. We go back downstairs.'

She clomped down the staircase diagonally, in the way that women with too-high heels do, heading down to the kitchen. This vast flagstone room was also dazzlingly bright, with gleaming copper pans hung from ceiling racks. It was lit by great side windows that overlooked the hills. Set in the back wall was a similar carved wooden door to the one upstairs, but so small that you'd have to bow your head to enter, and also locked.

'No keys for this either,' Julia complained. 'I don't understand.'

'What's behind there?' I asked.

'This is what I wanted ju to see,' she said. 'There are four doors to the back of the house, two *liddle liddle* ones on the left and right of the ground floor, one here and one in the other drawing room. Then the full-size door in the middle of the first floor hall you just saw, and also a connecting door in the master bedroom. The back is interesting. For the servants, ju see. At least, I guess. Wait. We check the other door.' She led the way around to the door situated behind the drawing room, and tried the handle. 'No key for this one but I think is open.'

She put her formidable pink shoulder against the door and gave it a good shove, but nothing happened. She stuck her fists into her hips and stared angrily at the paintwork. 'What is this? Why does this not open? Is like they have put furniture behind here.'

She bent down and peered through the keyhole. 'Is no good, is dark, is always dark back there. Wait, I have a light.'

I thought she'd have an app on her mobile, but instead she dragged a colossal metal torch from her pink handbag and shone its lighthouse beam under the door.

'Ah, I see now. Someone has moved the dresser. Why would they do that?' She pointed to the floor. I could see that something heavy had been dragged from its original place, through to the other side of the connecting door. The legs had created jagged rips in the dark polish of the boards.

'We can't get into the back of the house?' I asked.

'Is no big deal, nothing special back there,' Julia said airily. 'I'll get this open for ju. I'll have Jerardo move it when he gets a chance. He's the gardener. He is old but strong. Not so fresh,' she waved a hand over her formidable nose. 'So ju should stay maybe six feet away from him. He has been here for a long time, I think. This house is built over a hundred years, like 1910 or something like that, but the architect he was – what is it – when you are kind to everyone, even the stinky poor people?'

'Humanitarian?'

'Yes, something like that I think, or maybe cheap. So he build the servants' quarters like a copy of the main house, only much smaller, less than a quarter as big I think, just two floors and no light at all because the back of the house is right against the mountain, yes? Besides, they are servants, they work hard and go to sleep, they don't need light. To be honest ju can't do much with it, maybe store stuff I think. Is cold back there because of no light. I've been back there once and is lots of furniture the same, only not so nice I think, and no electrics. But anyway I have no keys to show ju.' She stared angrily at the door. 'I don't understand because there is no-one here strong enough to move that dresser, so how they do that?'

'It's okay,' I told her, 'I already know how I feel about the house.'

Julia pulled her grimace again. 'You don't like it? Is not a lot of work if you keep the gardener and the housekeeper. I don't mean to call her *loca*, she is just don't touch this don't touch that like it was hers. And a face like you want to hit with an axe. So what you think?'

'No, I love it. I'd like to show it to my husband. But I think the price is going to be far too high.'

'Yes, yes, the price, but it is not high ju see because the house has foreclosed to the bank, they need to get it off their books so they will definitely take a lower price, ju wait and see. Spain is in a mess, the *politicos* are all crooks and deserve to die.'

'So the last owner –'

'He got old and went bankrupt and then he got sick and went crazy, and then he went to a home. A very nice home, they say, in Marbella, and he was well cared for. He was *muy anciano*, very old. He had a long and happy life here but his brain dried out and there is no-one else to take over the house so it went to the pigs at the bank. And ju can get it from them. Yes?'

'Yes,' I agreed. 'Perhaps we could. I've never seen a house like this before. Certainly not in the architectural digests.'

'What is *digests*?'

'In books. The house, it's not well-known?'

'Ju don't see this before because the owner was private.'

'So he didn't want sightseers.'

'No, I mean *private*,' said Julia. 'You know what that means?' She waved her hand around her head. 'Crazy.'

CHAPTER TWO

The Arrival

UNFORTUNATELY, WHEN I got back to the hotel in Marbella I found that Mateo had already put in an offer on another house a few miles away, in a coastal town called Sabinillas. We had been viewing properties separately to save time, because he was supposed to be returning to his head office in Madrid on Monday and it was now Thursday. He told me had seen some extraordinary houses with elaborate tiles and painted ceilings. They had come onto the market because many of Spain's grand old families were running out of money and needed to sell up.

Mateo was a wine wholesaler. He imported sherry to London and New York. Most Thursday mornings he travelled from Madrid or Jerez to the UK and sometimes to the East Coast of the USA, returning the following Tuesday afternoon. I assumed he made good money, but he had the air of a man with inherited wealth. We never discussed money. He was old school about things like that. The kind of man who still seats a woman at a table before settling himself. I used to think that kind of behaviour was cheesy, but Mateo made it seem respectful.

After Julia dropped me off, I found him in the bar of the Hermosa and told him all about Hyperion House, explaining that the bank wanted to make a quick sale. He warned me that it was already too late, and my heart sank.

'What can we do?' I asked.

'You really liked the look of this place?'

'It's the one, Mateo. It's perfect. And the agent says we can get it cheap because they're desperate to get it off their books.'

'There's no such thing as a cheap house, even in the recession. Sabinillas has terraces and a sea view – I thought that was what you wanted.'

'I thought so too, before I saw this.'

Later we sat on the bed going through the papers. He studied the prospectus on his laptop and considered the problem. 'Maybe we could break the contract. It could end up costing money. Basically, it would be a bribe.'

Looking back, I must have been incredibly naïve. I said, 'What do you mean?'

'What usually happens is that the accountant makes a discreet exit from the room while business is concluded, and then cash changes hands. Welcome to Spain's famous grey market.'

'Let's go back and see it together,' I suggested. 'I'll get the keys from the agent. I know you'll love it.'

So, the very next day, that was what we did.

As we approached from the potholed road leading off the A-377, I remember being struck by the same sensation as before. At first glance the house didn't seem to be there at all. It was because of the cliff. It looked as if the rock-face had swallowed it.

Mateo opened the BMW's window and tried to catch glimpses of it between flashing firs and cork oaks. When he did, he saw what I saw – green wooden window frames set in pale stone, every pane of glass appearing to catch the sunlight perfectly, reflecting tall panels of gold. The frontage was like a stage flat, revealing no depth at all. Before either of us could understand what we had seen, it had gone again.

The radio station was playing Daft Punk's 'Get Lucky', and the song seemed disrespectfully loud in the stark, silent countryside, so I turned it off. I followed Mateo's gaze and looked once more. There was another break in the tree-line, again revealing the high stone walls inset with glittering windows, but it didn't seem possible that they could be the same walls, because the drive had curved around now and we were heading upwards, directly toward the house.

It didn't look quite so isolated from the rest of the world this time around. After leaving the motorway we had coasted along a dozen miles of undulating, deserted road, not the graceful lanes of Southern England that provided endless views, the stuff of childhood holidays, but bare blacktop causeways laid down across the land to link villages by the only routes that could cut through stubborn rock. You didn't alter the land here; you worked around it.

We hardly saw another vehicle, and this was the end of the peak tourist season. I wondered what it would be like in winter. Earlier we had stopped in a village so deserted that the only indication of life was the clatter of cutlery being used inside houses. Hyperion House didn't even have the benefit of being attached to a hamlet. The only houses within sight were derelict barns that looked as if they had been abandoned fifty years ago.

It wasn't surprising. The countryside had been slowly decanting itself into the cities as each new generation turned down rural life in favour of finding urban work. Who wanted to be a farmer and get paid peanuts by supermarkets when you could find a job in a city company, and hang out in the cool barrios of Madrid or Malaga?

I had done something similar in London, and had burned my fingers badly enough to know that I would never go back. It was a new start, and this time it would work because I had done something I'd insisted I would never do; the evidence was banded in gold on my left hand.

There was something indefinably theatrical about the building. I thought of the Adelphi, which had once been a separate district of London. Its main terrace was a block of twenty four houses, but it was fronted with a vast fake neoclassical façade. Hyperion House had something similar. It was as if the view had been folded back on itself in incorrect proportion, the better to be enjoyed by an audience.

I remember this distinctly; it was 11:00am. The sun was punching its heat down through a sea-blue sky, and the house was aglow with colour and light. But it still looked incorrect, an Alice in Wonderland dwelling that might suddenly play tricks on you, closing its doors, changing its walls and twisting its corridors until you'd never be able to find your way out. I thought nothing more of it at the time.

'Strange, isn't it?' said Mateo, glancing over and reading my mind. He drove with his left arm leaning on the door, so casual that he might have been at the tiller of a boat. *Why can I never appear as relaxed as that?* I wondered, but of course I already knew the answer. 'It looks like the windows are angled out slightly.'

'They have to be to make the whole thing work,' I said absently. 'The front appears bowed so that it catches the sun at every point, but it's not. The windows are offset at slight angles.'

'You noticed that?'

'Of course. It's what I was trained to do.'

'Sorry, I forgot.'

'Do you know how hard it must have been to build this kind of house here?' I said. 'It would have started with a spring, the discovery of water coming down from those mountains. A well would have been dug. The land would then have been cleared by hand, and the trees cut down with axes in early spring, in a way that would make them fall onto each other. After that they would have been left to dry out over the summer, so that the stumps could be burned and uprooted, and all the rocks would have been removed with chains and horses. The cliff could only be cut with pick-axes. Labourers would have been found in the nearest village, transported and probably housed here during the construction, an incredible undertaking.'

'I didn't think of all that.'

'And the result is a real box of tricks. Julia said the architect was crazy, but I got the feeling she thinks everyone is crazy, including the banks, the housekeeper and her husband.' I studied the vista, excited by it. 'The trees are planted with exactly measured spaces so that you catch perfect glimpses of it from the driveway, like a giant zoetrope.'

'You think it was planned that way?'

'I'm betting every last detail was planned. You'll be able to see more easily once we get inside.'

The road swung around to the left again. It felt as if we were closing on the house in a great spiral. But then the amber rocks parted and there it was in all its glory, framed in wild green planting. Hyperion House was too large for a family of three and was absurdly remote. *But look at it,* I thought, *so beautiful that it really does seem to be glowing, actually glowing in the late morning sunlight.*

'Check out the lawn,' said Mateo. 'It's like something you'd find in the Thames Valley.'

'The gardener's been with the house forever. Apparently you have to stand upwind of him. We don't have to keep the housekeeper on.'

'How are you with domestics?'

I laughed. 'I don't know. I've never had one. Would I be expected to lay down the law?'

'For all the good it will do you. If they've been with the house that long, they'll merely see us as tenants passing through. You just have to be gracious, and if you want to lay down the law switch to using their formal names, that usually works. Don't worry, I'm sure you'll charm them, and I'll back you up. You'll soon learn to be the lady of the house.'

'My god, what a bizarre idea.'

'Are you really sure this is what you want?' Mateo asked.

'I won't know until I've tried,' I admitted.

'It would be strange for you at first. I mean, it's pretty isolated. That's what's keeping the price low – well, that and the fact that it's an albatross for the bank.'

'I've checked out the distances. Ronda's not that far, and there are other towns. Estepona's on the coast, Marbella's not hard to reach and has great shops, and of course I can head over to London on EasyJet if you don't mind funding me,' I said.

'No, of course not.'

'And I'm sure I'll find myself a project, and Bobbie will be with me for a while at least.'

'I guess you'll make friends in the village. Gaucia is only –' he checked the mileage, '– seven kilometres away.'

'I know there are bound to be a few problems. I'm an inner city gal – I don't drive. For me, going to South London is always a culture shock. It's going to do my head in for a while but I'll find ways to cope. I promise I won't go mad and do a Mrs Danvers.'

'Good. One crazy woman in my life is my limit.'

'Are you referring to my mother or your ex-wife?'

'Okay, make that two. Anyway, you could easily learn to drive while you're here.'

'I have to learn to speak Spanish first. I can say *por favour* and *gracias*.'

'It's a start.'

We parked and crossed the drive. Elegantly framed by the cliff behind and entirely of a piece with itself, the house looked as if no-one had ever considered adding an extension or a porch for fear of spoiling the overall effect. It was a perfect example of urban rococo that might have been lifted from Barcelona's Gracia barrio and carefully reset here in the harsh countryside. It seemed to have been born in perpetual light, its façade aglow and warm to the touch. Only the sides were lost in the black shadows of the olive trees and the wall of rock that nursed its back. All around us I could hear birdsong and the buzz of bees, so many of them that I could actually see them swarming in the distance.

Around the edges of the sloping red-tiled roof, interspersed with the urns, were languorous caryatids and squat but friendly-looking gryphons with beaming infant-faces. Beneath these guardians ran a terracotta frieze of classical figures, a parade of healthy young men and women dancing through bounties of fruit and flowers. Okay, the paintings were a little tacky but they added to the overall charm of the place.

I sensed Mateo was immediately drawn to the house and found myself praying that he would love it, but the decision was hardly mine to make. I had no money of my own. I mean, we were married but we hadn't yet set up any joint accounts. I didn't want to rush him on that score – it would have seemed pushy and ungrateful. And I *was* grateful, for everything he'd done so far.

We reached the main gate and I dug out the keys, wondering if Julia had managed to get the doors to the servants' quarters open at last.

'Please do me one favour, and wait until you've been around the whole place before you say you hate it,' I pleaded.

'*You* like it,' he said simply. 'That's all that matters to me.'

I was always amazed that he could be so smooth without sounding glib and insincere, even when he was wearing his big gold cufflinks. 'It's better that you see it first,' I said.

Above, the gryphons looked down on us with benevolent smiles.

CHAPTER THREE

The Party

I HADN'T INTENDED to get married; I had just wanted to upset my mother.

What happened was this; we were at a party in Pimlico, not my usual neck of the woods, but Anne, my mother, was there on business. I remember watching three tanned and tightened wives in mini-dresses dancing very carefully to Katy Perry's 'Telephone', ageing hipsters living it up while the kids were at boarding school. Anne would have called them her friends, but they were nothing of the kind. One of them waggled a crimson-tipped claw at me to come and join them, but I declined the invitation. As if. I didn't belong there. They knew it and I knew it, but I was just about the youngest person in the room, and age opens doors.

The crimson claw was in her late forties and had a Swarovski crystal-covered Hello Kitty handbag hooked over her arm. She moved like she'd just had a hip replacement.

This is what happens to rich women from the home counties, I thought. *Their husbands go away on business from Monday to Friday and they regress into the needy teenagers they raised. If I ever move out of the city to do that, shoot me.*

I headed off to sneak a vodka, something I was expressly forbidden from doing by my mother. I'm not a child, it's just that I'd been down that road before and it had led to a few problems, and Anne didn't want me embarrassing her in front of her clients.

The kitchen was typical of a weekend apartment – tiny, white and steel and barely used – in contrast to the vast, stripped brick and oak beam parody of a castle refectory that our hostess, Sandy Fellowes, had back in Somerset. The men had been driven away here, some leaning out of the rear balcony to smoke, not quite pushed into the rain by their need for nicotine, but certainly hiding from their wives.

The party was for Sandy, who was turning fifty with a vengeance. At that moment she was locked in the bathroom doing coke with her personal trainer, which struck me as a contradiction in terms. Sandy had gone to secretarial college with my mother when such places were still popular, then failed upwards in publishing for a while, but the idea of a career had never really been in her plans. She soon married a man who handled wetland development in Brussels, which meant he was away for five weeks out of six, and Sandy now considered herself widowed in all but her bank accounts. Her screechy girlfriends were clustered in nearby Somerset villages and lived separate lives from their men, concentrating on the four S's: shopping, spas, salads and sex, none of which they could be bothered with at home. Occasionally they came up to London and stayed in clubs like Home House and The Arts, or in the last of the affordable Chelsea flats.

I was there because my mother needed accompaniment, being clinically unable to attend a party alone, and because she needed to work the room. Anne's reasoning was, as ever, barbed, 'It's not like you have anything better to do this weekend, is it, darling?' She ran an online auction site selling discount designer handbags, so it was business more than pleasure, even though the sideline allowed her friends to treat her with condescension, as the English do with all shopkeepers. She fawned around them, and laughed and joked like she was one of them, but everyone knew we lived across the river in Vauxhall, and not the nice regenerated part either.

I helped myself to ice from the gargantuan fridge that had no food in it – these were women who didn't eat, unless you counted Martini olives, nuts and romaine lettuce. I hoped the ice would disguise what was obviously a tumbler full of vodka, and when I closed the door there he was, just standing there, leaning against the wall, regarding me with an amused smile. The only man here in a suit and tie, Gieves and Hawkes, the colour of a summer midnight.

He said, 'Hielo.'

I said, 'Hello.'

'No,' he said, '*hielo*. Ice – in Spanish.' He pointed to my glass. 'I didn't think the English liked ice in their drinks.'

'You don't know I'm English.'

He gave a laugh. 'Really? *Really?* Forgive me but you are the most English-looking girl I have ever seen.'

I bristled, Englishly. 'I don't know what you mean by that.'

He shook his head. 'I'm sorry. I am from Madrid. We have the unfortunate tendency to say what is in our heads. Sometimes it gets us into trouble. We don't have the English way with euphemism.' He continued to smile and stare at me until I felt uncomfortable and moved away. He followed.

'Now I have offended you. Please, let's start again. I'm Mateo Torres.'

The kitchen had emptied out, so I relaxed. 'I'm Calico Shaw.'

'Calico? That's a very unusual name.'

'Isn't it though. My mother thought it was hip, but it's sort of insulting when you think about it, being named after a kind of cheap fabric that tears easily.'

'Well, I think it's attractive. These days everyone in London seems to be called Katie.'

'My friends call me Callie,' I told him. 'You have another accent underneath that very careful English one. American.'

'Well spotted.'

'I'm good at seeing what's going on underneath.'

'I'd hoped it had gone by now. I spent my teens and twenties in New York.'

'But you didn't stay.'

'No, I went home. Eventually everyone goes home, don't you think?'

'I don't know. I've only ever been at home.'

'So I was right. You're very English.' He took pleasure in proving the point, and touched his glass against mine.

'It's true,' I said. 'Until the Second World War, the average English person had only travelled three miles.'

'Is that right?'

'Yup. It's why there are so many accents here. Accents develop at home and vanish with travel.'

'Is this a specialist subject of yours?

'I qualified as an architect. Architecture is about knowing what places mean to people, and vice versa.'

'How long does it take to become an architect?'

'In total? Around seven years.'

'You don't look old enough.'

'Trust me, I am. Just.' He was still smiling at me. Beneath his very white shirt cuffs I could see tanned wrists and a silver Breitling watch, discreetly tasteful, the opposite of what everyone else was wearing. 'What are you drinking?'

He raised his glass and looked through the amber liquid at me. 'Sherry,' he said, as if it was obvious.

'I always think of the stuff my grandmother kept in the sideboard for Christmas.'

'No, this is very different. It has to be drunk cold and young. A good Manzanilla from Jerez – it means 'little apple'. Dryer than a Fino, very refreshing. Try it.'

I took a sip. The chill tang awoke something pleasurable on my tongue. I handed it back in approval. 'So what's the deal here?'

He looked at me strangely. 'What do you mean?'

'Well, you're obviously not visiting London with the Somerset mafia. Who are you with?'

He leaned forward confidentially. I smelled an aftershave, not the usual variation of lemons, something with musky bite. 'My wife. Tonight I'm just acting as her chauffeur.'

I chilled down a little, disappointed that he was flirting while his wife was in the next room. *Well, obviously someone like him would be married.* I said, 'I suppose it must be nice to always have your husband drive you around.'

'Ah, the English personality. Like the weather. A little warmer, a little cooler, you never know what affects it or where you stand.'

'I don't know what you mean.'

'Don't you. Well. It was nice to meet you, Callie.' He gifted me a wide white smile and took his leave.

Shit, I thought.

I was annoyed with him but more with myself. He was right; I'd asked the question and shown displeasure when he gave me an answer. There was still time to make it better. He was almost out of the door.

To this day, I don't know what possessed me to do what I did next.

'Wait,' I said. 'That's not me. This is me.' And I stepped forward and kissed him. On tiptoe, with my hands on his shoulders, pressing my lips over his surprised mouth. To his credit, he didn't jump away. Not at all.

When we returned to the lounge it felt as if everyone was staring at us, a pair of schoolchildren caught behind the bike sheds. Mateo was quickly joined by a well-preserved woman with an upswept lion's mane of blonde hair, a smart black New York dress and a proprietorial air, obviously the wife. She wore a necklace of heavy glass harlequin panels, matched earrings and nail colour, all sharp angles and edges. She looked as if she could easily leave a scar if she wanted to. The pair started talking together and moved away to the far side of the room.

Sandy Fellowes caught up with me as I was looking idly about, trying to piece the story together. 'Just what do you think you're doing?' she hissed, taking my arm and leading me out of earshot.

'What are you talking about?' I was about to pull myself free, and remembered that Sandy was my mother's biggest client.

'If you're planning to practise your seduction technique, you should try doing it in a room that hasn't got a glass door. You're a guest here, Callie. You were only invited because your mother and I go back a long way.'

'I don't have to answer to you.'

'You do when you're in my home, okay? With one of my guests.' Flecks of white had formed at the sides of Sandy's mouth; her coke jag was still peaking.

'It's okay, I'm going,' I said, breaking away. 'There's a little too much hypocrisy in this room for me.'

Sandy followed me. 'What do you mean by that?'

'You know. Everyone likes to pretend they have such perfect lives.'

'Well we all know how perfect yours has been, *lovey*, we've seen your wrists.' I instinctively touched the African bracelet covering the worst of the cuts on my left wrist. 'It's your mother I feel sorry for. She's the one who had to clean up all of your mistakes.'

I could have shot back at her – God knows I had enough ammunition – but I knew Anne would kill me. Instead I walked away, closing my ears. I'd heard it all before.

I found my leather jacket among the conspicuously expensive couture racked in the hall. I knew my mother would be in full flow right now. She never noticed anything when she had an audience and could smell purses being opened. It was better not to interrupt her.

'You're going already?' Mateo was there again, like some kind of magician perfecting his act by selecting the same member of the public twice.

I pushed my arm into a sleeve. 'I don't really fit in with this crowd.'

'Neither do I. Tonight is for the ladies, after all.' He smiled. 'And I must go to check on my daughter. Maybe I can accompany you?'

A daughter now as well. But I'll admit it. He had me at 'hielo'.

CHAPTER FOUR

The Courtship

I'LL ADMIT I was intrigued. I wasn't as trusting as I had once been, but I decided to give it my best shot.

It was just a short walk across the bridge to the flat where I still lived with my mother, but it had started to rain and he had an umbrella; another reason to accept the offer. We left Pimlico's streets of antiques shops and bijoux residences, heading for the grim modern apartment buildings of Vauxhall.

Mateo kept the conversation light and casual, but uninformative. He seemed honest, and I sensed he was free in spite of his intimidatingly elegant wife. In the lights on the bridge I took stock of him. He was a good foot taller than me, with a slender band of greying hair and distinctive black eyebrows that signalled his Spanish ancestry more clearly than any passport. A little heavy around the waist. Undeniably handsome, but quite a lot older. Gold cufflinks. Highly polished shoes.

He didn't speak until we were in the less than salubrious street where Anne had her apartment. I was embarrassed to be living at home again, and didn't want him to get a good look at the place, not after where we had just come from. Sandy's world. His world.

'To answer your unspoken question,' he said, turning to me with a smile, 'I was there because Mrs Fellowes and my wife are both on the board of the English National Opera Trust. It's the last stop on Maddie's European tour, spreading largesse before she heads back to New York. She leaves tomorrow. My daughter is going with her until the end of the school holidays. She loves having Bobbie come to stay, so long as she can return her.'

'So you're divorced.'

'I would have hoped it was obvious. I wouldn't have let you kiss me otherwise.'

'But you *were* flirting.'

He held out his hands. 'You have me there.'

'Your wife, is she American?'

'From Colorado originally. Maddie was very smart, very ambitious, now she's very successful and very driven. When I met her she had just arrived in Manhattan. But you know, New York is a city that takes over some people. Five years after we married I took her to Madrid. She hated every second of being there and told me she was going back to NYC. I said I didn't want to, so she asked for a divorce. Bobbie was seven. I think we had both realised by that time that our lives had taken a wrong turn. It was just over two years ago.'

I stopped before the building entrance. I couldn't let him come up because the corridors reeked of disinfectant and the flat was a mess. I said, 'I'd ask you up but my mother –' It was hard to explain the situation. I had more confidence with men of my own age. A sharp remark could always nail the young ones in place but Mateo was different. It was as if he saw who I was, and still didn't mind.

He had the good grace to gloss over my excuse. 'Are you doing anything the day after tomorrow?' he asked. 'If not, we could make a day of it. Saturday, I'm not working.'

'Neither am I.' I didn't tell him that I was not working any day.

'Perfect. Then I'll pick you up at ten o'clock.'

This time I agreed without thinking twice.

'Good.' He stopped and looked about himself as if mentally ticking off boxes. 'So – here. The day after tomorrow. Ten. Till then.'

I don't really remember much about the next few meetings. All I know is that the more I learned about Mateo, the more I liked him. He was generous and thoughtful, and had high expectations of life which he seemed able to realise without stamping on other people, and *that* made him very appealing. I soon learned that he could also be opinionated and stubborn and rather old-fashioned, but he understood his own limitations. Best of all he took everyone at face value, regardless of age and social standing, with the freshness and innocence of a younger man.

In a carefully chosen selection of expensive bars and restaurants, the kind he sensed I had never been able to afford, we talked late into each night about pretty much everything, although I was careful to avoid going into my past. I know it was cowardly, but I'd spent a long time building up my defence mechanisms, and they weren't easy to dismantle. Besides, Mateo was seriously old-school Spanish Catholic – albeit one with an eye for much younger women – and I didn't want to give him any reasons to think less of me.

We began dating in earnest. I realised that because of his job I would be spending a good deal of time alone, but he called me at the same time every night from wherever he had to be. I learned to be patient because I had never met anyone like him, and wasn't sure if I ever would again.

We made love on our seventh date. I tried so hard to please him that I made the whole thing awkward and embarrassing.

Seventeen weeks later, we got married. Yeah, I know, a shock to me too. Mateo's parents lived in New York's Upper West Side near his ex-wife, and showed their disapproval by finding excuses not to attend our wedding ceremony, which was performed at Islington Town Hall in North London. My mother came along with Sandy, and they spent the day finding ways to suggest that I wasn't good enough for such a saintly man. I stopped talking to Anne after she darkly warned me that Mateo would leave once he knew about my past. I'd wanted to tell him everything but it was complicated; being totally honest involved getting into something I could barely admit to myself.

Mateo's old college friend Darrell flew over from Jerez to be a witness, and gave us a beautiful wine cabinet which we had nowhere to store because I was still at my mother's and Mateo was split between a rented apartment in Madrid and a borrowed room in the old mayor's house in Jerez. I invited a pair of colleagues from my old practice, just to show that I wasn't entirely friendless. I met Mateo's daughter, Bobbie, and the relative proximity of our ages helped to make us instant buddies. She was a bright and enquiring almost-nine year-old, with all the openness and confidence I'd never had as a child, but there was a prim stillness about her, too, so that I was never quite sure if she was in the same room with me.

We spent a working honeymoon in Seville and Salamanca, and Mateo took me on a tour of the Rioja region, teaching me the differences in varieties of wine. During this time he often spoke of his family's birthplace and how he longed to go back there, and as I was anxious to distance myself from his first wife, I agreed to look for a house in Andalusia. He was delighted by the idea, so we rented a hotel room at the coast and began hitting the websites. We shortlisted around fifteen places, and as his time was limited we viewed some of them separately. It seemed amazing to me that I could make someone so happy just by agreeing to do this one thing.

I'd spent five years studying for my architectural degree and two more working in a domestic practice. Shortly after the partners had agreed their bank loan, the credit crisis hit us all hard. The staff took deferred wages while they tried to find new clients, but with a glut of defaulted properties on the market nobody was looking to build from scratch. Unable to pay our most basic bills, I watched in a state of panic as the enterprise collapsed around us. I was the youngest in the team, and the first to be let go.

After we went into liquidation, I was unable to pay my rent arrears and moved back in with my mother, where I spent my mornings fruitlessly searching for a new position and my afternoons sleeping on her couch. I knew it was a bad idea, and that we would end up wanting to kill each other within days, but I had no choice. The future I had mapped for myself hadn't panned out, and I needed to save money. I had no CV to speak of, and as finding work in my chosen field was proving impossible I wondered how long it would be before I ended up in some backwater office doing filing.

Marriage had been the last thing in my plans. Anne said that marrying in your twenties was what girls with supermarket jobs did, not ones with careers. My mother was full of advice about things that were too late to change. After my first dinner with Mateo, I had fought with her.

'Your first real date in over a year, and you've picked someone who's barely divorced?' she said, incredulous. 'He's a friend of Sandy's, you know.'

'His wife knows Sandy,' I pointed out. 'And at least he *is* divorced.'

'He's twice your age.'

'He's eighteen years older. It doesn't matter to me, and it certainly doesn't matter to him.'

'You could at least try to think it through. Especially after all I've had to put up with from you in the past. You know how easily led you are, all those ridiculous fads you went through. Remember the astrology, the Buddhism, the *spiritual realignment* or whatever it was? And where did any of it get you? Do I have to remind you?'

She really didn't, and of course did so at great length. I tried to stop her but she carried on over me. Whenever Anne started on the past, there was nowhere to escape to. The flat had one bedroom; I was sleeping on an incredibly uncomfortable DFS sofa in the lounge. She followed me from one room to the other, determined that I should be reminded.

'You didn't speak for over a year, Callie. Not a word to anyone. You cut off all your hair. All the weight you lost, the food you wouldn't keep down, those horrible marks on your wrists, you made yourself look so *ugly* –'

'And you make it sound as if I could help myself –'

'You could have done! You were always smart, too smart for me and your father. But you chose to do what you did. And in the process, you almost destroyed us as a family.'

There was no point arguing. We had been over it so often that the words had lost all meaning. Everyone should recognise there are fights you can't win, and leave them alone.

I moved out while the deal on the house was still going through. Mateo arranged for the rest of my belongings to be shipped over to Spain upon completion. He also paid seven months of back-rent on my old flat so that I could leave the country without first having to go to court. My meagre savings had evaporated after the collapse of the practice, and Anne had refused to lend me any more money.

I knew one thing; that I loved Mateo. But he was also my route to a better life, a happy life, and the solution was practical. I felt as if I was finally in control of myself.

I was twenty-six. He was forty-four.

CHAPTER FIVE

The Housekeeper

We moved in on the first day of September. I don't know how to describe those days – even now I only have blurred impressions.

Over and above everything else, there was the light, a wide, high pathway to the heavens. The landscape was a great rock tray tilted to the sun at the kind of angle you'd leave a drying rack. When I first arrived the ground was parched and cracked everywhere except in the garden, which was still watered by the spring that surfaced in a low stone well at the end of the property.

The lawn was an emerald Eden that looked Pixar-fake until I discovered that the spring meandered back and forth beneath it, keeping it lush and fertile. The voluptuous colours were misleading – a lattice of soft orange flowers was interrupted by translucent petals as delicate as dragonfly wings, trailing into the shadows of the cliff's spine, but the plants beneath were sharp and hardy, armed with twin thorns that dug deep into my flesh when I later tried to tear them out. In the early days Bobbie and I would sit out there listening to the drone of insects and fall into a fugue state, a dream within the dream of life.

I soon stopped thinking of Hyperion House as an architectural absurdity. It had been decorated in an urban style because it was wide and flat and had three floors. A low traditional farmhouse would have looked ridiculous cut into the cliff. The building intrigued me. There was something about it that was just beyond the edge of my understanding, something that didn't conform to the usual rules of architecture.

Although our voices were always shockingly loud in the house, it was never truly quiet. There were always birds chirruping outside, clocks ticking inside. The only time it ever went silent was just before something bad happened. I got to recognise that silence later, and dreaded it.

On that first day, as we walked from the great iron gates, we disturbed a cloud of saffron butterflies. I stopped to watch them dissipate, entranced. There was a green parrot shrieking in the trees. This wasn't my life; it was a nature film.

'The rest of your stuff should be here on Wednesday morning,' Mateo said, sorting through the keys, 'and Bobbie won't arrive until next week, so you'll have a little while to orient yourself.' For a fleeting moment I felt less like a new wife than an employee, being given time to settle in before starting my duties. It was a big house. I wondered just how much time it would take to look after it properly.

'I suppose I should carry you over the threshold,' he added, taking my hand, but I could see his heart wasn't in it and anyway, I had already protested the idea. 'Maybe not,' he agreed, 'but Senora Delgadillo might be disappointed. I think she already has an image in her head.'

'What sort of image?'

'Oh, I don't know, the young English bride, very pale skin, diamonds and a veil, something out of the magazines she reads. Not –' he looked over and indicated my baggy T-shirt, my tan, my faded jeans and scuffed sneakers. 'Not you.'

'I could whip into a twinset and pearls if you prefer,' I said, not without sarcasm. 'I don't want her to get the idea that I'm something I'm not. I want to be able to say "fuck" in my own house.'

'You wouldn't be you if you didn't swear a lot,' he agreed, stopping in front of the house. The front door was surrounded by purple bougainvillea and scarlet hibiscus. 'Although I'd rather you didn't in front of Bobbie. I'd like to make a rule about that.'

It was the first of the new rules in my life. 'I just have to get used to the quiet,' I said again. 'I could always hear police sirens in Vauxhall.'

'You won't find any police around here. Senora Delgadillo says there are two in Gaucia, but they won't drive out this far because they don't like to waste the gas.' In the weeks before the sale was completed, Mateo had been able to come up to the house several times while I was back in London, getting ready for the move. He already had a head-start on the village gossip.

'There are some locals around who keep an eye on things – I'm sure you'll soon get to meet them. They'll probably seem very private at first, but they'll come to love you. How couldn't they?' He placed his right hand flat on the front door and pushed. 'Shall we?'

It didn't smell like any old house I'd been in; no lavender polish, damp floorboards or cooking cabbage. Instead there was the scent of orange blossom, sun-hot wood and lemons. I stood at the threshold and breathed in the warm, fragrant air.

In the hall of midnight blue Castilian tiles, sunlight bounced off every surface. All around me, motes and midges glowed golden in the angled geometries of four great stained-glass windows. It seemed as if brightness was filtering in from everywhere; it flowed in pools across the floors and cast chromatic diagonals on the walls, so that they appeared to be lit from within. Windows are important clues to the purpose of a building. They provide personal vistas. These vast panes of glass were meant to raise serotonin levels, pure and simple.

On closer inspection, I saw that the bordering tiles were scattered with representations of stars. The sun and the moon were wrought in glass at opposite ends of the hall. Other representations of the heavens featured in the smaller panels and friezes, lunar symbols in shades of sapphire, solar signs in amber and citron, a cathedral of constellations, and all this in a hallway. It was like a church, designed to instil respect, wellbeing and a sense of calm.

'My God,' I said, turning about, 'how could I have forgotten the light? Look at it!'

'No wonder the old owner valued his privacy,' said Mateo. 'If this house ever got on the tourist trail...'

The astronomical theme continued into the rooms. With so much sky on display at every window, it was hardly surprising that the planets had been selected as part of Hyperion's design.

I walked further into the largest of the front rooms. Around the central table, half a dozen crystal bowls were transformed into rainbow prisms, and the carpets and tapestries appeared sewn with gold thread.

'It is especially good in spring and autumn, when the sun is lower,' said a woman's voice.

Even though her hair was leached of colour and worn in a tight chignon, there was something ageless about Rosita Delgadillo. She had the scrubbed look of someone in a Vermeer painting. Long-necked and small-featured, her skull-like face was free of lines or expression. Her white apron held starched creases and covered a black high-necked dress that must have been hot to wear every day. She wiped flour from her right hand and held it out. 'Welcome to Hyperion House.'

'Senora Delgadillo has been with the property a long time,' said Mateo, his eyes full of meaning. 'She's seen many owners come and go.'

'You make me sound so old,' admonished the housekeeper. She was not predisposed to smiling, but seemed tentatively friendly. 'I am very pleased to make your acquaintance.'

'I'm sure we're going to be great friends,' I said uncertainly. 'You speak English beautifully.'

'My husband was from your country, God rest him. Perhaps you would like to tidy yourself before dinner. You will find your suite prepared at the top of the stairs.' The interview was over. She turned and was gone a moment later. Mateo made a face.

'Apparently Rosita has a very precise list of the things she does, and the times when she does them,' he explained softly. 'She's already made it clear to me that she prefers not make friends with the owners. She says she'd rather consider herself a servant. I think she preferred life under Franco. She doesn't carry bags or do any heavy lifting. She's waiting for a hip replacement.'

'Does she cook?'

'Yup – and she says she'll teach you.'

'Oh God, I can see we're going to be gutting fish together,' I said, only half joking. 'Leave the cases. I want us to see everything.'

Mateo grinned. 'I went through the inventory and studied the surveyor's report, wasn't that enough?'

I playfully grabbed his hand and led the way. 'No, I want you to show me around properly this time. Come on.' Even the staircase and landings were bathed in brightly filtered light.

'Have you even counted how many rooms there are?' Mateo peered into the main drawing room.

'I made it twenty-two, not including the servants' quarters.' I pushed the first door wider. 'We don't have to live in all of them.'

'I seem to remember the ground floor has two drawing rooms,' Mateo said.

'The house was designed with distinct male and female areas, for the sake of propriety. The gentlemen's quarters are larger and a bit more sombre. There was probably a billiard table there once.'

'Hmm – maybe we should re-install it. I can see myself breaking out the cigars over a game.'

'Don't get any ideas about going back to pre-emancipation days.' I followed him into a vast, dazzling room dominated by its window. 'The view's the same from almost everywhere in the house,' I said. 'The light gets right in, all the way to the back. Sometimes it's reflected back by the mantelpiece mirrors. It's very cleverly constructed.'

I walked to the glass and looked down. My view was framed by two amber mountains, one topped with an honest-to-God ruined fort. Between them were miles of green fields, and in the distance beyond those lay a cobalt ribbon of sea that separated Spain from the coast of Africa, with the tilted rock of Gibraltar visible through the haze.

'That's Tangiers on the far shore,' Mateo pointed out. 'At night it's so brightly illuminated that sometimes it blots out the stars. What do you think?'

I struggled to find the words. 'It feels – connected to the world,' I said finally. 'I don't think I'd ever find it lonely here.'

'Even a London girl like you?'

'In London you're never alone for more than a minute, even when you feel completely isolated.'

Even though there was not another human being within sight between here and the coastline, the shape of the house seemed specifically designed to draw in sunshine and bright colours, and prevent loneliness. The mountain at its back reached out arms of warm rock that embraced the building, cradling it into the landscape.

'Okay, where to next?'

I checked the ring in my pocket. 'That's odd.'

'What?'

'The agent said there had been a mistake with the keys. She didn't have the ones to the servants' quarters. But they're not on the master ring, either.' I withdrew the set and counted them out. Numbers 15 to 18 were still missing.

We had purchased the house without seeing the small closed-off area at the back of the property. Although we had studied the floor plans together, the surveyor hadn't managed to gain access, and neither of us had been able to visit the house again before flying back to London.

'You can deal with this,' he told me. 'It will be good practice for you.'

I found Rosita emptying the oven, her face burnished to a coppery red by the flames. Above her, giant iron pans hung like instruments of torture. A lethal-looking *jamon* holder stood on the wooden worktop, its carving utensils still coated in shreds of dark meat.

'Rosita, the servants' section is sealed off and there are no keys on this ring.'

She set her trays down with a clatter. 'Yes. I keep them.'

'Why?'

'I have always done so.'

'Well, may I have them?' I asked with some curtness.

'The rooms never get any light, and there is no electricity, so there are rats. And the sinks – the taps never worked well. Sometimes there is standing water. It means there are – well, it is best to keep the doors shut.'

'Then surely it's time the rooms were aired and cleaned. When were they last used?'

Rosita had an evasive look in her eye that made me suspicious. 'There have not been any servants here for many years,' she said, clearly unhappy about being questioned in what she considered to be her domain.

I stood my ground. 'Then I don't understand what the problem is.'

'There is no complete set of keys. I will have to find them.'

'I'd like you to do so. I thought you were going to find a set for the surveyor.'

'I thought I had some copies but I could not find them. The master keys were never properly labelled, and were put in different boxes.'

'Well, I'll need to get in there sooner or later, because I want to see what needs repairing.'

'Nothing needs repairing,' said Rosita firmly.

'Senora Delgadillo, my husband and I bought the whole house, not part of it, and now we would like to see what we own.'

'Very well,' said Rosita finally. 'I will speak to your husband about it.'

'No, you can speak to me.'

Rosita sniffed in the subtlest of disapprovals, and continued with her work. I had an ominous feeling that this might turn into a battle of wills.

CHAPTER SIX

The Atrium

'SHE WON'T GIVE them to me,' I explained when I returned to the drawing room. 'She's been in charge of the place for so long that she thinks she owns it.'

Mateo laughed out loud.

'I'm glad you think it's funny.'

'I'm sorry. This kind of attitude is so typical, if you were from here you'd appreciate it. Don't worry, I have to talk to her about her wages anyway, I'll sort it all out then.'

'It's your property. You have a right to know what's behind those doors.'

'I'm sure we'll be disappointed. You heard the same as me; they're not habitable because there's no natural light. I'll leave you to go and freshen up for a few minutes. Then we can make a proper tour of the rest, yes?'

He closed the door softly, leaving me alone.

Is he expecting me to change my clothes? I wondered, scrubbing a mark from my old blue *Just Do It* Nike shirt. I couldn't change who I was, but decided to make a bit of an effort to look more like the lady of the house, at least to start with. I wasn't about to start creeping about the place in high-necked dresses and court shoes.

The shower was black-and-white tiled, with a battered tin head that pumped out a drenching waterfall. Outside, the temperature was rising into the high thirties, but the interior of the house remained pleasant and breezy.

Already my pale skin had freckled and was darkening to a smooth caramel. My chest had cleared its persistent passive-smoker cough and my recent nights at the coast had passed silent and uninterrupted. I had spent two weeks there, waiting for Mateo to conclude his business in the wineries of Jerez and Cadiz, so that we could travel to the house together.

I'm ready to start our life now, I thought, discarding my jeans and selecting the kind of simple, old-fashioned dress I would never have thought of wearing in London. *Things are going to be different from here on in. I'll make sure of that.*

As I unpacked, I took stock of the room. As in the drawing room, it was full of heavy dark *fin de siècle* furniture, with cushions the colour of bad meat, patterned maroon rugs, elaborate tiles and fussy cornicing, bookcases, sideboards, dropleaf tables, lots of hard, uncomfortable surfaces. Looking around, old words came to mind, words used to describe the finishes on old objects; *craquelure, patina, foxing.* Old school Spanish, I decided, pre-Franco, sturdy and built for generations to come. And yet there was also something paradoxically modern brought about by the pervasive light. Old buildings were usually repositories of shadows, dust and memories. This house had something I'd never seen before.

I looked up at the windows, sensing a difference.

What was it? Something had changed. Was it the angle of sunlight? A movement in the trees outside? Setting down my clothes, I walked to the window and looked out. A faint gust stirred the uppermost branches of the cork trees, fluttering the leaves. The window knocked slightly in its frame. I listened, and heard the smallest of movements, a shift of weight on a floorboard, a whispering displacement of air...

The clocks rang out, startling me.

One o'clock, time for luncheon. Not wishing to be late, I hurried from the room, my passage marked by chiming clocks. I felt like the heroine in an old novel.

There were timepieces everywhere, a matrix of measurements that included carriages, grandfathers, mantelpiece ceramics, shepherdess figurines with delicate inset dials, monstrous fat-legged ornamentals with convex fascias and high tinging ticks. They all appeared to have been wound and kept at the correct time. They weren't just correct but meticulous in their regularity, so that even their second hands appeared to move together. The ticking calibrated the passing seconds as if marking off life itself. The sounds followed me from one room to the next, one *tick-tock* being replaced by a *clop-clop*, that was in turn replaced by a *din-din* or *crick-crick*, each mechanism dividing the hours into quarters, minutes, half minutes, seconds, and it seemed even the sunlight had been ordered to keep time.

Making my way down the staircase in search of the dining room, I took a wrong turn and found myself in the octagonal glass atrium, with doors that opened to an internal greenhouse. The tall ceiling led up to a turret filigreed with copper tracery, mostly stained-glass irises and poppies in the art nouveau style. It looked – wrong.

'There you are,' said Mateo, smiling at me from the door. 'Rosita is waiting to serve. I guess the tour will have to wait until after we've eaten.'

I knew he was anxious to fatten me up. My mother had been only too happy to warn him. 'Of course you know she was terribly anorexic, and then it was – what do you call that thing where you throw up after you've eaten, darling? *Bulimia*, that's it. She had terrible breath and the acid ate the enamel off her teeth. Those are veneers, aren't they, sweetie?' *Thanks, mother.* Mercifully, Anne was back in Vauxhall, over a thousand miles away, and she could damn well stay there.

I looked down at the long table and saw Serrano ham and *croquetas*, *empanadas*, hake filets, clams and *txangurro relleno*. 'My God,' I said, 'she's cooked for a dinner party of ten.'

'Just eat what you can,' Mateo coaxed gently. 'Let Rosita see that you're pleased with her cooking. Show your appreciation, and then you can change her menu to suit yourself.'

I picked my way around the plates, pushing the food about without actually eating it. An old trick; I was an expert in hiding the amount I consumed.

After, we walked through the house taking note of everything. All the rooms were perfectly symmetrical, even down to the arrangement of their furniture, and each had its own broad slice of sunlight, either reflected in from the huge front windows or bounced through the angled glass atrium via the internal panels. It was as if the architect had sought to import happiness by banishing the very idea of gloom.

When Mateo asked me about it, I explained, 'The emperor Tiberius was so obsessed with light that he had a greenhouse constructed from sheets of selenite. He used to grow cucumbers that way. They were wheeled around in carts so that they could be kept in full sunlight all day long.'

'I thought your degree was in Edwardian architecture.'

'Yes, but you have to cover the entire history of buildings.'

'So, what does the architect in you make of this place?'

'I've only been here a short while. I haven't seen all of it yet.'

'All right. The part you've seen.'

'Well, it looks like it was constructed between 1910 and 1915.'

'Exactly right. 1912, but then you knew that from the report.'

'The building is – unusual.'

'Go on.'

'It's brick-built and on a hill, backed by cliffs, south-facing. There aren't many houses like this in the countryside, and the ones that exist have a specific purpose.'

'What do you mean?'

'They're art studios or museums or designed for growing plants. This one's different. It seems too urban somehow. Not at all self-sufficient. I expected to find the remains of a mill on the property, something used to grind maize or corn. The land is very barren, but someone was determined to grow a full garden, not a vegetable garden but one for looking at and strolling in, a flower garden. It doesn't make sense. Come with me.'

Taking his hand, I led him to the heart of the house, the atrium with its crystalline cupola. The colours were almost painful to the eye. Here grew pink blossoming agaves and palms, flowering succulents of every description, their budded stems flushed and fleshy, glistening with nectar. In the middle sat wide ochre rattan chairs and a long table piled with magazines, arranged on the shining red floor tiles.

We stood in the centre of the octagonal tiled floor and looked up at passing birds. 'This is odd. The glass turret was obviously added at a later date. See the welded joins?'

'What do they suggest?' asked Mateo.

'It was a private house, but I think it also had another purpose. At a guess I'd have said it was an observatory.'

Mateo grinned broadly. 'I knew you'd get it. The original architect was an astronomer.'

'What happened to the telescope?'

'What happened was the civil war. This area was Republican. Franco's Nationalists occupied the house and tore out the telescope, presumably for scrap. Nobody knows what became of it. The building was used as a strategic outpost because of its view. The furniture was placed in storage, and the soldiers who lived here damaged everything else. The couple who took it over bankrupted themselves repairing it.'

'So the telescope was housed where this atrium is now. How did you find that out?'

'My lawyer told me his great-grandfather had a photograph of the observatory. They used to drive past it before the war on their way to the coast. They could see the telescope sticking out.'

I pointed upwards, to a pair of perpendicular metal shafts that appeared to have no purpose. 'Those are the remains of the old steel struts that held it in place. The design looks English, a bit like a very small version of the one in Greenwich Park.'

'Anything else?'

'It was a smart move to turn it into a sort of greenhouse, but it sticks out. I haven't seen everything yet. But there *is* another anomaly. We failed architects like anomalies.'

'Where?'

'Back here.' I took his hand and led him out into the hallway, to the locked door set in its end. 'I can tell you that if these are servants' quarters, they aren't where they should be.'

'What do you mean?'

'It's a house built for a leisured class, so naturally they would have servants. But there would normally be passageways running down the sides of the dining and drawing rooms to the kitchen. Instead, the only access has been placed at the rear of the house. There's no way of unobtrusively delivering hot food or admitting callers. A house built to accommodate servants is like a theatre. The stages are the rooms used by the owners and their guests, and the backstage area is for the staff, who would have slept on in the smallest bedrooms on the uppermost floor. Between the two you have narrow side-corridors, so that servants can pop up unobtrusively, without having to use the main staircase. But here, the rear of the house was apparently given over to them. As far as I can tell, that's a unique arrangement. It must have been done for a specific purpose.'

'Maybe you've just found your project. I know how keen you are to start working again. Think you'd be able to write about it?'

'I'd only be able to do it if I could research the history of Hyperion, which is bound to be in Spanish, of course.'

'You said you wanted to learn. Here's your chance. Besides, something like this might keep you busy through the winter months. That's if Bobbie doesn't wear you out first. She's excellent at keeping herself amused – she's never been much for making friends of her own age – but she has a good line in asking awkward questions. Meanwhile, you still have a while to acclimatize yourself before she arrives.'

My face must have betrayed my feelings, because he asked me if something was wrong. 'I'm not sure I'll be much of a mother,' I admitted.

'You don't have to be. She already has a mother in New York. What she really needs is a friend. You know how much I have to travel. It's seven kilometres to the nearest village and you don't drive so you're going to be here –'

'I'm going to learn –'

'Let me finish. Bobbie has a dispensation that allows her to be taught at home, but it's not renewable beyond the end of October. The school is insisting that she boards so that she can catch up on the official curriculum. I've found a tutor, but she can only do ten hours a week. You'll have to fill in the gaps for a while, just until she can start at her new school. It shouldn't be too taxing for you.'

'I guess I could help her with her homework.'

'You're closer to her age than I am. I have no idea what she's talking about half the time. Do you think you're up to it?'

'I just hope she'll like living here.'

He took my hand and we headed back out into the brilliant front room. 'She already thinks you're wonderful. But you must say if it gets too much for you. It's a big house, you're a long way from home, and I won't always be around. We can call and Skype each other when I'm away, but it won't be the same as me being here.'

'I can manage. This isn't the 1950s. I did have a good job. I'd have it now if the company hadn't folded.'

'Yes, but your mother –'

'Don't take any notice of what my mother told you,' I said. 'I'll be better here than I ever could be in London, you'll see. Anyway, I'll have Rosita to help me.'

'Of course. I just want you to understand what you're taking on.'

'I understood that in the registry office,' I said. 'I'm not about to change my mind.'

'Good,' said Mateo. 'Neither am I.' He took my face in his hands. 'I know you didn't have it easy, Callie. Whatever it was that happened to you, it's in the past. I'll make sure this is a good life for us.'

I wondered what else my mother had said. I had tried to stay in the room with them whenever possible, so that Anne couldn't carry out any more terrorist attacks on my reputation. I gave him a reassuring smile, and we continued with our inventory of the house.

I wanted to tell Mateo everything, but even then I was afraid of losing him.

CHAPTER SEVEN

The Project

AFTER WE HAD worked our way through most of the rooms, I went up to our bedroom, intending to put away the rest of my clothes. The car journey had unsettled my stomach, and I had eaten too much just to prove to Senora Delgadillo that I was willing, so I lay down on the bed for a few minutes.

The mattress was immense and marshmallowy, the room thick-bricked and cool, with eggshell blue walls and a polished parquet floor. Everywhere were paintings of bombazine-clad women and stern-looking men with luxuriant moustaches, so overlaid with sepia tobacco residue that they were rendered almost invisible within their frames, like phantoms. Presumably they had been left behind because they belonged in the house, and would mean nothing to anyone else.

I sank down into the pillow but there was something lumpy beneath it. When I looked, I found a small wooden crucifix with a hook on the top. It had clearly been taken down from the wall, so I put it back up.

I had been expecting to feel at least a little disoriented and odd here, but the only sensation I felt was a soothing calm, a happy sense of homecoming, and I quickly fell asleep. *I'm becoming Spanish already,* I thought, *taking an afternoon siesta.*

At five he came to me. It felt as if I was still dreaming. From the corner of my eye I saw him unbutton his blue shirt and let it fall to the floor. I heard the rattle of his belt opening. The black trapezoid of his chest hair ended abruptly below his pectoral muscles, narrowing to a stripe of fur arrowing to his navel and below. If his body was toned by the natural forces of hard work, his hands were too smooth. They could only have known the touch of keypad, a phone, a steering wheel. He pressed them lightly against the side of my body to turn me, and lowered his lips to mine.

He was unlike anyone else I had made love with. My past sexual experience was a spontaneous, chaotic blur of late night fumbles and hungover mornings, after which I usually hated myself. Mateo was slow and deliberate, and if he was more intent on his own pleasure, it was because he knew it would please me. When he touched my breasts, my throat, the almost-flat of my stomach, it was with a sense of entitlement, but there was also discovery and wonder.

He took his time. I could hear birdsong, clocks ticking distantly, the rustle of bedclothes. When he finally entered me, it was as if he was starting a ritual of possession, a process in which I was complicit. The steady pressure of his body drove gently and steadily into me, filling me with a warm completion. I thought, *let it always be like this, don't let us ever become indifferent or lost to each other.*

After, we lay in each other's arms until I noticed the change.

At first it was so subtle that I couldn't be sure that my eyes weren't playing tricks. I sat up, moving so as not to wake him, and carefully disentangled myself from the white sheets. Stepping naked to the window and looking down, I could see that the sun was lower in the sky now, but was still before the windows. Outside, there was not a breath of air. The boles of the gnarled cork trees were partly in shadow, but the room was squarely flooded with light. It felt as if the sun was present inside me and without. Everything was warm to the touch. I thought then that the house liked us, that it wanted us to be here and to be happy.

I walked to the right-side pane, set further toward the ridge of the cliff, but found it also washed in sun-dust. The reason why became apparent. All of the foliage that might have blocked the path of the light had been removed in a great fan shape, so that no shadows could fall across the house. It must have been done years ago; the sawn boughs of the trees had long grown over.

Returning to the bed and gently stroking Mateo's arm, I watched as his black lashes parted. 'The house –' I began, but didn't know how to continue.

'What's wrong?'

'Nothing. Nothing at all. It's just that the light – it comes all the way through to the central atrium,' I said. 'All of the time. Like a trail.'

'I don't understand.' He sat up, fumbling for his clothes. 'Is that a problem?'

'No, but it's unique. I mean, in a house of this age. It must have been done for a reason. Can we – ?'

'Let me find my pants.' He searched around, dressing with infuriating slowness while I waited impatiently.

'The Hyperion Observatory must exist in some kind of catalogue,' I said, holding open the door.

'You want to start this right now?' He was still half-asleep.

'You said I needed to find myself a project, and I've found one.' I led the way back down the stairs, past the unsmiling Senora Delgadillo, her arms palleted with folded sheets. I wondered if she'd heard us making love.

The rooms spread out beneath us from the central atrium, shafts gilding the polished floors. I slid open a tall panel of glass that admitted us to the great octagon at the heart of the house.

I wanted to understand. After the telescope was removed, why did they replace it with a glass roof? 'The agent called it *La Casa De La Luz*, the House of Light,' I said. 'The house is self-fulfilling. Plants are phototropic. They always turn to face the light, so everything faces front. There are precedents.

Several similar Venetian versions were constructed in the 18th century to use the light from the Grand Canal, and there were some built in Paris, usually for the display of precious objects. The Italian ones were filled with collections of glassware. The sun passes across all of the windows, but it doesn't look as if the house was intended to display anything. Who would they show off to? If that was the purpose, the Hyperion Observatory wouldn't have been constructed in such an inaccessible place.'

As I passed between the plants, their foliage shining with a waxen lustre, I became aware that there was something missing. I tried to think it through. Astronomical observatories were built long before telescopes were invented. They'd been around since the third century in Alexandria, when the movement of the stars was studied with the naked eye. Then the Caliphs built them in Baghdad in the 9th century. French and English telescopes were invented for the purpose of learning about navigation, but they didn't arrive until the early 17th.

'Are you sure there was even a telescope? Do you think it could have been some other kind of apparatus? Those struts needed to come all the way down to the ground floor, but there are no sloat cuts.'

'What does that mean?' Mateo asked.

'It's an old theatrical scenery term, obsolete now. A wooden slot that you can slide something through. The wood on the ground floor is original; it's never been planed and filled, so the only supporting arms were those two rods up there. Which means it probably wasn't a telescope, because the old ones weighed a ton. It must have been something else. Look.' I pointed to the small brass brackets that stood around the edges of the room. 'Your lawyer's great-grandfather thought he saw a telescope, but there was something else held here.'

Mateo had folded his arms and was watching me with interest. 'I can't believe your practice went under with you as an asset.'

'The bank wouldn't budge. We were doing everything right, we just got caught in the downturn. Hey, maybe the agent has a history of ownership or something. We have the address of the last owner, right?'

'No, we have the address of his attorney.' Mateo studied the replaced glass atrium, a neat copper-edged octagon cut into the roof. 'The nights are very clear here. The warm dry air would have been perfect for stargazing. Surely that's enough to explain the location.'

'But there must be a record of the building somewhere, and a history of the architect. You think maybe in Gaucia?'

Mateo led the way out, stopping at a door constructed under the main staircase. He fished about for a switch but found nothing. 'Rosita says they never got around to fitting electricity in the basement,' he said. There were candles and matches on a side-table. Inside was an antechamber, the first room we had encountered without natural light.

A hatch in the floor had weighted handles attached to either side, and rose to the touch with hardly any application of strength. 'If you think the telescope-thing is weird, you're going to love this.'

A stone staircase led us down. The temperature dropped as we descended. We were now under the house. There was a chair and an ornate wooden desk, French-looking, and the central core was still here, an octagonal column of pale stone seemingly hewn and transplanted from the cliff itself. Around it, in a room that reminded me of a factory floor, stood a filigreed mechanical network of polished brass gears and cogs. I smelled earth and oil. In earlier times you would have heard more ticking and clicking and whirring down here than the noise made by the clocks above.

'Oh my God,' I said, 'it's a master clock. There's a calibrated brass ring around the edge of the cupola. I think there would have been a rod going from here up to the roof. They only had to look up to read the time by the stars, and set the clocks.' The gear system was in excellent condition, probably because the hatch to the room was airtight.

'You know, I have a few contacts in New York who would probably consider publishing a book on this,' said Mateo. 'I'm there in a couple of weeks, I could have a word with them. What do you think?'

'How soon can I start? Today? Now?'

He smiled again. 'I love it when you get excited.'

'You hardly know me yet.'

'There's plenty of time for that. We have our whole lives ahead of us.' He embraced me with great tenderness. 'I hate the idea of being away from you. These trips won't last forever, maybe a year, just until the company is better established.'

'I can live with that.'

We headed back upstairs. The burst of setting sunlight as I emerged blinded me for a moment. I stood in the hall waiting for my vision to return. *It's not about being able to see the stars,* I realised, *it's about the light.*

Mateo appeared at my side. 'What?'

'How do you know I'm thinking of anything?'

'You're always thinking. I can see it in your eyes. It's funny,' he said. 'The first time I met you, I assumed you were just another uptight county girl. The second time, I saw a *little* bit of the wild child there. After that, intelligence.'

'Yeah, I'm a complicated lady,' I said.

'You're lucky. It means the world will always hold fresh hope for you.'

I walked toward the outer rooms, running my fingers lightly over the gilt frames of the paintings. 'All the rooms are kept in sunshine, right until the moment the sun disappears.'

'So?'

'Why? The rear rooms must be in permanent darkness, which means they're cold and uninhabitable. I want to see inside them. Will you talk to the housekeeper before you go?'

I walked across the great reception chamber to the entrance and pulled open the front door, shielding my eyes from the sunlight. 'Come and see this,' I called. Carved into the wooden lintel above my head was an inscription. 'It's in Latin. *Felicitas in Solis Animabus*.'

'What are you doing?'

'Hang on.' I had a translation app on my mobile, and tapped in the phrase. '*Happiness only in their souls*.'

'Sol can also mean sun.'

'Okay – *Happiness lives within sunlight*. Or *Happiness only in sunlight*. Think this was put there by the original architect?'

'I imagine so.'

'He wanted to live in everlasting sunshine,' I explained. 'A bit of a romantic notion, but quite common throughout history. Persian sultans were mortally afraid of shadows. They equated them with death. They constructed their courtyards so that no part was ever in darkness. They were inbred and isolated, and very sensitive. They hated noise of any kind. There's a story that someone accidentally shattered a pane of glass in the Topkapi Palace and a Sultan dropped dead from fright.'

'It's good that the house always remains in sunlight,' said Mateo. 'Your mother told me that when you became a teenager you started to hate the dark. She said you used to have panic attacks –'

'I told you to ignore anything she said.'

'It's okay, there's no shame in that. Everyone's afraid of something.'

'I can't imagine you being afraid of anything.'

'As it happens, I'm scared of wasps. There – not so tough now, am I?'

'At least you can see them and move out of the way. The dark – you don't know what's in it.'

'Well, you could never be frightened here,' said Mateo. 'Don't you see? From now on, you'll live your life in sunshine. The house is built in the lee of the mountains. There are no shadows. I sensed it the moment I stepped inside the door, and I could see you did too. Rosita says that even the cut flowers she sets out in the dining room stay in bloom longer because of the light. So let this be my gift to you.'

'Everlasting sunshine.' I pressed my head into his chest and tried not to cry. In the last few years I had become lost. Now I felt as if I had been found and brought home.

CHAPTER EIGHT

The Staff

THE NEXT MORNING, Mateo took the car down to Estepona for a meeting with some supermarket managers, and as I had very little to do until my belongings arrived, I decided to start work on my project immediately. I began with Senora Delgadillo. I found her on the first floor, ironing.

Rosita appeared to resent the intrusion of the new wife into her private service area, and pointedly set the iron aside, staring ahead and awaiting instruction.

'It's all right,' I said, 'please don't stop for me. I just thought it would be good to get to know you a little. Mateo says you've been with the house for a very long time.'

'I was born here,' she replied, 'as was my mother before me.' She sprinkled water and smacked the iron onto white linen, snaking it, hissing, through the creases.

'Then you must have seen many changes.'

'Not really, no. The house is the same as it always was. But it will be good to have everything working again.'

'Why, what's wrong?'

'The lights are always going out. Senor Torres tells me he will pay to have the electrics repaired. Also, many of the roof tiles are loose and cracked. This he will fix. And the garden buildings need clearing out. He says he will do this also.'

I was surprised that Mateo hadn't mentioned his plans to me, but there was no reason why he should tell me everything.

'He says you will write a book about the house. I hope people will not come here to stare.'

'I don't think you have to worry much, it'll be an academic book, and we're not exactly on the beaten path. Of course, the perimeter walls are still in place, so you can't see much from the road. And I don't suppose anyone is able to get in.'

'This was built as a family home, and it will always remain so. It is a very happy place.'

'So it appears,' I said. 'There has to be a catch.'

Rosita set aside her iron. 'What do you mean?'

'It's just so perfect. It's hard to believe that in this day and age you can still find such a home.'

'Spain is suffering through very hard times, Senora. Many great houses are falling into the hands of *guiri*.'

'I don't know what that means.'

'The tourists from your country with the fair hair and the red faces. They are *guiri*.'

'But surely if they restore these beautiful old properties and keep them from being ruined it's a good thing?'

'Only if they truly understand what they are doing.'

'Your country has seen bad times before and survived.'

'If you mean the *Generalissimo*, not all of us saw them as bad times, Senora Torres.'

'But he kept dissidents in concentration camps, he censored everything, he used the death penalty and forced labour –'

'He was a good Catholic. And he brought us the Spanish Miracle, many good years for the people of Spain.'

I could see it was time to change the subject before I got into trouble. 'There are so many clocks in the house, will I need to wind them all?'

'I take care of the clocks. A lot of them now have batteries. Jerardo changed them over for me. He is the gardener, also the handyman.'

'There must be a lot to do in a property of this size,' I said, deciding that a little female solidarity was called for. 'I'll need your help and advice. I think my husband is quite old-fashioned. He'll expect me to run the house, and I'm rather nervous about that.'

Rosita warmed a little. 'You must not be. The rules of Hyperion House are very exact. The rooms without light stay locked. As for the rest, every night the lights are lit ten minutes before sunset, according to the timetable. The clocks are kept working so that the lights can be turned on at the right time and can remain lit through the hours of darkness. I make sure that the rooms in use stay bright at all times, until the owners go to bed. This was what we always did here, and it is something I will continue doing.'

'What was the last owner like?'

'I don't like idle talk about my employers,' she cautioned. 'But he was not an easy man. When he first came here he was not happy, but in the end he was very sorry to leave, even though he was dying. You may find the house hard at first,' she warned, smartly cracking her sheet and folding it away in the cupboard behind her. 'But I think in time you will come to care for it.'

I noticed a catch of reservation in the housekeeper's voice. 'Why would I find it hard?'

'The light can be – confusing. This area is lonely. During the winter it is very quiet, a few farmers perhaps, no *turistas*, and for those from the city the country darkness can play tricks on the mind. But you must not worry. I promise you will be very happy.'

'I must let you get on,' I said, rising. 'Thank you very much for the advice.' *Well, she was a bundle of laughs,* I thought, heading downstairs. *I can't wait for the long winter evenings when Mateo is away on business. Perhaps we'll play cribbage together, whatever that is. Perhaps I'll start hitting the bottle again, like Jack Nicholson in the Overlook.*

I went outside to take a walk around the grounds.

It still astonished me that such a sunbaked area could have yielded so magnificent a garden, even with a spring beneath it, but shade was afforded by the surrounding trees that lined the property, and there was a complicated watering system consisting of a network of fine black plastic tubes over the flowerbeds. They looked new, and had been discreetly inserted around the edge of the lawn as well.

I found Jerardo in a small summerhouse of white peeling wood, in the farthest corner of the grounds.

Short and tanned to the colour of the tree-trunks, he was so old that it hardly seemed possible he could still manage the gardening. He was bent over some seed pots, looking as though he belonged on the lawn of one of my mother's Somerset friends, possibly as a gnome.

When I entered he ignored me, continuing to dig into the soil with his fingers. The room smelled overpoweringly of sour sweat and earth, but I tried not to let my distaste show. I waited. From the corner of my eye I could see a bright green lizard perched on a rock with something yellow in its mouth. The butterfly fluttered its wings feebly, and then the rest of it vanished into the lizard's maw in a single swift movement.

I thought that Jerardo would rise and show some deference to the new lady of the house, but nothing happened. Finally I gave in.

'You must be Jerardo.'

He turned to look at me. Cloudy blue eyes were set in a heavily lined face. The sun had drawn itself over his skin.

'I'm told you're the gardener and the handyman for the house.'

He looked at me blankly.

'My husband talked to you.'

He continued to stare.

'Do you speak English? *Usted habla Ingles*?'

Still he remained silent, watching me. I was trying to work out what to do when he opened his mouth and pointed. At the back of his throat was a waggling pink stub like a block of luncheon meat. It was clearly not a deformity; his tongue had been cut out. I tried not to look startled.

He seized my hand and put my fingers in his mouth, so that I could feel the hot dry stump wriggle beneath my touch. I yelped and snatched my hand away, but he took it again, dragging me from the summerhouse and leading the way between rows of corn at the rear of the garden. I allowed myself to be pulled along, annoyed that Rosita had failed to warn me adequately.

Jerardo cut across the lawn, which was segmented into four equal squares by paths of ochre sand. At the centre stood the stone sundial topped with the statue of the naked young man holding the black and white disc above his head. Releasing my hand he gestured at it, then pointed toward the house, but it was impossible to understand what he wanted me to know.

'It's very beautiful,' I said, not knowing what else to say. He shook his head violently and pointed again to the line of shadow at the edge of the house. I stared in the direction of his raised hand, but I hadn't brought my sunglasses outside, and couldn't understand what he wanted me to see.

He grabbed my hand once more and placed it on the bronze figure's arm. The sun had heated it so that it felt almost alive. I wondered if the sun had touched Jerardo, too, and quickly removed my fingers, leaving the gardener alone in the centre of the absurdly emerald lawn, its green geometry too perfect for this harsh climate, this wild and wilful land.

CHAPTER NINE

The Village

WHEN MATEO RETURNED I sat him in the drawing room and told him what had happened. I was surprised when he started laughing. 'I'm sorry,' he said finally, 'I should have warned you about Jerardo. I'm used to people like him. Don't worry, he's not crazy, he's just spent too many years in the sun and too much time by himself to ever develop social skills.'

'What on earth happened to his tongue?'

'Ah, *that*. You should come to the village with me next time, you'll hear all the gossip. The story goes that when he was very young his father supported the Republican rebels and spied on his countrymen in the village. Some of the boys from the *Movimiento Nacional* didn't take kindly to the idea that Jerardo's old man was relaying their conversations to his pals in the workers' party up in the hills, so they kidnapped the father and son. They made his father watch while they laid the boy on a table in the village square and hacked out his tongue with a can opener. The pair couldn't stay there, so the owner of Hyperion House took them in, and Jerardo stayed on after his father died. Even now, when he drives his van in for supplies, he won't stop for more than a minute.'

'My God, how awful.'

'Well, feelings ran deep about the war. It divided villages and split families apart.'

'He tried to show me something but I didn't understand.'

'Just let him do his thing. If there's anything you don't like, tell Rosita. She'll relay it to him. Remember, you're the boss around here.'

'I'm not just going to be the lady of the house, Mateo,' I warned. 'I want to get back to work and make something of myself, even if it's as an architectural writer. I have plans – I can't just sit around.'

'Of course you do, but let's take it one step at a time. Get used to this place first. Exert your authority, make all the changes you want but respect the past. That's how we do things here.'

'You mean the paintings?' Rosita had warned us about not moving them. 'I'm starting to kind of like them. They belong in the house.'

'It's your call. I know Rosita won't be happy when I send in my man to take the remaining bits of equipment out of the basement. I've told her we're going to improve the electrical supply, and she's fine with that. This isn't France, where everything's frozen in the past. We adapt, but I'm sure we'll find our own way of doing it. Come on, let's have some dinner. Rosita went to the fish market this morning and is preparing something special.'

'How does she get there?' I asked, knowing that the market took place every Tuesday in Gaucia.

'There's a farmer over the ridge who picks her up. She does his mending in return and cooks him the odd meal. Everyone helps each other here. You'll soon see.'

The great table in the dining room had been covered in old lace and laid out with thick white china plates filled with sea bass, squid and clams. Bowls of salad, inky black rice, fat long-stemmed onions called *calçots*, and stacks of tomato-bread sat between the piles of steaming fish. The sheer amount of food on display robbed me of hunger.

'Rosita still cooks as if there was a big family here,' said Mateo, reading my mind. 'We can leave what we can't eat for her and Jerardo. Anyway, we need to fatten you up, remember?'

I wished my mother had never mentioned my eating problems. 'I'll do my best,' I promised, and began to serve. 'Jerardo doesn't look like he's had a hot meal in years – or a bath – but I'll ask Rosita to share the food out.'

'Maybe he has a family of his own stashed away somewhere,' said Mateo. 'A bunch of tiny gnome-like people in the potting shed. Did you get a chance to take a proper look around the rest of the house?' He accepted a platter of soft white squid carapaces.

'I thought I'd start with the grounds and work my way in,' I told him. 'There's a small barn full of insects and rotting hay behind the well. Oh, and the statue on the sundial, I presume it's meant to be Hyperion's son, Helios. I looked him up. Hyperion was one of the Earth's twelve Titans, 'The High One'. Helios was the physical incarnation of the sun. He's mentioned by Keats and Shakespeare, and he's in Marvel Comics. I haven't found any reference of him holding the black and white disc though, but it must represent something; yin and yang, perhaps, the world held in balance.'

Mateo laughed. 'It sounds like you've already made a start on the book.'

'I've got the kind of mind facts stick to. I could bore you for hours with the history of windowsills. I want to get a real feel for the place first. It's quite disconcerting to look at the house, get on with something and look back a few minutes later.'

'Why?'

'The shadows don't move,' I explained. 'That's when you notice the perpetual flat light. I really need to uncover the background history. I ran a few internet searches today but they didn't lead anywhere. Usually you'd expect to find something.'

'I guess the family really did manage to protect their privacy. There was nothing about the original architect?'

'I only know what Julia told me. The property had been posted on her website for over a year. Despite its grandeur, it's not a very prepossessing building when you photograph it in harsh light, and there's the problem of the location and the price, so they had virtually no interest. Then it reverted to the bank when the owner stopped his payments.'

'Right now every bank in Spain is keen to dump their property,' said Mateo. 'Did I tell you there was a stipulation in the contract that wouldn't allow them to lower the asking price? There's other stuff as well. It turns out Rosita and Jerardo are still getting their salaries paid through a bequest in the will of the owner-before-last, and it's not due to run out for another five years. How weird is that?'

'It's no different to France,' I told him. 'You buy a house and discover you also have a part-share in an onion field two miles away. I think it's going to be very good for us, being here.' The walls were angled in shafts of golden light, and it cheered me just to look at them. 'And Bobbie. Rosita's got her room ready. I can't wait to get started on everything.'

'Good, I was hoping you'd feel that way,' said Mateo. 'Why don't we go into Gaucia tomorrow morning, and you can see what the village is like. There's someone I want you to meet. It'll be your last chance for some peace and quiet before Bobbie arrives. She's very excited about seeing you again.'

'I wish I'd been able to see more of her before the wedding,' I said. With deliberate bad timing, Mateo's ex-wife had whisked his daughter away to France before the celebrations, returning her only for the day.

'Don't worry, if I'd thought for a second that the two of you wouldn't get on, I'd have brought her back to meet you again, but she's a very easygoing child. There won't be any problems.' I found his confidence in me astonishing. It was one of the things I loved most about him.

The next morning we rose early and headed into Gaucia.

The tiny town was tucked into the base of the mountains and, according to my Dorling Kindersley guidebook, wasn't famous for much; it produced raspberry-coloured gin and small plates of dried acorn-fed ham, and there were tiny, brightly coloured birds on all the telephone poles. The houses were whitewashed and shuttered against the searing heat, and had blue and yellow geckos painted on the walls, and were edged about by orange trees in earthenware pots. The wives washed their front steps and balconies first thing every morning, just as the wives of England once had. Wherever we walked I could hear someone talking or sweeping. Apart from that, the place was silent. Apart from a couple of vans parked outside shops, there were hardly any cars.

However, there were a couple of small tourist hotels here, and a few ex-pats. The Spanish children played ball games in the street and the English ones stayed inside on their Playstations. The local bar manager told us that by May it was usually so hot that you could cook an egg on the iron plate that covered the town fountain. The best hotel had eight rooms, there was a square where the older boys hung out and fishtailed their bicycles past the café, a church the English never attended except at Christmas, and a restaurant the locals wouldn't use because the owner once cheated his neighbour in a game of cards. Everyone knew each other.

Celestia was a tall, elegant Englishwoman, a former artist's agent in her early seventies who had passed most of her life in Marylebone. She had moved here to Gaucia because of a divorce, a devotion to bullfights and a passion for chain-smoking cigarillos. She knew everyone in town, including the man who had once robbed her house. She gave his children money to show that he had been forgiven, and her displays of largesse brought a certain amount of distant grave respect. She told me that she did not miss Marylebone in the slightest, because who in their right mind would, but she did on occasion miss England.

'How do you two know each other?' I asked as we sat together in the shaded town square drinking thick dark *cortados* and sharp orange juice.

'Oh, I met Mateo's mother centuries ago in London,' said Celestia, delighting in spraying smoke everywhere. 'She warned

me against moving here. She said, 'I'll tell you what happens to people when they move to Spain. All they do is drink and read, drink and read, then they slowly fall apart. It ruins them. Drink and read. It'll happen to you too. That's what always happens."
She gave a throaty laugh. 'God, I could think of a lot worse ways to go than that, couldn't you? I sold up in Marylebone, had the name of a lover tattooed on my right buttock and grew my hair long, and now I sit here at Eduardo's reading and drinking and watching the world go by.'

I liked her instantly. I thought, *if someone like her can reinvent herself, and just take off for another country without looking back, I should be fine.*

Celestia apparently had a better connection with the locals than any of the other ex-pats. Eduardo doted on her and I suspected that he undercharged her, just to make sure there was someone always sitting outside his cafe. The ladies of Gaucia acknowledged her in the scorching streets as they passed each other on the way to the bakery, even though they clearly thought she was mad. If the English wanted to live in Spain, why not choose a town caressed by Atlantic breezes, like Cadiz? Why burn up here, spending half their lives behind thick, cool walls or bobbing about in swimming pools like greased ducks?

'I'd have loved to have been in London for the Diamond Jubilee,' Celestia confided. 'The Queen has always been in my life, right from when I was little. But I do love it here. The *guiris*, those ghastly straw-hatted tourists in blazers who come and sit in the square of a summer morning, rustling their out-of-date English newspapers and drinking beer all day, they don't stay long. Mercifully the budget airline passengers are a good sixty kilometres away, frying themselves in oil at the coast. I first came here with my parents when I was ten. I never dreamed I'd one day move here.'

I saw my new neighbour through a cloud of pale blue smoke, puffing away, filling her ashtray and topping up our glasses, and could not imagine her as a little girl. 'You'll have to come and visit my little house,' Celestia instructed. 'You can see Africa from my upstairs rooms. It's dark and cool there, and my garden has a small pool you can use whenever you like.'

'That's very kind of you,' I told her. 'And you must come and visit us at Hyperion House.'

'Thank you. I had a feeling I might drop dead before I ever got to be invited inside that place. Mateo, you're a very bad boy.' She arched an admonishing eyebrow at him. 'You should have told me you were buying Hyperion House. I could have warned you off it.'

'Why?' I asked. 'What's wrong with it?'

Celestia airily waved the question aside. 'Well, I suppose it's not the house so much as the past owners. They have a bit of a history with the simple folk here.'

I looked at Mateo. 'Is there anything I should know about?'

'No, I'm sure you'll be a new broom. I daresay you'll eventually hear stories though.'

'What kind of stories?'

'Screams in the night, bloodshed, suicides, prayers and madness. The usual sort of thing for this region.' Celestia raised her carafe. 'Top up?'

CHAPTER TEN

The Window

THE YELLOW TAXI got as far as the gates, but Jerardo would not allow the driver inside. I was slowly coming to realise that there was a territorial line between 'us' and 'them'. I had to go down to the edge of the property and help Bobbie bring up her bags.

'It's okay,' she said, 'I can manage.' The red nylon holdall was almost as tall as she was. Bobbie was small and dark and had her father's deep-set caramel eyes. I had only seen her mother that one time, at Sandy's party, but it was clear who she took after.

'Don't be silly, let me help you.' I grabbed the bag and lifted it. 'What have you got in here? It weighs a ton.'

'Course books, mostly,' Bobbie told me. She was wearing a ridiculously old-fashioned outfit for an almost-nine-year-old, a round straw hat and a skirt of tiny brown flowers with a shapeless grey-green top, the sort of clothes a certain kind of New York mother would dress her child in. I knew I'd have to take her shopping. 'I guess Dad explained I have to be educated at home until I can move to big school. We get tablets when I go there.'

'Tablets?' I must have looked alarmed because she started laughing.

'Electronic ones.' She had the precise tone of a privately educated English girl but there was a trace of an American accent beneath it, betraying the fact that she'd been moved around. 'Are you going to be here all the time?'

'Of course,' I said, 'why wouldn't I be?'

'Mummy says you won't make it through the first winter.'

'Does she now? We'll have to prove her wrong, won't we? My full name is Calico, but you can call me Callie. That's what friends always call me. Your full name's Roberta, isn't it?'

'I only get called that when I've done something wrong. Everyone calls me Bobbie.'

'Then I'll have to make sure I never call you Roberta.'

'Dad says there's a teacher coming.'

'Yes, she's called Julieta, but she doesn't start until Monday, so we have time to get to know each other.' We walked side by side up the drive, the sharp morning sun beating hard on our bare necks.

'I've seen pictures of the house.'

'Did Daddy show them to you?'

'No, it was on the website. You know, the agency. They've taken it down now that it's been sold. I like computers. I want to work in IT when I'm older. Mum doesn't think it's a job for a girl.'

'All the more reason to do it, I say. You'll have to teach me. I don't know how to use my new laptop yet. Your father just bought it for me, and it's very complicated. I want to be able to Skype him when he's away, but I haven't been able to set it up.'

Bobbie flashed a grin full of painful-looking metal braces. 'I can do that for you, easy peasy.'

'Do those things hurt?'

She shrugged. 'Mum made me get them. She wanted to straighten my hair, too, but I stopped her.'

'Good job too. You can be yourself here. I hope you're hungry. I have a feeling there's going to be a huge welcoming meal for you.'

'Have you found the maze yet?'

'No, I didn't know there was one.'

'Yes, it's in the back of the garden behind the trees. It's made of beech-hedge and it's very difficult to get out of. It has a little wooden house in the middle that you can turn around to confuse people.'

'You know more about the house than I do. How did you find out about it?'

'The gardener showed it to Daddy. Didn't he tell you?'

'No, he must have forgotten.'

'What are you going to do while I have lessons?'

'I'm going to write a book about the house.'

'Maybe I can help you with it. Are you going to get it published?'

'I certainly hope so.'

'Have I got a bedroom near you?'

'It's right next door, and it's lovely and sunny. Come on,' I said, 'let's get Mrs Delgadillo to make us some lemonade to sharpen up your appetite.'

'You must call her Senora,' warned Bobbie. 'And you can't use her first name to her face. Daddy told me she doesn't like it.'

'Did he? Well I'm in charge as well, you know,' I said cheerfully, 'so we'll see about that.'

There was still so much to take stock of in the house that I had not even thought about getting the former servants' quarters unlocked. After helping Bobbie to unpack her clothes, I left her with her father for a while and went downstairs. Slipping outside, I walked around the perimeter of the house. I had no plan or purpose, other than to fill in time before lunch, so I went looking for the maze.

Mazes are always disappointing to adults, unless they have hidden meanings. Some of the bigger ones do. When they're seen from above they can reveal symbols which are hidden at ground level. I know way too much about mazes. The most famous ones are probably the medieval Christian pavement labyrinths. The hedge maze at Hever Castle is designed to be appreciated from the battlements. They're usually made of yew or beech, and people tend to think they're exclusively English, but I'd seen videos of a really maddening one in Seville, where the hedges are grown to adult height. Unfortunately ours was low and threadbare, with an octagonal wooden house at its centre which could be turned on its axis to face any direction. I could hear a buzzing inside it.

There was no lock that I could see, so I climbed the three steps and pulled at the door handle.

I found myself faced with a single room about seven feet high, and just one small square window. The little house was empty except for a bag of fertiliser, a shovel, some flowerpots and a large grey papery sack hanging from the rafters. As soon as I saw this, I realised I had been hearing it ever since I drew close. The air near the rafters was dark with hornets. One landed on the joist near my right hand, a great black insect with feathery feelers and an acid-yellow hieroglyph on its jointed, shiny back. There were a great many types, and this one looked particularly lethal. I knew that its stinger would be engorged with poison. As it crept forward, it seemed to me that the spike quivered with the anticipation of entering flesh…

'Jerardo!' I called, fleeing the maze-house. He was standing at the end of the hedge watching me with bemusement. 'Please can you get rid of the hornets' nest in there? My husband hates them.'

He looked back over my shoulder, to where the hornets were pouring in and out of the dark doorway on an insect freeway, and shrugged hopelessly.

'Just find a way to get it down, please, and burn it.'

He shook his head violently, as if nothing could ever be disturbed in the house. But this was where I drew the line. 'I mean it,' I told him, 'I want you to remove it. Get someone in to help you if you have to. They only use their nests once, so if you get rid of it they won't come back to the same spot. Wait.' I dug out my cellphone and thumbed open the calendar, picking a day. I turned the screen to show him. 'Do it on this morning, will you? Mr Torres will still be away in Madrid. I don't want him to be anywhere near here when you do it. I'll arrange to have the doors and windows shut, and I'll keep Bobbie inside. But I want it done. You'd better write down the date.' For a horrible moment it occurred to me that he might not be able to write, but he finally nodded and stumped off to his shed to make a note.

I returned to the house. The bricks around the door were warm beneath my hand. The temperature in the darkened back part had to be much lower. I thought it would probably be ideal for storing wine, and we could put Darrell's wedding-gift cabinet in there. Mateo had amassed a good cellar, but at the moment it was still stored at his head office in Madrid. I followed the edge of the building until I reached the border of light and shade. Surprisingly, there were windows at the rear the same as those on the front, but very much smaller, so that the house appeared to be a distorted mirror image of itself. They faced into the narrow alley formed by the sunless cut of the mountain, and were blocked with interior shutters of dark green wood.

I still couldn't get inside. I was growing tired of Rosita's delaying tactics – I'd become sure by now that she was doing it deliberately. I couldn't imagine that there was anything she didn't want me to see. It was about ownership and power; if I couldn't get into all of the house, she'd still be in control somehow. Of course, I couldn't tell Mateo this because it would play into his old-school beliefs that two women left alone would end up fighting. I had a suspicion he believed that all we talked about was men when he left the room.

The alleyway between the rear wall of the house and the cliff face was only just wide enough to enter sideways. By sliding myself in, I could reach the back window. There was a gap in the centre of it, just where the shutters met, so I pressed my face close and cupped my hands around my eyes, trying to see in. It took a minute to adjust but soon I could make out the interior.

It was decorated, but had fallen into disrepair. I had an impression of browns and greys, an old-fashioned gate-leg table with a filthy green baize cloth, a vase of tall, dusty peacock feathers, some overstuffed armchairs with tattered antimacassars.

A tall mantelpiece of pale marble, a gilt mirror with diseased mercury-glass, more clocks – the room was a stunted, shallow mirror image of the one on the sunlit side. But I saw a spot where we could put a wine cabinet, beside the fireplace.

Something puzzled me. Why would servants want to live in a dark, miniature version of their master's house? Perhaps it had been a misguided attempt to make them feel more at home. I couldn't imagine the number of unthinking slights and small cruelties they put up with, but then I came from a time when the very idea of servants was regarded as distasteful and demeaning.

I suddenly noticed that the birdsong had died away in the garden. Perhaps the house blocked sound from this side. I was about to move my face away from the glass when something flashed across my vision. A moment later it had gone, or at any rate, stopped.

Then I became aware of it.

Someone standing in the dark, to the right of the fireplace, keeping very still, as a child might do when it tried to hide. I felt sure I wasn't imagining it, a tall shape, vaguely human in form, but when I looked again it was gone and there was only a darker shade among the others, and I could only assume I had somehow managed to cast a shadow into the room.

Except.

Except the peacock feathers in the vase on the table were still faintly waving in the sudden passing movement of the dead air.

Yeah, right, I thought. The movement had to be caused by a draft under a door, a crack in a window. The house was airy. Perhaps even in those closed, claustrophobic apartments something was bound to move.

It was ridiculous that we couldn't get in there. I decided that if Rosita wouldn't give me the keys, I'd have a locksmith remove the locks from the doors. I remembered her warning that the unusual behaviour of the light would play tricks on me, and stormed back inside the house, dusting myself down. Mateo was just descending the stairs.

'Is there anyone else here, apart from Rosita and Jerardo?' I asked.

'No, of course not,' he replied. 'Why?'

'It's just that – I thought – it doesn't matter.' I pushed the idea away and smiled sweetly instead. 'Is Bobbie settling in okay?'

'She's going to be fine. She's already talking about taking trips into the countryside with you, so you must have made a good impression.'

'She's adorable. She seems very bright for her age.'

'Trust me, she is. But you have to watch out for her – she'll run rings around you if you let her.'

I remembered myself at that age and smiled. 'I can handle it.'

He looked at me for what seemed like a moment too long, as if he was about to question my reply, then headed into the drawing room.

I thought about the other side of the house and for a brief moment an old fear rose inside me, urging me to run away. Like a cliff edge that would draw a vertigo sufferer toward it, the darkness moved a little closer, demanding investigation. I knew that if I didn't deal with the problem at once, a black iceberg of fear would rise up and stay there. *Do something positive.* I headed to the kitchen, where I found Rosita preparing lunch.

'Senora Delgadillo, I'm going to make a study of the house, and I need a full set of keys to the other rooms,' I said firmly. 'I must be able to open every door.'

'I'm afraid that is not possible,' Rosita replied without looking up.

'Why on earth not?'

'Some of them are lost.'

'You mean you haven't been inside at all?'

'We restored the rooms after the soldiers were garrisoned here during the war, then we closed them up. I told you, there was a full set of keys but some went missing.'

'Well, how many rooms are sealed?'

'The ones on the first floor. I can probably find the keys to the ground floor rooms.'

'Very well, I'll start with those.' According to the floorplan, there were rear stairs leading up to the rooms above. 'I'll find a locksmith to deal with the others.' I held out my hand.

Rosita looked at the outstretched palm before her, then went back to kneading dough. 'I'll look for them after lunch, and speak to Mr Torres.'

'Senora Delgadillo, Mr Torres is my husband. You don't need to get his permission.'

'I've always got permission from the master of the house,' said Rosita stubbornly.

'You have a mistress too. I'd like a full set of the remaining keys, as soon as you have a minute to find them.'

I turned and walked out of the kitchen, but could feel a tic in my neck, my pulse rising in anger. The last thing I wanted was to start playing games with this woman. Of course, it wasn't about her at all. I know that now.

CHAPTER ELEVEN

The Architect

IT HAD BEEN arranged that Bobbie would take lessons from a woman who lived in Gaucia. Her name was Julieta Cortez. She was a schoolteacher in her mid-thirties, and had been made redundant after the local school reduced its size two years earlier. The plan was that she would come to the house every other day for four hours, and that in between these times she would Skype Bobbie with assignments and Q&A sessions. I agreed to supervise Bobbie's coursework and tests to make sure she had done everything.

The plan was to try out the system until the mid-term break and if Bobbie hated it or slipped behind in the curriculum, or felt the need to go to a school to be with children of her own age, then she could be boarded at the coast earlier, in Estepona. It had been Bobbie's decision not to board, but she agreed to go if homeschooling proved too difficult.

Julieta could not have looked more Spanish if she tried. She was pretty, with large dark eyes, but thin and sallow, as if she had never sat in the sun, and wore dark loose clothes, greys and browns, or sometimes deep greens. Like Rosita she rarely seemed to smile, but was always courteous and pleasant. On the rare occasions that she did find something funny her laughter seemed forced, as though she was laughing because others expected it of her. I worried that there wouldn't be enough joy in Bobbie's life, and then I worried about myself. I was sure I'd miss going out for a drink with the girls. Back in London, a few of us had met up every Thursday night. Somehow it didn't turn out that way; I hardly missed them at all.

It seems strange to say this, but there was always the house, the way it hurled sunlight so extravagantly into every room, making everything sparkle and come alive. It made up for so much that Bobbie and I always seemed to be laughing about something. At least it did in the early days, when I refused to believe what was happening.

I'm getting ahead of myself, and this has to be laid out clearly.

Bobbie arrived in September and a few days later I set out to make an inventory of the contents of the rooms. Rosita insisted she was still having trouble finding the keys to the servants' quarters, and I hadn't yet been able to track down a locksmith in Gaucia. Celestia told me that they usually had a man drive up from the coast, but he was on holiday. As a result, I had no choice but to accept Rosita's promise that she was looking for the remaining keys. After all, I couldn't imagine why she would want to delay opening a few poky derelict rooms.

I started making notes on the main drawing room, and soon spotted another anomaly. The house appeared to have been constructed according to strict principles based on pairs, twins, opposites and doubles. For every statue there was a matching one, every chair was one of two, every ornament had its mate, every tile and section of cornicing had its opposite number. This determined symmetry had a curiously calming effect, as if it was impossible to find anything alone and out of place. I could only assume that the architect had planned this, too.

Mateo announced that he would be making an extended trip to Madrid and Jerez, to work out the terms of a new deal with the Tio Pepe company, and why didn't I make a start on the book now that we were all fully settled in the house?

On the following Thursday morning he drove to the airport in Malaga for the first flight off the stand, and dropped me off in

Gaucia. The town was hot and silent, as always, with only a few women passing me on their way back from the bakery with their daily breadsticks. Celestia was not yet in the square – she rarely got up before ten – so I had coffee alone at Eduardo's café while I waited for the library to open.

Finally, a short but rather handsome young man in heavy black-framed glasses came past to unlock the doors of the small white library building, and ushered me inside. He told me in impeccable English that his name was Jordi, he ran the library every day except Sunday and Monday, and he would help me by translating anything I needed. He also suggested that if I was looking for a Spanish tutor he could probably teach me as he wanted to improve his English. It was a small library in a small town, and he was bored. I asked him if he had any books or documents on houses in the area.

'We keep most of the records for the region, but there are gaps,' he replied. 'Many of the people here are, well, private. They don't want everyone to know their business. There are basic documents required by law, and others of regional interest.'

I looked around the half-empty, spider-infested shelves. We were alone in the building. 'Who comes here?'

'Tourists, mostly. We keep old magazines and crime novels. That's what most of them leave behind when they go home – paperbacks and a bottle of sun oil. What are you looking for?'

'Documents relating to a building called Hyperion House. It might have been listed as an observatory.'

He smiled in recognition. 'Many people around here know of it, but not many have ever been there, or been inside.'

'Why not?'

'The family was not *simpatico*. If people took pictures they broke their cameras.'

'You mean recently?'

'No, no – a long time before I was born. The old stories, they get embellished and retold. Let me see what we have.'

He climbed a lethal-looking wooden ladder to the upper half of the hall's only records case and descended with several ringbinders that had clearly lain untouched for several years. 'You can have a look in these,' he suggested. 'If you have no luck there are others we can search, but they are kept in the annexe beside the remains of the convent, where the older documents are stored. Nothing will be in order anymore. Nobody's been in there for years.'

I took the folders to a table and set to work. My first find came half an hour later, a general entry in a description of the region from an English magazine called *Spanish Traveller*, dated 1967:

> 'The Hyperion Observatory was designed at the very end of the Victorian architectural era by the astronomer Francesco Gabriel Condemaine, but did not complete construction until 1912. Condemaine was a brilliant engineer and considered the house his greatest achievement. Its fixed telescope operated until 1938, when it was removed by soldiers representing Spain's Nationalist Party. The house is privately owned and not open to visitors.'

It appeared I was wrong about the telescope and that there had been one after all. I checked my iPad to see if there were any articles on Francesco Condemaine and came up with a few brief entries that mostly repeated each other's information. One was on a website called *Spiritual Senses* that seemed mainly to be about astrology, not astronomy;

> 'Francesco Gabriel Condemaine – b.1887 – d.1917
>
> The Anglo-Hispanic architect/astronomer understood that good architecture could improve the lives and maximize the happiness of every social class. A firm believer in the power of sunlight to restore mental health, he was employed by in the Welfare Department of the Spanish government to redesign the Santa Isabel State

Mental Hospital in Marbella, creating large windows that would admit more light and fresh air to patient's rooms. Construction of the hospital ran over-budget, and further plans were shelved amid controversy and accusations of misappropriated funds. His only realised project was the Hyperion Observatory in Andalucia, Spain, which is privately owned. Condemaine was killed at the Battle of Passchendaele in 1917.'

Another appeared in an online data entry assembled by the University of Malaga, which I was able to run through a translation app:

> 'Francesco Gabriel Condemaine married his wife Elena in 1906. Six years later, he finished building their new home, the Hyperion Observatory. The couple had twin sons and a daughter. Although Spain remained neutral during the First World War, Francesco was half-British, and enlisted to fight on behalf of the allies, much against his wife's wishes. In May 1922, Elena Condemaine was deemed unfit to take care of her family, and was subsequently taken to an asylum suffering from an unspecified mental illness, where she died a year later. The Hyperion Observatory was inherited by Francesco Condemaine's cousin and his family, who lived there until 1937, when the property was requisitioned by Spanish Nationalists.'

'How did you get on?' asked Jordi.

'There's not much to go on,' I replied, 'but I have the architect's name and dates now. I can try some other stuff online.' Thanking him for his help, I headed out to the town square, where I found Celestia on her first glass of sherry and her first pack of cigarillos. She had tied her long auburn hair up in a bun and looked like a mad and rather wonderful gorgon.

'Hello there,' she called, imperiously summoning the waitress. 'Come and sit with me. This is a nice surprise.'

'I just came to use the library,' I said. 'It's in a bit of a sad state.'

'It's dreadful, isn't it? How can you have a Spanish library without Cervantes? Just old issues of *Hello!* and some dog-eared Harry Potters, nothing for a grown-up to read. We had hundreds of copies of that *Fifty Shades of Grey* thing. We burned them at the spring *feria*.' She released a spirited cackle.

'I was trying to find something on the history of the house. There wasn't much to go on.'

'You're probably better off talking to some of the locals. You'll need an interpreter, though. Not many of them speak English.'

'Jordi has offered to help teach me.'

'I bet he has. You should watch out for him, like all Spaniards he has wandering hands. Lovely little bum on him, though. Smart, too. He's completely wasted here. Speaking of charming men, your husband is *such* a dish. There aren't any decent men left around here, not that I care. I'm past that sort of thing. And Roberta – I find most children repulsive but she is delightful. How is she settling in?'

'It's all just a big holiday to her at the moment,' I said.

'Children are so *accepting*. And you?'

'Doing better than I thought,' I said. 'It's such a beautiful house.'

'You'll have to learn to slow down a bit, though. The sun takes its toll. You'll find that having a kid around makes you take things slower, otherwise you run out of energy around lunchtime. When the heat hits forty here I get terrible dizzy spells and the only thing that will shift them is a lie-down with an iced towel. I suppose you have some staff to help you out?'

'Yes, a gardener and a housekeeper, Senora Delgadillo.'

'Oh, she's a miserable old cow. We're not good enough for her, apparently. She only comes into town for supplies and hardly bothers to talk to anyone. That's the trouble with those old housekeepers, they start acting as if the houses they look after belong to them.' She wagged a nicotine-stained finger at me. 'You mustn't let her do that. Let her know who's boss.'

'I'm trying to, but it's not easy. Bobbie's having a tutor from here, Julieta Cortez.'

'Julieta's a good sort. She had a hard time feeding her family after they shrank the school, so I'm glad that she has some work now. The younger generation doesn't want to live here anymore.'

'But it's so pretty.'

'Yes, and it's also cut off from the action. The sons and daughters all want to live at the coast, where the nightlife is. Of course, nobody can afford to move there now, not since the crisis. Spain is so different to France and Italy. One always feels everything in Amalfi and Provence has been explored to death. The Frogs rip you off for dinner and wine then insult you behind your back, and the Eyeties blatantly rob you. Just when you think you've discovered an unknown corner, the villagers pop out to flog you tablecloths and napkin rings. But here there are still good people and quiet towns in regions that hardly anybody visits. They spent years getting out from Franco's shadow, then the unemployment crisis started all their troubles again.' She ground out her cigarillo with a vengeance.

'I must get back,' I said. 'Bobbie's teacher has to leave at noon.'

'How are you getting there? Shall I order you a taxi?'

'Oh, I'll walk,' I said.

'I don't think that's wise. It's very hot out there.'

'Honestly, I'll be fine – it won't take me long.'

'Well, if you're sure...'

I left Celestia leafing through an old *Sunday Times*, dappled in light beneath a fluttering tree, a picture of summer contentment.

I set off along the winding blacktop, but after half an hour I began to realise that I had seriously misjudged the heat and the distance. The blue-hazed views from the road down over the valley were astonishing, but the sun was relentless, and I had brought no water with me. I reckoned I was still less than halfway there when I began to grow dizzy. The hard bright landscape hurt my eyes. There was no wind, no breath of air, and no car passed. There was only the relentless abrasion of crickets.

Sinking to the low wall at the edge of the road, I shielded my eyes and watched for vehicles, feeling unnerved and foolish.

After a few more minutes I saw a wavering dark vehicle in the distance. It was Jerardo, passing in his smashed-up van on his way back from buying gardening supplies. When he saw me sitting on the wall, he pulled over and opened the passenger door. My shoulders and face were burning. If I ever decided to do that again, I knew I would need to be better prepared.

At that moment I came to understand just how cut-off we were at the house. With Mateo gone there would only be females here now, plus a mute gardener, and whatever passed in the shadows at the back of the house.

CHAPTER TWELVE

The Other Side

MATEO HAD BEEN away for three days, but Skyped me every night before he went to bed, and often called during the day when he was between meetings. As always, he was courteous and attentive, but I could tell work distracted him, and he didn't really listen as I told him the news of the day, which usually amounted to bits of regurgitated gossip and perceived slights from Senora Delgadillo.

I had started to make up detailed floor plans for the house, but was missing some of the equipment I needed, and had sent away for some old-fashioned scale rules and compasses. I liked using CAD but still enjoyed the feel of tools and graph-paper. Meanwhile I continued to catalogue the furniture and antiques. None of them seemed to be especially valuable, but they suited the rooms so perfectly that I had no desire to rearrange anything or throw it out, not that Rosita would have let me.

While Bobbie proved almost impossible to wake up in the mornings (especially annoying, as her tutor arrived early), I found it difficult to get to sleep. I left the curtains open so that starlight could fill the top half of the windows in the master bedroom, but I missed Mateo. It seemed to me that he had become far more loving and sexually attentive since arriving at the house, which only made the nights without him worse.

Downstairs all the clocks still marked the night-hours, although I had managed to mute the one in the bedroom. It was odd sensing that the door at the end of the hallway led to a small version of our bedroom that no-one had lived in or even seen for years. Rosita had *still* not located the keys, and they now they had come to represent a test of wills between the pair of us.

On that third night without Mateo I checked the clock and saw that it was only 2:47am. Activity in the house naturally followed the path of the sun, so bedtimes were earlier than I was used to. I lay back, allowing the peacefulness of my new life to wash over me, listening to the distant ticking, the rustle of trees outside the window.

And beneath these sounds, something else.

I pushed myself up on one elbow. There it was again. A trapped cat, or a girl crying.

'Bobbie?' I called.

I listened again. Silence. Then something that sounded like a swallowed sob. Pushing back the sheet, I slid out of the high bed, padded across the floor and into the hall, positive that the sound was coming from the other side of the door at the end. I pressed my ear against the connecting door. The sound was fainter now, not dramatic, just stifled and fearful. I heard the softness of a sigh, the scrape of a chair leg.

There was somebody else in the house, I was sure of it. I tried the door, knowing that it was still locked. Returning my ear to the panel, I listened again.

Bang – It was as if a fist had hammered against my ear on the other side of the wood. I jumped away from the door in shock, my ear ringing. But I found myself approaching again.

The crying had stopped. It was silent on the other side. Whoever had been there had left.

Oddly, I didn't feel scared, just puzzled more than anything. I went back to bed and instantly fell asleep this time, waking at seven with the sense that I had probably dreamed the whole thing. Or perhaps just choosing not to think about it.

* * *

'The keys,' I said, holding out my hand. 'I need them right this minute.'

'But there is not a full set,' Rosita insisted. 'And the master instructed me to keep the doors closed during all the hours of daylight because he did not want you to –'

'I'll decide where I can and cannot go in my husband's absence,' I said, holding firm. 'Let me have all the keys you've found so far. You won't be blamed. I'll inform Mateo that it was my choice. If you don't, I'll break the door down.'

Senora Delgadillo's lips narrowed to a thin line. 'Very well.'

She found a small footstool and made a big production of climbing on it, feeling around on the top of a freestanding kitchen cabinet and taking down a cigar box, which she handed to me with theatrical reluctance. Inside were a great many rusted bands of keys, mostly old iron flagstaffs. The rest were modern brass Yales for new locks that had been added since we moved in. I looked at them in dismay.

'Is there any one set you use as the master keys?'

'These.' The housekeeper fished the largest ring out of the box. 'But they are not all here. Perhaps among the loose ones…'

'Thank you.' I decided that Rosita was only doing her job, and softened a little. 'I don't want to disturb anything in the rooms, I'm not going to modernise them, I just need to see inside.'

None of the keys were labelled. As I was determined not to have her trailing behind me with a disapproving expression, it became a painstaking matter of trial and error to get any of the doors open. There was no point in trying the door in the drawing room, as it had the chest of drawers holding it shut, so I headed up to the first floor landing and the elegantly carved art nouveau door. It took over half an hour of fiddling with various loose keys, pressing and testing each bit against the tumblers in the keyhole, before I felt one turn over and unlock. According to Rosita, the key did not exist.

I carefully pushed open the door. A spear of light bounced from a mirror on the other side and sloshed into the room, as if someone had thrown yellow paint across the floor. The air was dusty and thick – there were no open windows, doors or grilles on this side. I breathed in. The room smelled old and unlived in, of camphor and dried lavender and damp. The dust was so thick that the patterns on the carpets and tablecloths had been lost. Small grey clouds formed behind me as I walked.

But it was perfect. Mateo's wine racks could sit in here. I imagined them filled with rare amontillados. The room was a copy of the one on the sunlit side, as I had suspected, just much smaller and meaner-looking, the wood cheap and far less solid, a room probably deemed ideal for servants. It was disappointing to find no secrets or surprises.

I felt an old familiar sensation stirring, something I hadn't felt in a long time. I knew I was testing myself by stepping into the shadows. It's a strange thing, nyctophobia. You're not born with it. It can start at any time. It comes and goes, and it's one of the only phobias you can transmit to other people. But it can also disappear without warning. My horror of the dark lasted for just over a year. During that time I couldn't even step outside the house at night, and in London it doesn't even get properly dark. Then one day I awoke to find that the feeling had gone.

The answer now was to leave the door ajar, admitting a shaft of reflected light that provided me with a path I could stay on. I wanted to go further and dig around in the drawers of the desks and dressers, but something stopped me. It was enough for now. I could see that nothing had disturbed the dust. Retreating, I was pleased to leave the room and lock it again.

I repeated the exercise in each of the rooms. In every one I could open, I found the same interiors, the same tables and chairs, but cheap ornaments stood on the sideboards and the mirrors were spotted and ruined. It was as if one half of the house had been cloned from the other, but its twin was smaller, sicklier, shabbier, designed to suit the second-class status of service. These meaner rooms seemed newer in some indefinable way, as if copied at a later date.

In the servants' dining room, there was one difference. On the table where the meals would have been laid out there was a doll collection, the dusty figurines arranged in order of height. Seven ugly, puffy-faced dolls, probably Edwardian, corseted in adult clothes, with movable eyes and dry plugs of real hair. There was no match for them on our side, and I assumed they had once belonged to the waiting staff. I didn't touch them for fear that they would fall apart in the desiccated atmosphere. There was an odd smell here, of a bitter vinegary herb, something I couldn't quite recognise.

The only door I couldn't get open was the one that connected to the drawing room. The chest of drawers had been pushed hard against it, and was too heavy for me to budge. I knew the rooms had to be connected between themselves, otherwise the servants would not have been able to get up to their bedrooms or reach the toilets, but there was no space between the house and the cliff-face for proper staircases, and I didn't fancy creeping about the mean little passages and dark stairs that had to be back there without Mateo, so I decided to wait until he was home.

'Senora Delgadillo, who did you work for before we arrived?' I asked the housekeeper when I went to return the keys to the cigar box.

'I was employed by various members of the Condemaine family,' she said, 'until the last one had to leave and the property was sold to Senor Torres.'

'So it always remained in the same hands?'

'Yes, until there were none of them left.'

'Did they die in the house?'

'Sometimes.'

'Have there been – tragedies – here?'

'No. Never. This is a happy house. It always was.'

'No-one else can get into the other side, can they?'

'Of course not.'

'So we are alone.'

Rosita turned to me with her customary impatience. 'Senora Torres, if you wish to ask me something, please be clear and say it.'

'It's just that I thought I heard someone moving about in one of the other rooms.'

'I told you. Hyperion is an unusual house. You must expect unusual things. The cliff behind it heats up during the day and cools at night. There are bound to be noises.'

Which was entirely unhelpful, and pretty much what I had expected her to say. The wood was old and expanded in the warmth, so it cracked and popped. What else could there be, the suffering ghosts of those who had lived here before? I wasn't living out some movie in which the heroine finds that the previous owner was a mass murderer, or that his wife was a witch who'd placed a curse on all future residents. It was embarrassing to even think about such things.

'But the room that connects to the drawing room has a chest of drawers wedging it shut. Who put it there?'

'I never go back there, Senora, so I would not know.'

'Nevertheless, someone has put it in place for a reason. Can you think what that might be?'

Rosita sighed. 'I think perhaps that lock does not work. It is to stop the door opening by itself.'

'By itself?'

'There are breezes in the house when we open the windows – sometimes the doors slam.'

She would not give any further answers, and I could think of nothing else to ask her that would settle the matter, so there it ended.

The sun continued to pass across Hyperion House, centimetre by centimetre, the flowers feeding from the light and blossoming, smelling ever sweeter, the warmth spreading over the floors and walls, the dust motes dancing in the light as radiant as crystals.

I went back to my drawings, went back to helping Bobbie with her studies, or to the computer where I had started compiling my history of the house and its precedents, anything to take my mind off the idea of someone – or something – living beside us in the part of the house that lay in permanent darkness.

CHAPTER THIRTEEN

The Thread

MATEO CAME HOME and the three of us went down to the coast, enjoying the last of the summer sea. I felt as if I had been blessed with a new chance in life – an opportunity to get back on my feet and bring an end to my rootless existence. With my problems behind me, I was suddenly happy and untroubled. We swam and ate and lazed around. Mateo was solicitous and charming. His old-fashioned ways made me laugh; he ushered me through doors, dusted off a beach bench, paid for the ice creams with exaggerated courtesy. We took candy and seashells back for Julieta, and Mateo had bought duty-free cigarillos for Celestia, and life went on.

But on the last evening of that week, I took the bunch of keys from the cigar box again, and substituted a big rusty ring of old keys I had found in the summerhouse, carefully folding the originals inside my sweaters in the bedroom wardrobe. I felt like a traitor to the house, but I was entirely within my rights.

During that happy time, there was only one further incident that bothered me.

Early on Saturday morning I was sure I heard the crying again, this time coming from behind the locked connecting door in the kitchen. I managed to get to the keys and open the door while the lament was still in progress, but when sunlight entered the room it stopped at once, as if ashamed of public exposure.

As I was coming back out I heard Rosita enter the kitchen, and froze. For some illogical reason I did not want her to find out that I was entering the rooms, so I waited while she set down the lunch dishes and went back out.

Bobbie had been playing in the next room, and said she'd heard nothing at all. As a committed atheist I believed in science, not ghosts, but I couldn't explain what I thought I was hearing. There were days when I felt like removing the Catholic icons that dotted the sideboards and taking down the paintings of weeping virgins that covered the walls, but I knew it would upset Mateo. I decided not to mention my experiences. It would only make me appear weak and prone to excessive imagination. And besides, my days were filled with the project and the house. And Bobbie, who was always drawing or painting or making bread with Rosita, or cutting out bits of cardboard to construct marionettes, a throwback child uninterested in television or the iPad Mateo had bought her. The sun that made us all so happy was also slowing me down, just as Celestia had predicted. I took siestas, and began working late at night when the house was cooler.

Mateo finally managed to move the chest of drawers with help from one of the truck-drivers who ran vegetables to Gaucia, and they cleaned the room behind the drawing room, fitting it with a new key, so that all of the servants' area was now accessible, although we conformed to the rules and kept the doors locked. Mateo installed the cabinet and had his wines brought down from Madrid. The temperature in the back of the house was perfect for them.

With my husband walking behind me as reassurance, I paced my way through the servants' rooms. There were four, three of which roughly corresponded to rooms on our side, and I mentally named them the Half-Dining Room, the Half-Kitchen and the Half-Bedroom. The fourth, at the end of the first floor corridor, had a more irregular shape than the others, but I was sure we could find a purpose for it. Above was the Half-Attic, with a low sloping ceiling and tiny square windows that looked out onto the dark rocky outcrops of the cliff, which was no more than six inches away at this height. A stale smell wafted up from the narrow space between the house and the wall, as if something had crawled in there and died.

There were other spaces, too, cramped corridors and what appeared to be a tiny bathroom, but it had no windows and I decided to tackle it at a later date, when I felt up to clearing the grime from a hundred-year-old sink and toilet.

We made very few changes to the main part of the house. Every time we moved a clock or a painting or lifted a rug, the room seemed to be thrown out of balance and we guiltily shifted everything back into its rightful place. On the rare occasions that we did make an alteration, Senora Delgadillo noticed and her face froze.

If there were any hairline cracks in this perfect world, they were too fine to show. It was true that Mateo was more frequently absent than I had expected him to be, travelling between Southern Spanish vineyards and cold Northern cities on business, and that he was often so wrapped up in his work that he seemed distant and uncommunicative. It was also true that sometimes I felt isolated, only catching up with my friends on a laptop screen. Mateo's mother remained antagonistic toward me, and his ex-wife simply hung up when I answered the house phone. I had intended to accept Jordi's offer of Spanish tutoring, but so far I hadn't been able to set aside the time. I spoke to Mateo's publisher friend and the book started to look as if it might become a reality. I began to make career plans once more.

Then everything started to change, and I came to look back on this as a golden time, when all was well with us.

The second Thursday in October was Bobbie's ninth birthday. 'What would you like to do?' I asked her as we sat together in the reading room one afternoon, sorting through old magazines.

Her face lit up. 'Could we have a party?'

The sun was a little lower in the sky now, but it was still warm. Only the shadows had started to chill down, so I thought we could have it outside. 'That's a great idea,' I told her. 'Who do you want to invite?' Bobbie had made friends in Gaucia, and although they had asked her over, they had never come here.

'I can make a list and we can paint cards to send them.'

'Okay, let's get started right now.' We found boxes of coloured pencils, glue, glitter and cotton reels, and made cards the old-fashioned way instead of typing them in online.

'Why don't we ever open up the other rooms?' she asked as she sketched out her design.

'Because it's always dark in there, and there's no electricity,' I explained. 'And the wines are very valuable and can't be disturbed, so we can't have you playing in there, in case all the sediment gets shaken up. Sediment is –'

'Dust in the bottles. I know. Don't you get fed up with sunshine?'

'No, because I don't like the dark.'

'Why not? It's dark when you go to bed.'

'Yes, but when Daddy's not here I sleep with a nightlight on. And Rosita keeps all the clocks wound up, so she always knows when to turn on all the lights.'

'I don't mind the dark. The room behind your bedroom is one of the dark ones, isn't it?'

'There's a tiny room there, yes.'

'I know because I can hear it.'

'What do you mean?'

'I can hear water dripping. Rosita says there's standing water in the servants' bathroom, and that means leeches. She says I can't go in there.'

I laughed. 'I'm sure she didn't say there were *leeches*.'

'Yes, she did. They suck your blood.'

'I really don't think she meant that.'

'Yes she did,' Bobbie insisted. 'We need envelopes and stamps.' With the subject of blood-sucking leeches smartly written off, it was clearly no longer on her roster of interesting topics.

'I'll go and see if Rosita has any.' I headed off to the kitchen, where the housekeeper stored the stationery supplies. I was going to tell her off for filling Bobbie's head with images of ghoulish creatures living in stagnant pools, but she wasn't there.

I stood in the kitchen, listening. It seemed to me in that instant that the birds had all stopped singing. When I returned, Bobbie was still sitting on the floor of the drawing room gluing tinsel onto cards. Her sheet of silver stars glittered in the afternoon sunlight. A faint draught blew from under the door that connected to the matching room on the other side.

'I can't do this.' Bobbie was trying to thread some red sparkly cotton through a piece of cardboard cut into a star.

'Here, let me.' I held out my hand and she gave me the thin spindle of cotton.

'Can I get some lemonade?'

'Of course.' I watched her go, and began threading the card.

I didn't want Bobbie running in the hall – the floor had just been polished and was slippery – and turned to admonish her when the spindle slipped between my fingers and bounced onto the wooden floor. Before I could grab it, it rolled away, unspooling. A door slammed. Bobbie was still in the hall, heading for the kitchen. I looked up in time to see the spool disappearing under the gap beneath the connecting door, leaving behind the strand of cotton.

Rising from my chair, I picked up the end of the thread and absently pulled it back toward me, but it started coming undone because a moment later I had several feet of thread in my hand, so I kept pulling.

Quite suddenly, the thread stopped and tightened. Dropping to my knees, I tried to see under the door, but there was only blackness. I pulled again.

Something pulled back. I rose with a start.

Wrapping the thread around my fingers I pulled hard, but whatever was on the other end pulled harder still. The stinging thread sliced into my fingers, but I could not let go. I hung on, but finally it snapped and I fell back, watching as the crimson cotton snaked under the door and disappeared from sight.

CHAPTER FOURTEEN

The Birthday

YOU FIND RATIONAL reasons for unexplained events. I told myself that a rat had got caught in the cotton. The thread had snagged on some piece of furniture, and the rodent had run, tightening it. What else could it be? I always thought I had a logical mind, despite my mother telling people I had 'too much imagination'. I never wanted to be the imaginative type. I need rational explanations and I seek practical solutions to problems. It was one of the things that first drew me to architecture.

But the explanation for this – although not the scientific one I sought – was already lodged in my mind like a burning needle: *There is someone living in the other side of the house, in those cramped little rooms full of cheap furniture. Someone who hides when I enter, but who wants to be let out. Someone with a desire, a thirst – for revenge or forgiveness or just to be heard. That's why the chest of drawers was in place – to keep them in.*

After I cleaned my cut index and middle fingers and put on a pair of plasters, I went upstairs for the keys. My plan was to explore the rooms once more. I unlocked the door in the kitchen and went round, keeping close to the entrance.

I failed to find the cotton reel. It had vanished. But a faint tracery of scarlet could be discerned, snaking its way across the floorboards. The chiming clocks reminded me that darkness had settled all around us now, and I suddenly needed to get back to the safety of the brightly lit side.

As she climbed into bed later, Bobbie watched me in puzzlement. 'Are you alright?' she asked, sounding very grown-up.

'Of course,' I told her. 'Why wouldn't I be?' I followed her eyes to my hand. 'This – it was nothing, a silly accident. I'm just tired, that's all.'

She didn't look as if she believed me, but gave me a kiss and slid down into bed.

'Does your mother usually read you a bedtime story?'

'No, I'm too old for that,' Bobbie said, pulling a face. 'I prefer to read my own books.'

I saw the Kindle on her bedside table. 'What have you got on that?'

'I like short stories. I've got Robert Louis Stevenson and Guy de Maupassant.'

'That sounds a bit adult.'

'There's Horrible Histories too. I read a lot when we're in New York. Mummy's always working and she doesn't like me watching TV. She doesn't let me go out by myself because she says New York is full of crazies.'

'Well, it's good that you read a lot, but you need real experiences too,' I said. 'We'll take some trips. You can go wherever you want.'

'I'd like that.' With her hair brushed back from her forehead and her chin just over the blue coverlet, she seemed tiny and fragile. I gave her a kiss.

'Tomorrow we'll look at a map and see what there is to see. Good night, sweetie.'

'Good night, Callie. Leave the night light on.'

WHEN MATEO RETURNED and saw the plasters on my fingers, I lied and told him it had been my fault, an accident while we were making the cards. I explained that we were organising a birthday party, and I made sure that Bobbie backed me up.

'I wish you'd told me before you decided to make the

invitations,' he said. 'I won't be here on Saturday. I have to go to Paris. We have a stock shortage problem with the supermarkets.'

'It's okay,' I said, 'we'll make it for the day after.'

'I can't get back until Monday night.'

'But we have to hold it over the weekend, Mateo, she's so excited about it, and it's the only time her friends can come.'

'There's nothing I can do. Right now I'm in danger of losing a big order from Carrefour. I'm the only one in the department who can renegotiate the contract. Why don't you go ahead with the party, and we'll have another one when I get back? It'll be mostly mothers anyway. I'll give Bobbie a special day out.'

I agreed, but it was hard hiding my disappointment. I broke the news to Bobbie, and as she seemed happy with the idea of having two birthdays, I let it go. I didn't exactly have a choice.

The Saturday of the party arrived. Rosita and I hung decorations of coloured crepe around the summerhouse until it looked like a giant cake, much to Jerardo's disgust, and we tied red and white balloons on as many of the overhanging branches as we could reach. I kept the maze off-limits because Jerardo hadn't got rid of the hornets' nest yet, and we laid out coffee, iced lemonade and cakes on a trestle table, setting up games on the lawn.

I had removed the two plasters from my fingers. The cuts had not been deep, and had healed invisibly. Bobbie's friends arrived bearing presents, accompanied by their mothers. It seemed that the husbands of Gaucia were in short supply when it came to children's parties. Celestia turned up bearing the largest bottle of gin anyone had ever seen. Jordi looked in with a book of poetry wrapped in gold foil. Few of the mothers spoke any English, so they sat smiling indulgently at me as we cut cake and played Blind Man's Bluff.

I was determined to keep the children occupied. Bobbie and I had written out a timetable of races – egg and spoon, sack, three-legged – funny old games we had culled from an ancient set of English children's encyclopaedias in the attic, and a host of puzzles and catching games that seemed to delight the children. I imagined my great-grandmother must have once hosted similar parties, and the thought was comforting. One girl called Liana wore an elaborately frilly purple polka-dotted dress complete with a little *mantilla*, and seemed determined to beat Bobbie in every game. Soon the air of playful competition started to developed a mean edge.

The mothers sat in lawn chairs facing away from the house, looking down to the magnificent garden. They knew Jerardo but were loathe to compliment him for his handiwork; the old stories had left deep scars. Rosita served drinks and spoke only in Spanish, excluding me from the conversation.

We were lining up the children for a balloon-passing game when one mother called out 'Liana?' Everyone looked around, but she was nowhere in sight. It seemed we were missing one precocious little girl.

'Perhaps she's gone to the loo,' said Celestia, disrespectfully flicking her cigarillo stub into the flowerbed. 'Do you want me to go and look?'

'No, it's all right, you stay there. Tell her mother to search the garden.' I went inside and walked to the foot of the stairs, listening. But for the clocks, the house was silent. Everyone else was outside. Rosita was still sitting with the other ladies.

'Liana?' I called. There was only ticking. 'Liana?' I waited, my head cocked on one side, listening carefully. There was something like the scuff of a shoe, a drag, then a thump.

I opened the door to the drawing room but found it empty. 'Liana?' I listened again.

There came a sudden thin, terrible scream of pain from behind the connecting door in the kitchen. I tried the handle but knew it was locked. I ran upstairs to get the keys, and as I passed the staircase window overlooking the lawn I saw Rosita and Liana's mother heading for the house.

Grabbing the keyring from its hiding place in my sweater

drawer, I took the stairs two at a time back down, just as the women entered the reception hall.

'It's all right, I've got them.' I held up the keys to Rosita, hoping that she wouldn't realise I had brought them from upstairs.

'Please, give them to me,' said Rosita as we headed for the kitchen.

'No, I know which one it is.' I found the key quickly and stood before the door, twisting it in the lock. Liana's mother was calling to her. The terrified girl was crying steadily now, a thin continuous wail of distress.

As the door creaked open she fell out into our arms. The hem of her frilly dress was torn and there was a vivid red scratch up her leg that had bloodied her white stocking. Some drops of blood had dripped onto her white shoes, too, staining them scarlet. The girl cried to her mother, speaking rapidly in Spanish, and pushed her way outside.

Her mother turned angrily to me. 'She says she got lost coming back from the toilet, that something grabbed at her and tried to hurt her. She says *the other people in the house* tried to hurt her.' She ran on to look after her little darling.

Rosita touched my arm. 'The doors were locked, weren't they?' she asked. 'Senora Torres, the doors *were* locked.'

'Of course they were,' I cried, confused. 'She's lying. She had to have got in some other way.'

Rosita looked me in the eye. 'Do you want to go out there and tell her mother that little Liana is lying?'

'No, of course not, but it's just not possible that she got in through the door. You saw me – I had to unlock it! We should go and see how she is.'

The mothers made a big fuss of the girl, changing her white stockings for a fresh pair. The scratch on her leg was not deep, but it ran raggedly from her ankle to her thigh and looked much nastier than it was, especially to a little girl as vain and imperious as Liana. After it had been bathed we gave her extra cake and lemonade, and soon the child was playing with the others again at the bottom of the garden, but the mood had altered. She was using her ordeal to exercise control over the other children.

'Don't worry about it, darling,' said Celestia, trying to comfort me. 'The mothers around here have nothing else to do but dote too much on their children. If you ask me, she got lost and snagged those ridiculous clothes of hers on one of your more baroque pieces of furniture.'

'But I don't know how she got into the back of the house. We keep the servants' quarters locked.'

'Then let's have a look.' Celestia rose to her full imposing height and walked around the house, searching for the room's corresponding window. 'What's this?' she said, waving her cigarillo in the direction of a small grey wooden panel set beneath the window, half-hidden behind the flowering border. I had never noticed it before. Squatting before it, I pushed at the board and found that it swung inwards. 'A dog-flap,' I said, surprised.

'You see, darling, there's an explanation for everything. She wriggled inside, it was dark, she got caught up on something with a sharp edge and couldn't find her way back out. Let's go and repair the damage, otherwise the fair ladies of Gaucia will turn this into a drama they can feed on for months to come. And whatever you do, stop apologising. It makes you too English.'

We rejoined the group, but something had changed now. Liana was still limping in an exaggerated fashion, and dropped out of the games with a dramatic wince of pain, clearly enjoying the experience of having pulled the attention away from the birthday girl to herself. The party broke up soon afterwards.

'They'll never come back,' I said miserably. 'I know it. They'll think the house is cursed or something.'

'Nonsense,' said Celestia. 'But they might use it as an excuse if you upset them in the future. That's the way it works around here. All information is put to work. They have long memories when it comes to storing knowledge they can use. But that can sometimes work in your favour, too. Come on, let's show them we're made of stronger stuff. Let's have a drink.'

After everyone had left, including Celestia, who cadged a lift with the last of the mothers, being too tipsy to drive herself, Rosita and I tidied up the garden in the dying light.

'Did you explain to them about the dog-flap?' I asked, stacking up the paper cups.

Rosita's face was grim. 'Yes, but they did not believe me.'

'Why ever not?'

'They don't like the house. The Condemaine family – it goes back a long way.'

'Let me guess. The civil war.'

'Yes. The last members of the family, and some of the families in the village – well, they took different sides.'

'Even now, in the twenty-first century – it's ridiculous that they should remember such things.'

'Perhaps to you. But for many people in this region it was a matter of life and death. People were lost, many were betrayed. It changed everything.' It seemed a glass of sherry had loosened Rosita's tongue. As she rose with an armful of streamers and paper plates she asked, 'Senora Torres, are you sure the doors were locked?'

'Of course I'm sure – why?

'Come, I will show you.'

She led the way back to the window. Setting the party paraphernalia down, she lowered herself onto her knees on the path. 'Look.' She reached behind the plants and pushed at the wooden flap, stretching in as far as she could, knocking on something. 'The last owner had a dog, but when it died Jerardo bricked up the inside to try and stop the rats from getting in. He never got round to removing the flap at the front.'

'So Liana couldn't have got into the back of the house this way.'

'Not, it's not possible.'

'But all four of the doors were locked,' I said. 'I know because I tested them all before the party started. Somebody must have opened one from the inside.'

'There was nobody inside,' said Rosita firmly.

I looked back at the shuttered window just as a cloud dimmed the sun, and a chill traced its path across my neck and shoulders.

CHAPTER FIFTEEN

The Owner

THE MORE I drew the house, the less I understood about it.

The inked ground-floor blueprints were now almost complete, and I was working on a range of accompanying sketches. Mateo had provided me with a full set of diagrams for the telescope mechanics, but they looked wrong somehow, as if the equipment had been constructed for another use. For a start, there was no traditional eyepiece at its base, or any kind of step for the viewer to stand on.

The answer to one question continued to elude me. Why did Francesco Condemaine feel the need to sink his fortune into a building so clearly unsuited to the location? If he had designed it purely as an observatory, the telescope could have been placed within an astrolabe and turned according to the alignment of the planets. I felt sure he had created the structure for another reason, one that had to do with the darkened rooms.

I found a photograph online of a formally-dressed, stiff-necked young man, more Spanish than English, standing behind his wife, who was seated with her hands folded in her lap. In those days the sitters had their necks placed in braces to keep them still for the camera's slow exposure, and you could just see the clips holding Senora Condemaine's head in place. What was unusual about the photograph was that both she and her husband were smiling. Usually in pictures of this age everyone looked awkward and stone-faced.

On the following Tuesday, when Mateo was back from his Paris trip and was able to look after Bobbie, I returned to the shadowy little library at Gaucia. Once again, Jordi climbed the wavering wooden stepladder to help me find folders related to the observatory.

'I wish you could have spent more time at the party,' I said.

'I wanted to.' He removed some catalogues from the upper shelf. 'Saturday is really the only day I'm busy here.'

'Did anybody said anything about it to you?' I asked, trying to sound casual.

'You shouldn't worry about things like that,' he replied, stacking the catalogues so that he could reach the volumes behind.

'So they have. What did they say?'

'If I tell you, you have to take it as a joke.'

'Okay, hit me.'

'They think it has *una maldicion*. You know, a curse.'

'Oh my God.'

'But you shouldn't worry. Everything here either has a curse or a blessing on it. They may all have smartphones and flat-screen TVs but some part of them still checks the weather for signs and omens. You should see the stampede for lottery tickets when word gets out that there's a special lucky number for the week. And when a blackbird lands on a chimney – obviously that's a sign of death.' He shoved the catalogues back. 'Well, there's nothing more here.'

'What about in the annexe?'

'Possibly. When the owner of a house dies, it's common for the surviving members of his family to add a little history in the form of a bequest of private papers. People like to be remembered. I could go and take a look tomorrow – I can't leave the library today.'

'Could I have a look?'

'I suppose so. You just need the key, but I can't tell you where anything is. It's the old white barn next to the ruins of the convent. It'll take you a while to go through it all.'

'I have nowhere else to look, Jordi. Let me at least try.'

He handed me the key and I made my way over there.

The last of the nuns had died of disappointment in 1983 and the Santa Maria convent finally fell down. The man who had robbed Celestia's house was the town's builder, and instead of removing the rubble he just painted it white. Poppies and lavender grew up between the rocks, and myrtle and wisteria and big green bushes with thick dark leaves that nobody knew the name of.

I managed to open the lock on the front door, but Jordi had forgotten to warn me that there were no windows or working lights inside, and I found myself unable to step into such complete darkness. After hovering at the threshold for a few minutes I was forced to give up, and relocked the door. When I returned the key, Jordi promised that he would take a look for me, if I could leave him a list of the things I was searching for.

The diurnal shadows slid over the village like ghosts fleeing the heat. I had promised to call Mateo when I needed a lift back to the house, but decided not to bother him just yet. It upset me that the mothers of Gaucia were making up stories about Hyperion House, and I wondered how I could make amends. I headed to the town square and asked Celestia what she would do. My friend was sitting in her usual place at the café table beneath a stratocumulus of smoke, silent and thoughtful. She considered the problem for a moment.

Finally, she tapped her cigarillo and said, 'I think we need to ask Maria Gonzales what to do.'

Maria Gonzales was about a thousand years old and knew everything. She ran a strange, dusty shop that sold organic honey, dried shrimps, wind chimes, homeopathic medicines and shawls, but at the back there was an internet café of sorts comprising three ancient Dell computers and a table covered with out-of-date alternative healthcare magazines.

Apparently she and Celestia held village meetings that started with coffee and glasses of Oloroso and ended up encompassing most of the older ladies. Given that they spent the whole of the afternoon there and the Oloroso was 22% alcohol, it was a wonder they managed to walk home without falling into bushes or getting run over.

The meeting began in earnest, conducted in a strange, disjointed tangle of Spanish and English, with introductions made and glasses raised. Finally it was decided that there would be a dinner on the evening of a Saint's day, and as there were plenty of those they would be able to pick a date that was suitable for everyone. Mateo, Bobbie and I would all be invited. It would help to put the party behind us, and replace the stupid notion of the curse with a happier memory of a fine evening. There would be drinking and dancing, and the children would throw fireworks at one another and frighten all the babies, and hopefully everyone would have a good time without getting their fingers blown off.

Feeling slightly the worse for wear I called Mateo, who drove into town and collected me. We were just driving off through the hot white streets when I glanced in the rear-view mirror and saw an extraordinary sight. Running towards us, her black skirts, raggedy yellow cardigan and necklaces flapping, was Maria Gonzales.

'*Parada!*' she shouted, dashing after the BMW and actually running alongside it. Maria threw me a package as if passing a rugby ball – she had a strong arm on her for an old lady – and I caught it, thanking her.

The incident stuck in my mind later because it was the most energetic thing that had happened in the village since we had arrived. Presumably Maria Gonzales returned to her shop to sit in the cool gloom among the pots of organic tomato marmalade and string sweaters, her energy spent.

I sat with the packet on my lap.

'Well, what is it?' asked Mateo.

'I need scissors,' I said. 'It can wait until I get back.' But there was a part of me that did not want to share whatever was inside the packet with my new husband. I didn't want him to think that I was turning into one of those village wives.

When I arrived home, I went into the drawing room and tried to open the parcel, a thick rectangle of brown paper knotted with proper unbreakable string. And having finally got it open, I found myself in possession of something entirely unexpected.

The set of smudgily photocopied newssheets had been printed out in English for the ex-pat community in the region. Titled 'The Anglo-Andalucian', each one no more than four pages held together by a single staple, the first was dated May 2004, and the last dated to the August of the previous year.

It was thoughtful of Maria to give them to me, but I didn't really want to read a newspaper where world events had secondary importance to the details of wine-tasting nights, fiesta preparations and problems with parking spaces. After idly flicking through them for a few minutes, I was about to put them in the bin when an item in the Obituaries column caught my eye.

> 'Sr Amancio Lueches was taken from Hyperion House, his private residence just outside of Gaucia, to Estepona's Santa Theresa hospital. He was suffering from dehydration and malnourishment, but the doctors were unable to save him. He is the last remaining member of the respected family who had owned the former observatory for almost a century.'

I looked to see if there was anything else, but no luck. The piece was three years old. With the freesheet in my hand, I went to find the housekeeper. 'Rosita, did Senor Lueches become sick here in the house?'

Rosita was vacuuming the stairs, and in no mood to be interrupted. 'Yes, as did many other members of the family. The nearest hospital is far away. People prefer to be in their own homes when they grow old.'

'Well, I wish you'd told me. What happened to him?'

'I don't know. I was on my annual holiday, visiting my sister in Valencia. Senor Lueches was very elderly, but he was perfectly capable of looking after himself. He did not want to live any longer. He stopped eating and drinking. All of the food I had left for him was untouched.'

'You must have felt terrible when you came back and found him in such a state.'

Rosita looked at me in surprise, as though the idea that I cared had never occurred to her. 'He'd had a long and happy life. He loved this house, all of the family did. He'd hardly ever had a day's ill-health. But he had lost his wife, and missed her terribly. Sometimes an elderly person can sense the shadows gathering. Who would not want to leave, knowing the time was right? He went to the hospital but they could not save him. It was what he chose for himself.'

'But this was *three years* ago. What did you do?' I asked.

'My arrangement is with the house. Jerardo and I are paid in perpetuity by the estate.'

'So you stayed on, even though there was no-one to look after.'

'I look after the house, not the owners,' said Rosita. 'The house does that.'

CHAPTER SIXTEEN

The Nest

I RETURNED TO the drawing room and scanned through the rest of the newssheets. There was one other noteworthy item, a column entitled 'Places Of Interest', which gave a capsule description of the Hyperion Observatory, noting that it was privately owned and not open to the public.

> 'The house owes its unusual symmetrical shape to the fact that it was once an observatory. Its architect, Francesco Condemaine, picked this sunny, peaceful spot with clear skies for his fragile wife, Elena, because she suffered from a fear of the dark, and in this lovely spot the moon is famous for its brightness. It was said that he so loved her that he wrote her a letter every single day of their lives together.'

'Don't you see?' I told Mateo later that evening as we sat with Bobbie having our meal. 'It explains everything. He loved her so much that he built a place where she could live in permanent light. He put in all the clocks so that the servants could make sure she never had to suffer from her phobia.'

Mateo put down his fork and smiled gently at me.

'You knew,' I said, thunderstruck.

'Of course I knew. Why do you think I wanted you to see it? It was me who pointed it out to you on the website, remember? A friend of mine in Malaga heard it had come on the market.'

'I'm very touched.' I turned to Bobbie. 'Your father is a very kind man.'

'I know,' said Bobbie. 'He once let me have so much ice cream I was sick on the way home.'

'If you want to get some now, it's in the freezer,' I told her. 'Tomato and basil, or black cherry. But not too much.'

'Do you know how proud you make me feel?' said Mateo once Bobbie had run off to the kitchen. 'I know things weren't easy for you before we met. I wanted to give you the life you deserve, a truly happy one, just like Senor Condemaine did for his wife. Seeing you and Bobbie together just makes me feel surer than ever that I did the right thing.'

It was ridiculous, but I found myself close to tears. 'There was a time when I thought I didn't want to live,' I admitted. 'I'm so grateful you found me.'

'You don't have to be grateful. I'll never let anything bad happen to you, I swear.' He cupped my chin in his hand and kissed me tenderly. The clocks had begun to chime. The sun was setting behind the trees, and the last of the golden light was being exchanged for the soft glow of the dining room lamps. We played games late into the night, the three of us.

The next morning, Mateo went to Jerez for a meeting. He promised he would be back in time for us to spend the weekend together as a family, and I made a note of his return on my phone.

Meanwhile, I continued to be fascinated by the way the light fell throughout the observatory and its grounds, with each area perfectly divided by shadow and light. The mirrors, the windows, everything was positioned exactly so that the sun would find its way into the remotest corners. The only vaguely similar building I had ever visited was the Sir John Soane Museum in London, where mirrors and windows could be pivoted to send daylight in all directions. It seemed that the sundial statue in the centre of the lawn had been constructed on the same principle as the house, as it seemed to point into the sunlit drawing room.

Late on Friday afternoon I took a break from work and went into the garden to find a lounger and read an architectural digest for a while. Bobbie was upstairs with her tutor, taking lessons in Greek mythology and Spanish history. Rosita was tackling the laundry, a task she grimly performed using the hardest and most complicated methods imaginable, with a heavy, heatable iron and a tub of boiling starch. I assumed that Jerardo, never easily found at the best of times, had gone into the village to drink with his cronies.

I heard cicadas and drowsed in the late summer warmth, and when the architectural book slid from my knees I didn't try to catch it. My limbs felt heavy with the heat, and time passed. The sun lowered itself to the edge of the mountains. The shadows began to creep across the lawn.

Something woke me – the crack of a twig, a sudden rustle in the bushes. I blinked and sat up, trying to focus. I'd had a little too much sun; my face felt hot and tight. It took a few moments to unblur my eyes and focus. I could hear buzzing.

I turned around in time to see a black mass of hornets swarming overhead and passing into the maze-house like an airborne ink-blot. Jerardo had failed to get rid of the great papery grey nest, and I had forgotten to chase him up.

I found the gardener in his shed, reeking of alcohol. 'Jerardo, you have to get rid of that thing,' I instructed. 'Do it now, while Mr Torres is still away. I'll go into the house and make sure all the windows are shut. I see you're burning leaves at the end of the drive, put it on that.'

I went into the house and warned Rosita, Bobbie and Julieta to stay inside until I gave them the all-clear, then watched as Jerardo donned a beekeeper's hat and gloves, and went off into the maze house.

He emerged carrying a nest that was almost as tall as he was, with a massive angry cloud of hornets around him. I knew that although it was huge it weighed almost nothing, and without it, the hornets would build another somewhere else.

Jerardo carried it to the fire and set it onto the burning leaves. The smoke only served to enrage the hornets more, and I realised that I should have had him spray the nest first, but I'd been so annoyed that I just wanted the job done.

The insects rose and fell back in a furious drone that was so loud I could hear it through the closed windows. Even Jerardo had beat a hasty retreat and returned to his shed, pursued by a few of them.

The great grey globe quickly caught alight, and the hornets went into a frenzy. Looking through the smoke and flames, I was horrified to see the BMW approaching. The door opened and a figure made its way up the drive. Mateo was home early. He always left his schedule in the shared diary. I realised I couldn't have put the right return date in my phone.

He reached the top of the path and cut around the edge of the house toward me, fingers of shadow touching him from the trees. He was wearing his sharp blue business suit and blue tie, his black hair slicked back to reveal a trace of grey at the sides. He smiled. If he'd noticed the burning nest just a dozen yards away, he didn't appeared worried. Then I realised why; he couldn't see it from where he was, and was about to step into its path.

I ran to the window and knocked loudly on it, feeling something move, a faint and distant juddering beneath my feet, like a mild electric shock. I immediately thought; *earthquake*. I'd read up on stuff like that; there were a great number of minor earth tremors recorded in Andalucia every year. Through the glass, Mateo looked as alarmed as I did. He was almost on top of the bonfire now, which was just behind the hedge he was about to pass.

I tore open the catch on the window and yelled. 'Mateo, go back and stay in the car – there's –'

He heard me and looked up. I saw his head tilt – he hadn't shaved – his caramel eyes rolling up to spot somewhere above us. I followed his gaze. An immense cloud of frenzied hornets had risen from the nest and now dropped to envelop him.

Everything seemed to happen in slow motion. I ran out into the hall, heading for the front door, and pulled it open. The top half of Mateo's body was completely obscured by black carapaces, legs, wings. The drone was deafening. There was nothing I could do; if I went any closer to help him, they would attack me.

Mateo took a few paces toward me, and suddenly dropped onto the path so heavily that I heard his knees crack. It was as if someone had kicked him in the backs of his legs.

I couldn't let him suffer like that. I began running toward him. He lay still on the amber sand of the pathway, the hornets scribbling an angry cloud across his hands and face. As I dashed forward they suddenly cleared and lifted, dispersing into the sky, heading away from the bonfire smoke and off the property.

I reached him and turned him over. There were still at least twenty hornets swarming and crawling over his face. One was struggling to pull itself free from his left eye. I slapped it away, leaving its venom-filled amber spike half inside his pupil. Others were crawling out of his mouth, having stung his tongue and gums. There were hornets in his nostrils and ears. I knew they had the ability to sting many times over, and as I beat them aside one buried its stinger into the back of my hand. Mateo's face had already turned black. Crimson welts were rising on his throat and neck. He was no longer breathing. The poison had closed his air passages.

I pulled his tie loose and ripped open his white shirt, trying to give him air. His right shoe suddenly drummed against the sand, the sound loud and shocking, then stopped. I knew enough to recognise that he was in respiratory arrest, and would most likely be suffering a cardiac seizure. I interlocked my hands flat on his chest, over the lower part of his sternum, and pressed in a pumping motion. When this had no effect I tried artificial respiration, but first I had to remove dead insects from his mouth.

In between these frantic actions I called out for help, but I remembered that the windows were all shut fast, and that it was unlikely anyone would hear me.

Hyperion House, where nothing bad could ever happen, had shut out my cries of terror.

CHAPTER SEVENTEEN

The Return

LATER IT WAS hard to recall the precise order of events. I'd read that it was best to perform artificial respiration and CPR at the same time, but to do that there needed to be two of you. There was nothing more I could possibly do for Mateo by myself. His eyes were swollen with poison, his head thrown back, mouth wide.

Climbing tipsily to my feet I lurched away. The last of the hornets left Mateo's body and drifted off into the sky. A few lay crushed on the path. The garden was completely silent for a few moments, as if we were sealed inside a bubble. Then the birds returned and started chirruping again.

I ran inside, looking for Rosita. The ground fled from beneath my feet. I think I fell once or twice. I searched room after room in increasing confusion, calling out, but the vacuum's whine was coming from somewhere upstairs, drowning my cries. I crashed into the large dresser at the entrance to the kitchen, dislodging plates, then turned and followed the sound, running along the passage.

Upstairs I found the vacuum cleaner still on, its hose lying dropped on the rug, but no sign of Rosita – somehow we had missed each other in the labyrinthine house.

A pounding dizziness settled over me and I fell back hard against the wall, sinking down to the floor. The sinus pain punched hard, blinding me, a deafening high-pitched whine resounding in my ears until I could neither see nor hear. Quite how long I remained like this was hard to tell, but when it finally subsided I was able to rise and find my way unsteadily to the top of the staircase. I took the steps carefully, gripping the bannister until I reached the ground, then ran straight into the arms of a dark figure blocking the hall.

As I twisted and turned, shouting and trying to break free, I realised who was holding my arms.

'What's the matter?' Mateo asked, alarmed. He was still dressed in his blue business suit and tie, and smelled of airline air. His hands gripped me gently but firmly. 'Breathe – take a breath.'

Unable to speak, I seized his wrist and pulled him back toward the entrance of the house, out onto the drive, virtually dragging him to the path. I pointed down, unable to look.

When I did, I found the sand clean and dry and unmarked. There was no body. There weren't even any crushed insects.

I hauled him with me to the bonfire, where the remains of the empty hornets' nest still lay smouldering among the interlaced branches and dead leaves. 'I asked Jerardo to burn the nest while you were away,' I said. 'I put your return time in my phone calendar but I got it wrong. I saw you – there was an earth tremor, and the ground shifted. The hornets went crazy –'

'I just got here,' said Mateo, confused. 'I was going to call from the airport but – what's going on?'

Tearing myself free, I kicked at the sand in fury, then turned on him. 'I'm not crazy, I wasn't dreaming, I saw you die, Mateo! Right here!'

He looked puzzled. 'Where were you?'

'I was in the sun-lounger reading.'

Mateo went back to the chair and bent down, picking up my architectural digest. 'Your book's on the floor. Did you fall asleep?'

'No, yes – I don't know – I must have done.'

'And you had a bad dream.'

'No, I got stung, look –' I turned over my right hand and showed him the crimson bump of the hornet's sting.

'You should put something on that,' he said. 'But listen, Bobbie and Julieta – wouldn't they have come running if there had been an earth tremor?'

I pushed past him and ran back inside, shouting. 'Bobbie, come down here!'

Bobbie appeared at the top of the stairs with a pen in her hand. 'Daddy, you're back early.' She ran down and hugged him. 'Do I get a present?'

'Airport gift only, I'm afraid,' said Mateo. 'It's in my carry-on.'

I knelt beside Bobbie. 'Did you hear anything?'

'When?'

'Just now – a minute ago.'

'No. We were doing Myths of Ancient Greece, and Julieta is letting me paint a picture. Do you want to come and see?'

'In a minute.' I looked up at Mateo beseechingly. 'I'm sorry, I don't know what could have happened. I'm sure I was awake –'

'You may well have been,' Mateo agreed. 'The sun plays tricks. Maybe you had a little heat-stroke and dreamed you were awake. What do they call that thing, where you become aware that you're having a dream and you can change the outcome?'

'Lucid dreaming,' I muttered, pressing the heel of my palm against my forehead.

'Right. There's your answer. The hornet stung you and you had a nightmare.'

'But I saw it all so clearly –'

'My flight got in a bit early, I thought you'd be pleased to see me.'

'I am, I just –'

'I haven't eaten anything. I'm starving.'

'Rosita will – I just have to –' I had seen him die, and he was talking about eating. I turned and fled off into the garden. I found Jerardo, and he mimed an explanation of carrying out my wishes with the nest.

Everything was as it should have been, as it had always been.

CHAPTER EIGHTEEN

The Doctor

'PUT OUT YOUR tongue please.' Dr Javier Areces stared at it impassively. 'Lovely, nice and pink. It's a good indicator of your immune system. There doesn't seem to be much wrong with you.' In the waiting room of his Estepona office the usual assortment of tourists fidgeted. They'd come off motor-scooters, landed badly in swimming pools or had fallen asleep in the sun.

I told him, 'I haven't been sleeping very well.'

'Do you keep regular hours?'

'Yes. My husband's often away on business. I have trouble getting to sleep when he's not there. I wake up at dawn every day.'

Areces took a penlight from his top pocket and shone it first into my left eye, then my right. I had taken a taxi to the hospital without telling Mateo the real reason for my visit. I'd told him I was getting some mild sleeping tablets. I didn't want him to worry.

'Are you sensitive to strong sunlight? You know the light is very different here.'

'I don't know. Maybe.'

'Sunshine affects the brain by interacting with melatonin and serotonin,' said Areces. 'When sunlight hits your eyes, your optic nerve sends a message to reduce the production of melatonin, the hormone that helps you sleep. It raises the level of secretion when the sun sets. The opposite happens with serotonin, the so-called happy chemical; when you're exposed to sun, your brain increases it. And when the sun's ultraviolet rays touch your skin, your body produces vitamin D, which helps you maintain the serotonin level so that we slow down and sleep during the dark hours, and stay up during the day. This is called the human circadian rhythm.'

'Yeah, well something's messing with my circadian rhythm.'

'You're probably just having trouble adjusting to life in such a bright landscape. It upsets a lot of ex-pats.'

I had never thought of myself as an ex-pat. And I hated Dr Areces' condescending attitude. I had come out here to be with Mateo, not for any other reason.

'I sometimes have a problem with the dark,' I said. 'I don't always feel comfortable in it.'

'Does it frighten you?'

'I was diagnosed with nyctophobia when I was fifteen.' *Just like Elena Condemaine,* I thought.

'Oh, that doesn't really mean anything,' said Areces airily. 'Most phobias are irrational, but fear of the dark is quite understandable, especially in a place where the light and dark contrast so strongly. It's probably exacerbated by your disruptive sleep patterns. You know, we really don't need to sleep for eight hours at a single time. You can split the sleeping part of your schedule into two halves each consisting of four hours and you'll feel just as good, if not better, because the first hours of sleep are the deepest. That's why we take siestas. You need to give it some time, make sure you wear yourself out during the day. Don't just sit around. What did you do in London?'

'I was working in an architectural practice.'

'And here?'

'I'm trying to research a book, and looking after my husband's daughter – and the house.'

'So you're not commuting anymore, you don't have the camaraderie of the workplace, life has suddenly slowed down a bit for you, I expect.'

'I suppose it has.'

'Physical work is good – and you should get some regular exercise at set hours.'

I looked around the dazzling white office. Most Spanish hospitals were having a really hard time. Areces was Mateo's doctor and had a private practice, and it showed. 'I've had lucid dreams,' I told him, 'well, thinking I'm awake when I'm still asleep. Hallucinations.'

'Hm – any accompanying headache?'

'Yes, a bit, like neuralgia.'

'Buzzing in the ears?'

'Yes.'

'It sounds to me like it's all part of the same problem. I imagine there's nothing much to worry about, but I'd like you to monitor it for a while and make a note of the time, intensity and duration of the sensation if it returns. As for your fear of the dark, you're lucky – it's one of the few phobias that can be confronted and got rid of. And get on with that book of yours. Talk to people. Busy minds need to be filled.'

I knew how doctors worked. I could hear his tone lightening with deceptive casualness. He turned over my hand. 'You've been stung. The cuts – they've been there a long time?' He had spotted the scars on my arms.

'Since I was fifteen.'

'Well, perhaps when you have time, you can provide me with a few more details on your medical history. Were you hospitalised?'

'A couple of times, yes. Overdoses.'

'Trouble at home, I expect.'

I decided, with a sigh, to get at least part of the thing out. 'I went through a difficult time with my folks. My mother tried to have me sectioned. My parents had been talking about divorcing for a number of years, and I wanted to go with my father, but we fell out. Then I was stuck with my mother, and she had always hated me for coming along and messing up her career – her words, not mine. My father died of lung cancer when I was seventeen, and two years later I got pregnant.'

'Did you have an abortion?'

'Yes. I was studying to become an architect at the time. I haven't told my husband.'

'Why is that?'

'Well what do you think?'

'Because he's Catholic.'

'That's right.'

'Well, I've heard much worse. And it's good to know these things,' Areces kept the same casual tone, making neat little notes in his folder. 'I'm going to write you out a prescription for a light sedative. I don't think we need to do anything further for the moment, but check back with me if you have any more of these – interludes. If they get worse we may have to take some kind of precautionary measure.'

As I headed across the sunbaked tarmac to the bus-stop I decided that Dr Javier Areces was nice but useless, and I wouldn't be seeing him again. Mateo was back at the house because Julieta was off today, and someone needed to stay with Bobbie. Besides, if I'd told him he would have insisted on coming in with me, and I was determined never to let him find out about my past. He didn't go to church regularly, but he'd told me he sometimes took confession in Gaucia. I'd never been with him, and he had never asked me. I thought it was likely that he would never have married me if he'd known about the abortion.

When I arrived back, I found Bobbie and Mateo in the kitchen in matching aprons, helping a clearly irritated Rosita to make a fish stew. 'We're doing your dinner,' said Bobbie excitedly. 'We're making *mantecados* next!'

'We may not have enough anise,' Mateo warned, guiding his daughter's hands. 'We'll have to find a substitute. How did you get on, darling?'

'He's given me some very mild pills,' I said. 'He says I'm adjusting to my new environment and that it'll soon pass.'

'Well, that's a relief. You look a little tired. So it was nothing to worry about, was it? Why don't you take a nap, and we'll call you when dinner's ready.'

Mateo was right. I suddenly felt profoundly exhausted, and slumped into one of the big chairs in the atrium to rest for a few minutes. It was a beautiful day. All the doors and windows were open. I could hear birds twittering in the garden, and Bobbie and Mateo laughing in the kitchen, occasionally scolded by Rosita. All was right with the world.

But I also knew that in the dark half of the house, something was alive.

CHAPTER NINETEEN

The Presence

'I HAVE SOMETHING new for you,' said Jordi, dropping to his haunches and pulling out a red leather book from beneath his desk. As usual, the Gaucia library was cool and deserted, but for a stack of rainbow-coloured plastic toys and playbooks where the local children's group had met. 'I had a look in the annexe for you and found this. I think it was published by Senor Condemaine's cousin, the one who inherited your house.' He slid the slim softcover volume across the desk to me.

I found myself looking at a monograph published by Marcos Condemaine in 1926. It looked as if it had never been opened. Inside were elevations of the house and a small photograph of its telescope system. I could see from just a glance that it wasn't a telescope at all, just something that roughly conformed to the shape and size of one.

'Could I take this away with me?' I asked.

'Please, be my guest, it's not even registered in the library index. I don't think anyone ever got around to filing it. Take it for as long as you wish. Hell, keep it, it probably came from Hyperion House in the first place. You're the only one it would mean anything to.'

'I wonder why the cousin inherited.'

'I'm sorry?'

'Elena Condemaine had three children. Surely one of them should have inherited the house when they came of age.'

'Perhaps they were moved away when their mother was committed.'

'I suppose you're right.' I turned to the back section of the monograph. 'There's a piece missing, look.' I held up the folder for him to see. Part of the binding was bare. The pages that had occupied it had either fallen out or had been ripped out. The previous page was headed: *The Birth of the Hyperion Society.*

'Jordi, do me a favour and keep an eye out for some pages on the Hyperion Society, would you?'

'Sure, I'll have another look,' Jordi promised. 'The missing bit's probably dropped down the back of the shelves.'

I walked through the town square and found Celestia in her usual position, poring over the faded pages of old newspapers with a large red wine beside her on the sun-dappled table, a cigarillo balanced lightly between her fingers. There was a wonderful smelling of frying prawns coming from one of the nearby houses.

'My dear, you're almost a stranger these days,' she complained. 'Do come and sit. You missed the meeting about arrangements for the fiesta. The ladies were terribly disappointed.'

'I'm sorry,' I said, 'I've been busy with the house. It takes up a lot of my time.'

She peered at me suspiciously. 'Are you quite all right? You look rather worn out today.'

'I haven't been sleeping very well.' I accepted a glass of wine and took a sip. 'But I'm getting on with things. I went to see Jordi. He's been finding me documents about the house for my project.' I showed Celestia the folder. Today the café tables were being served by a chaotic, rather plain young girl called Lola. As she was clearing the next table she peered between our shoulders at the pictures of Hyperion House.

'*Ay, es malo*,' she said, shaking her head with a grimace. 'You are the one from London, yes?'

'I come from London, yes,' I told the waitress, who looked vaguely horrified.

'London where they all run around going buzz buzz, like bees?'

'Yes but we live here now,' I explained. 'You know this place?' I showed the waitress a picture of the house.

Lola squinted at the picture – she was supposed to wear glasses but apparently made more tips when she left them off. '*Si*, I know this from my grandmother,' she said, tapping the picture with a crimson nail. 'Very bad things there.'

'Oh, for God's sake don't take any notice of her,' Celestia warned. 'She thinks there are bad things everywhere. Crossing herself and knocking out the Hail Marys every five minutes, this one. Somebody backed their truck into Maria Gonzales' shop the other day, bashing a hole right through to the organic jams. Lola was down there in a trice sprinkling holy water all over the place, weren't you love?'

'*No entiendo,*' said Lola.

'Yes, she doesn't *entiendo* when it suits her,' said Celestia drily.

'Why does she think the house is bad?' I asked, waiting while Celestia translated in loud, terrible Spanish and listened to the answer.

'She says dead people live there. What she means is that the house is over fifty years old and therefore must be haunted. I'm afraid she's a bit simple.' She mouthed this last word at me rather than saying it aloud. 'Don't let her bother you.'

'Maybe she's right,' I said without thinking. 'Several times I've gone up to my bedroom and found a small crucifix under my pillow. I put it back on the wall, and a few days later it reappears in the bed. And there have been – events. Things I can't explain.'

'Really? How mysterious! Don't tell me you believe in haunted houses.'

'No, of course not. But sometimes I'm sure I can feel the presence of the old owners.'

'I suppose that's bound to happen a little – after all, you're living amongst all their old furniture. Can't you refurbish and make the place your own?'

'Mateo likes the way it looks,' I told her, 'and to be honest I do too. But sometimes I feel as if they're there in the other part of the house, just beyond the edge of my sight. I see – things.'

'What sort of things?'

'Movement. Shadows – I don't know. You know how you can sense someone's presence in a room even when you can't see them.'

'For Heaven's sake don't tell Maria, she'll be getting the priests out to exorcise the place.'

I checked my watch. 'Speaking of which, I have to get back in a minute,' I said. 'I got a lift into town with Rosita and her priest. He must think God has higher plans for her, because he picks her up whenever she asks him. She should have finished by now.'

'Oh, just as it was getting interesting. You are happy up there, aren't you?'

'Yes, very much so. It's a bit cut off, and I do miss the city. I Skype my friends in London and they're all jealous of me. They complain about the lousy weather and their long working hours and say I'm so lucky. But on some days I wish I could change places with them, just for an hour or so. I'm sorry, I shouldn't have told you.'

'Don't be silly, you mustn't let things get on top of you. You really have to learn to drive, you know. Then at least you'll be able to go down to the coast occasionally.'

'I know, and I haven't learned to speak much Spanish, either, but I'll get around to doing both soon, I promise.'

'Good, then you'll be able to drive into Gaucia and keep the ex-pats from sending me mad,' Celestia said. 'They come around to my living room to watch the highlights of the cricket, because I'm the only one with an illegal Sky box, but last time, just as everyone sat themselves around the television – *poof* – the signal vanished. And *this* one –' she jerked her thumb back at Lola, '– said the Devil had taken the picture away. It turned out that the man who once robbed my house had chosen that particular moment to swipe my satellite dish, so we all got drunk on Manzanilla and Sprite instead. Then I went next door and took it back. He's a rogue but I do rather love him.'

When I returned to the house, Rosita went off to start preparing the evening menu, and Bobbie went to the atrium with Julieta to write an essay about flowers. Mateo was working in one of the top floor rooms, where he kept the company's accounts. After every trip he needed to log his expenses and update the order files. Everything in the house was calm and orderly, structured around meal-times and lessons and sunsets, just as it should be. But I had started to feel like an imposter, lying to my husband and pretending all was well when it patently was not.

I skirted the patch of path where I had seen Mateo lying, the shiny black bodies of insects standing out against the amber sand. Heading to the reading room, where I'd left my laptop, I took out Marcos Condemaine's monograph and studied the telescope system. I managed to find some diagrams online of telescopes made in the same era, and compared them to the photograph. There was no doubt about it; whatever Francesco Condemaine had built in the atrium, it wasn't a telescope. It looked more like a projection system, or an instrument designed for drawing something down, but there was no precedent that I could think of for such an object.

An idea was forming in my head. It seemed to me that if you put a drawing table underneath the device, you could project and trace whole constellations, but for what purpose?

For some reason I was unable to explain, it felt linked to what I thought I had seen in the servants' quarters. I needed to go back in there.

A couple of days earlier Rosita had found where I'd hidden the keys and had silently returned them to the cigar box in the kitchen, but I had every right to take them, and did so openly, reminding her that I needed to make plans of the entire house, not just the main part in which we lived. By now I knew which doors the keys opened just by looking at them, and had full access to the other side, but the far back part was still too dark for me to venture into comfortably. I knew that apart from the four main rooms there was another toilet there, and a connecting passage to the servants' sleeping quarters under the eaves. It was an attic space that could hardly be counted as a room, but I would have to go and measure it if I wanted to provide the book with complete blueprints. I also knew that it involved going through the room where I had seen someone moving. Finally I decided that my curiosity was stronger than my fear, and I'd do it.

My opportunity came the following morning, when Mateo and Bobbie announced that they were going to go with Rosita on a shopping trip to Estepona. She was making monkfish in ground almonds with an onion and saffron sauce, and complained that the grocery store in Gaucia always overcharged her for their spices. I begged off, complaining of a headache. Mateo offered to stay with me, but I insisted he went along with them.

I hated the idea of lying to him, but I needed to understand whether it was me or the house, so that I could fix what was going wrong. What I had was too precious to lose without a fight. As soon as the BMW was out of sight, I walked toward the drawing room with the key to the connecting door pressed hotly in my pocket. It was the perfect time to go into the other side, if I could keep my nerve. I needed to look again, to prove to myself that there was nothing out of the normal, that it was just my mind playing tricks.

Standing before the door, I inserted the key into the lock, turned and pushed. The stripe of sunlight fell across the polished boards, lighting the dustballs that scudded away from my feet. I stepped inside, took a rolled TV guide from my pocket and wedged it under the door so that it couldn't shut behind me.

Fighting the urge to run away from the penumbral corners of the room, I slowly advanced inside.

CHAPTER TWENTY

The Lost One

Mateo and Jerardo had shifted the chest of drawers over against a wall, so that the little room was now crowded with furniture. I had brought a laser measurer and a small LED torch which was attached to my keyring, but the beam from this was very narrow, hardly more than a pencil of light. I needed to test my ability to withstand the dark, to know that there was a possibility of overcoming the panic I felt every time I realised that the edges of the room could not be clearly seen.

There was no need to take any more detailed measurements of the cool, dim rooms – in floor space they were exactly one third the size of their sunlit twins. So long as I could still hear the sounds from outside, I found that I could slowly advance inwards. There was a familiar odour, one which I had come to associate with these rooms, of rotted flowers, their soft pulpy stems steeped in ullage, the smell of something once fresh and beautiful that had gone bad.

Before me was a cabinet, identical to the one on the other side except that this one was pine, not teak, and was covered with cheap china ornaments and framed photographs. Tilting each of them in turn into the light cast by the open door, I saw the same groupings; stern couples posed for the flash, the women in stiff black bombazine, the men in high-collared shirts, arrangements of children including three that must have belonged to Elena Condemaine, a pretty, smiling girl of about seven, and two boys, identical, around nine or ten. It seemed odd that they should be in the rooms that belonged to the servants. Why would they not have had pictures of their own families? Then I remembered that back then photography was still the province of the wealthy. I set each one back in its rightful place, uncomfortable with the idea of disturbing anything that had remained untouched on one spot for a century, but took the one of the three children to show Mateo, whose sense of *noblesse oblige* prevented him from ever noticing such trifles.

There was a scuttle of a rat; I recognised the sound, a pattering of clawed paws. It didn't bother me particularly, but I thought it would be a good idea to get an exterminator in soon.

At the rear was a low door leading to a narrow staircase. The passageway was small and mean, bare boards and roughly plastered walls. It led to two box-rooms and a tiled bathroom which I assumed all of the servants would have shared. I leaned back against the cool tiles of the sink and shone the penlight beam around the walls. There really wasn't much to see. There was not even much dust, because the place had been kept sealed. I felt something flutter against my hand and turned the torch around in time to see what looked like a piece of chewing gum elongate itself toward my wrist.

There was another already on my arm, and it had left behind a thin streak of blood. I yelped and picked off the slippery grey creature, examining it. As I did, it stretched and swung around, trying to bite me. I was surprised at the speed with which it moved. I could see two sets of tiny hooks like pin-points, set on either end of its body. When I dropped it onto the sink it flipped over, end to end, like a Slinky. It climbed the sheer sides of the bowl in seconds and disappeared into a wet corner.

I had never seen a leech up close before. You expect anything that looks like a slug to move slowly. I placed my finger above it and watched as it stretched and waved about like an antenna, desperate to reach me. There was something grotesque about its obviousness, as if I was automatically expected to forgive its uncontrollable thirst for blood.

I knew that they produced an anaesthetic in their bite so that they could continue to feed from their host without being noticed. They also had an anticoagulant in their saliva, so they could carry on feeding until they were fully gorged. Then they would drop from the body to seek water, in search of a new host.

I wasn't at all squeamish, but I decided to stay the hell out of the bathroom. Shutting the door behind me and making sure that my bare arms were clear, I made my way back down the stairs.

This time when I entered the drawing room, I noticed other differences to its counterpart; there was a cheap pewter music box with a ballerina, some ugly gilt-framed landscapes, the brown craquelure of their canvases rendering them completely indecipherable, a standard lamp with dusty orange tassels. A modern steel wine rack had been set in place by Mateo. In the corner was what appeared to be a moulting stuffed dog, some kind of terrier – I was spending more time in the room than I'd intended, and now I noticed how far away the door seemed. I presumed it was because of the shuttered windows that I could no longer hear the birdsong or the ticking of the clocks.

A bubble of panic began to form itself and rise the surface.

The silence. Suddenly I knew I was no longer alone. Someone else had come into the room. My heart rate was increasing. I took a step back toward the door and the light, all the time peering forward, trying to see into the blurred far corners. *This is absurd,* I told myself, *there's nothing here that can hurt you. It's just your imagination. Get a grip.*

As I dug out the little LED torch and turned it on, the clasp holding it to my house keys opened and they fell off the ring onto the floor. I knelt and felt around for them under the table that stood to my left, but there was only dust. I tried not to think of whatever had been on the other end of the cotton thread.

My fingers spread out, feeling only furry dust. Then I touched something.

Cold, dead flesh.

Someone else's hand.

It grabbed my fingers tight and pulled. Screaming in fright, I pulled back even harder, but it wouldn't let go. I pulled with all my weight, and the fingers released me, slithering damply away over my hand.

Moments later I had grabbed the keys and was back on my feet running for the door, but the thing was also getting to its feet from under the table. Now I saw it rising in the penumbra, a creature consolidated from the very shadows; a ragged figure with a gaunt grey neck and collar-bone, and arms so thin they might have been branches. It wore an oval mask made of fine white china, on which were painted narrow red lips in a high-curved smile, and rouge spots where the cheekbones should be. It was held in place by aged leather straps, passed through slots at the sides of the mask. Ragged, unkempt tufts of hair stuck out from above its ears.

The poor thing moved awkwardly, like someone old and in terrible pain, its knees together, elbows out, every step taken as if passing over broken glass. No ghost this but bone and sinew, like old footage of someone in a concentration camp, helpless and utterly lost.

I knew I should stay and confront it, to understand why it had picked me, but I couldn't. Panic overwhelmed me and I ran for the open door and the light and safety, but I had to stoop to remove the rolled-up TV guide from under the door and I was suddenly sure that it was right behind me.

I lashed back and fell out into the light, and there right outside was Bobbie, home already, her face enquiring, and as I crashed into the child I was convinced that the thing would try to follow me out into the sliver of shadow cast by the open connecting door, but I had already fallen against it, shutting the creature back inside, and was fighting to turn the key in the lock, to hear the tumblers fall into place and seal the that dark soul in its prison once more.

To stay forever in the dark, away from us.

CHAPTER TWENTY-ONE

The Proof

'YOU KNOW WHAT happened,' I insisted angrily. 'You saw it too.'

Bobbie stared back at me, mute and uncomprehending.

'But there are scratches on my hand, see?' I held up my right hand so that Bobbie could examine the scarlet stripes on its back. 'You think I did these to myself?'

'You did the ones on your arms,' she replied with calm logic.

'Where did you hear that?'

'Daddy told me.'

'That was different, it was a long time ago and I was very upset, and Daddy shouldn't have told you such a thing.'

'I asked him. My daddy doesn't lie.' The way she said *my daddy* caught at my throat. I wanted to say, *But this was from the thing in the room, it grabbed me just like it grabbed the thread.* I didn't want to frighten her, I swear, but I had to know the truth. 'You did see it, didn't you?'

'There wasn't anything there.'

'It was right behind me! It tried to come out but I shut the door.'

'I didn't see anything.'

I grabbed her shoulders. 'You're lying. You know you saw something and you won't admit it. Why won't you tell the truth?'

'Stop it!' Bobbie put her hands to her ears. 'There wasn't anything there!' She ran out into the garden. I let her go, knowing that she was safe so long as she stayed in the sunlight. Whatever it was that inhabited that room, it was unable to leave the sunless part of the house. I was sure it wasn't alone. There were others. That was where they lived, where they had always lived. But why was I the only one who could see anything? Why hadn't Bobbie seen it as well?

My dream of Mateo's terrible death, perhaps that had only been a dream but this was real. The scratches on my hand proved it, surely.

I rose and turned to find Mateo coming into the house armed with shopping bags. 'I'm sorry, but can you two play your games a little more quietly today?' he said. 'I could hear your screams from the driveway and I've got to get on with the accounts this morning.'

'I'm sorry,' I said, slipping my hand behind my back. It was the same gesture I had used when hiding my scarred wrist.

He stopped. 'Is everything okay?'

'Of course. Why shouldn't it be?'

'I have to get everything updated before the London trip, so – you know.' He smiled and patted the air with his palm. 'Just keep it down for today. If this one goes well I was thinking maybe you should come with me for the next one. You could catch up with your friends.'

My friends.

I hadn't told him that half of them had already started to forget me. The people with whom I used to work all seemed too busy or preoccupied with their own lives to return my calls. I was the one who had got the handsome new husband and the beautiful house. They were still single and going to work in the rain, trying to pay their credit card bills, fighting off wage cuts and redundancies. I had expected to miss London more but I didn't, not really. If I was honest with myself, the last thing I wanted to do was stand around in crowded bars listening to their online dating horror stories.

Besides, I was accumulating a horror story of my own – something was crawling out of my head, ignited by a condition of the house that I could sense but not understand.

Mateo gave my forehead a light kiss, clearly still thinking about the problems in his order books. 'Call me when dinner's ready?' he asked. 'I get a little buried inside myself when I'm trying to do the figures. Maths was never my strong point.'

I watched him head back upstairs, so solid and sure of his place in the world, and wished I could be the same. I was being shaken out of the light and into darkness. And I still had no idea why or how.

Outside, the sun was low in the sky, trimming the tops of the cork trees with gold. Bobbie sat on the lawn, surrounded by her books and pencils, scribbling with angry, studied preoccupation. I knelt down beside her, but when I reached out to touch her shoulder she flinched and moved away.

'Bobbie, I'm really sorry,' I said. 'I didn't mean to frighten you like that.'

'You didn't frighten me,' said Bobbie stiffly. 'You frightened yourself.'

'What do you mean?'

'By going into the dark. You don't *like* being in the dark so why did you go in?'

'How do you know I don't like the dark?'

'I heard you talking with Daddy.'

'No,' I admitted, 'I don't like it. I know there's nothing to be afraid of really, it's just a bunch of dusty little rooms. I have too much imagination. But I thought I could cure it by going in there a bit further each time, until I stopped imagining that there was anything to be scared of anymore.'

'Why do you get scared of the dark?'

'It was just something that happened a long time ago, honey. Maybe it was always there, I don't know. But I can make it go away.'

'Is that why you never learned to drive?' Bobbie asked. 'In case you got stuck in a tunnel?'

'Maybe – I don't know. But I never meant to shout at you like that, sweetie, and I never will again.'

Bobbie set down her pencil. 'Promise?'

'I promise.' I hugged the girl to my chest, and everything felt good again. It would be good just so long as I dammed up my over-active imagination.

'Off you go now,' I said with false gaiety, 'get those dirty hands washed ready for dinner. I'll bring your stuff in.' I watched as Bobbie scampered off into the house, and felt more ashamed than ever for allowing my fears to spill over in front of the girl who had accepted becoming my step-daughter without a single qualm.

I examined the nails of my left hand, looking for proof that I had scratched myself, but there was nothing. As I gathered up Bobbie's books and pens, I realised I was avoiding the shadow-shapes of the surrounding bushes, as if there was something in them that could hurt me.

I started to head back to the house with my arms full but the books slid from under my elbow, falling onto the grass. As I knelt to pick them up, I found I was at the spot where I had imagined Mateo's death. My fingers reached out to touch the grass, retracing the moment. Here he had fallen, here I had run to him, here I had slapped the hornets from his mouth and eyes – and here they had landed, Their segmented bodies had dried out now, but were still lying deep at the roots of the grass. I could touch them, feel them between the blades and the sun-hardened soil.

The hornets. Positive proof that *something* had happened.

CHAPTER TWENTY-TWO

The Enemy

Two days later, just before Mateo was going to London, I got another shock when my mother turned up virtually unannounced.

'I'm in Malaga visiting a friend of Sandy's about a new line of accessories,' she explained on the phone. 'I can be there in a couple of hours. I rented a car from Sixt, it's a ridiculous little thing – why do Spaniards all have to be so short? – and I have to go almost right past your front door, apparently.'

I found it hard to imagine that Anne had even the vaguest idea of where we lived, but no doubt her rental was equipped with GPS. I knew that my mother would have a host of reasons that would prevent her from staying the night, but I offered anyway. 'God no, darling, but bless you. I have to dash back, but I'll stay for a spot of lunch. Can you manage that? Don't go to any trouble, a bit of salad will be fine. Is Mateo with you?'

'He's going to be at a winery until about five,' I said. 'But if you stay you'll see him, and Bobbie's here.'

'Oh dear, I suppose it's always just the two of you during the day. Isn't that lonely?'

'Not really, there's her tutor and the housekeeper, and the gardener.'

'Heavens, quite the lady of the house. How times have changed. Are you managing? Not too much for you? Don't tell me now, save all the news for when I see you. Won't be long, *ciao*.'

I could feel myself becoming annoyed already. Anne knew which buttons to push and worked them mercilessly. *You can afford to be gracious,* I told myself, *she's lonely and bitter and won't stay for more than a few hours. You can survive her for that long.* But I called Mateo at the vineyard to warn him that she might still be here when he returned.

I spoke to Rosita and we hatched a plan for a summer salad with ham and chicken, the sort of bland non-Spanish food Anne secretly favoured, although Rosita insisted on adding *padron* peppers. The house was flower-bedecked and looked beautiful. My mother turned up just after noon in a canary-coloured Seat. She was dressed in a lacy, impractical white frock designed for someone considerably younger.

'What a strange-looking house!' she said, coming in and kissing the air in front of me. 'With the cliff right at the back like that, and the funny little glass turret in the centre. But the planting's lovely. I'd have thought it would all dry out around here. It must take an awful lot of upkeep.'

I took her on a truncated tour of the house, carefully avoiding the locked servants' quarters, lingering instead on the furniture and paintings. I could tell she was pricing everything up as she walked about. I wanted Anne to be pleased for me, but knew that she was too selfish for that.

'I hardly passed a single other car on the road,' she said, feigning a fit of exhaustion. 'It's all so terribly barren and *desolate*. What on earth made Mateo pick such a lonely spot?'

'Actually it was me who chose it,' I said defensively, 'It's not very far from the coast, and there's a village nearby. I've already made friends there.'

'But Calico darling, there's no *culture*. I mean what on earth do people do of an evening? How's my darling little girl?'

Bobbie was staying back in a corner of the drawing room, and had to be drawn forward to accept a branding kiss. 'Look at you,' Anne cooed, 'so big and grown-up, and that colouring, so very Spanish, with the dark eyes and such severe hair.' Bobbie was on her best behaviour, but was visibly anxious to get away. Rosita served lunch, but she and Julieta wisely left to eat in the peace and seclusion of the atrium, the invisible lines of class making themselves felt.

'I was thinking that perhaps Roberta would like to come and stay with me in Somerset,' said Anne as we finished our salads. 'You'd love it, there are horses and lots of other little girls like you. And as you're not at a proper school you could come whenever you like.' It wasn't the right thing to say, or the right way to say it. Bobbie remained silent.

'I don't think that's a good idea,' I replied. 'Bobbie's being tutored here for now, but she's about to start school at the coast. And anyway, Mateo wouldn't like it.'

'He wouldn't or you wouldn't? Why would you want to deny me the pleasure of having a little visit? It's not as if you're going to have any children of your own, is it?' She topped up her glass for the third time.

'Bobbie, why don't you see if Senora Delgadillo has left some chocolate cake in the kitchen?' I said. The girl slipped gratefully from her chair and ran off. 'Why did you have to say that?' I asked.

Anne's eyes widened in mock-innocence. 'I was only stating a fact, darling. You remember what the doctor said. After that terrible termination and all those complications, it's hardly likely you'll ever be able to conceive. We all have to make choices in our lives. You always did make the wrong ones.'

'I just wanted to be happy. That meant getting away from you.'

'Hm. I suppose you probably regret having had the termination, and now you like to think of Roberta as your own daughter. That's only natural. Oh.' Her stare held an ill-concealed look of triumph. 'Mateo doesn't know, does he? Of course, you wouldn't have told him. Surely there are no secrets between the two of you?'

'He mustn't ever know,' I said quietly, staring down at my plate.

'Because he's a Catholic, I suppose. I thought they were more modern these days. Particularly after all those skeletons have fallen out of their own cupboards. I mean, they could hardly be critical of anyone else, could they? Well don't worry, your secret is safe with me.'

No it's not, I thought, *it can never be. Not if it gives you some power over me.*

'Speaking of which, are you still on your meds? You know how you get if you stop taking them. You always had an overactive imagination.'

'It wasn't my imagination, and you know it, mother.' I had been determined to say nothing about the past, but it was a matter of self-defence now.

Anne raised a hand to stop me. 'Please don't start all that again. We've been over it a hundred times.'

'And yet you still won't admit the truth, even to yourself.'

She turned and held my eyes. 'Your father left because he knew he was ill, and he wanted to spare us the pain of watching him die.'

'And why do you think I stopped eating before he left? Why do you think I cut myself?'

She sighed. 'You chose to do it. You entertained these – fantasies –'

'I wanted to make myself ugly. I wanted to be so unbearable to look at that he would never try to touch me again.'

'Yes, I've heard all this many times before. I thought perhaps that now the poor man was in his grave you could finally let it rest.'

'Why did you always believe him over me? I'm your daughter –'

'And he was my *husband*. For Heaven's sake can't we speak of something else? It's a lovely sunny day.' She drained her glass of rosé and refilled it.

'As you wish.' I let silence fall between us.

'You're happy here?'

'Yes, very much so.'

Anne looked longingly at the garden and made a show of checking her watch. 'Perhaps I could stay for a while, if Mateo's back at five. It would be nice to see that deliciously handsome profile again.'

In that instant I knew what she was up to. 'You're not having Bobbie come to stay,' I said. 'You're just playing your usual games.'

'Don't be ridiculous, darling, why would I do that?'

'I don't know. Perhaps you just want to get back at me –'

'For what? For doing drugs and getting pregnant and falling down the stairs at some drunken party? For trying to kill yourself?'

'For accusing my father –'

'Why is it that all little girls accuse their fathers these days? They've read about it in the papers and create false memories to blackmail their parents –'

'– and for denying you grandchildren.'

'I wish you could hear yourself, Calico. All this dreadful pop-psychology. I only wanted what was best for you. If only you hadn't spent so much time trying to hurt me. You were always your father's girl.'

'And the only way he could get away from you was by dying.'

'That's an evil thing to say. Poor Mateo, I don't suppose he had an inkling of what he was getting himself into, thinking he was marrying a blushing English rose.'

'I think it's time you left,' I said, rising from the table. 'I don't need you trying to poison my husband against me.'

Anne had one last weapon to use. 'I don't suppose,' she said imperiously, 'that you told him you were sectioned.'

'I got sick because you refused to admit what was happening right under your nose.'

'No, Calico, you made yourself sick because you simply couldn't handle the real world.'

'Well I'm married now and I have a step-daughter, and I'm handling this world perfectly well,' I said. 'I have friends and a life and people who treat me with honesty and respect, which is more than you ever gave me.'

I think Anne's slap came as a shock to both of us. She stepped back from the table, looking at her open right palm.

I rose and moved away, my hand to my burning cheek. A plate slid off the dining room dresser behind me and split in two on the boards. Moments later my mother had put on her coat and was leaving in a display of theatrical temper, and as I watched her rush out to her car I was just glad that it was over once and for all.

After all the years of pretending that there were still ties between us, there was no more need for us to try and behave like mother and daughter. We were enemies.

I went to the door, expecting to hear the car crunch gears and speed away, then returned to the dining room. My hands shook violently as I cleared up the broken plate and binned the pieces. To calm myself, I went to sit in the glass atrium. When Bobbie finally came back and woke me an hour later, it was evident that she had not heard our argument, and all was right once more.

I decided that if I spoke to Anne again – and I would, because in a month or so she would pretend we had never fought and would Skype me to chat about her work – I would always keep a wide, cold ocean between us.

CHAPTER TWENTY-THREE

The Storm

'I HEARD YOU were coming to see Maria,' said Jordi, holding open the door into the little library. 'I'm glad I could catch you on the way.'

'I guess it's impossible to do anything in this town without everyone knowing,' I said, following him into the gloom. It was a pleasant kind of dimness, not like the smothering dark deep inside Hyperion House.

Jordi pulled back the shutters from the small window nearest the books. 'We have nothing else to talk about here. I found the pages you were looking for. Here, *The Hyperion Society.* It had fallen behind the shelf.' He proudly handed me a tattered final section to the monograph. 'It was written and published by Marcos Condemaine for the British Architectural Library.'

I turned it over. 'Did you read it?'

'Sure. He wanted to explain the principles on which his older cousin built the house. The Hyperion Society was basically a bunch of philanthropists who believed they could improve society by studying the alignment of the stars.'

'Studying alignments? You mean they were astrologers?'

'Maybe not so much astrologers, as the followers of Hyperion,' he said with a shrug. 'I don't know what that means either, but maybe you can find this out.'

'Some kind of philosophical group, perhaps. Something founded on Greek ideals?'

'I don't know. There are still some pages missing but I think they've gone forever. We have rats in the annexe, they chew through everything.'

I gave the matter some thought. 'Elena Condemaine died in an asylum and her cousin Marcos took over the house until Franco's men requisitioned it. It would be useful to know why her children didn't inherit.'

He grinned. 'Don't worry, I will keep looking for you.'

'That's really kind of you, Jordi, but I don't want to take you away from your work.'

'There is nothing to do here,' he shrugged. 'It's more interesting to help you.'

I took the booklet and headed through the baking white streets to Maria's shop. My knowledge of Hyperion House remained frustratingly opaque. The previous night I had sat in the dining room with Bobbie and annotated what I had written so far. There were too many gaps in the story to write a full history of the building yet. I felt uncomfortable in the drawing room, knowing that something on the other side of its connecting door brought my worst fears to life, even if they turned out to be only in my imagination. I was scared of the dark, but there was a more disturbing place inside my head.

Maria Gonzales had a laugh like dried leaves being swept up, the result of smoking herbal cigarettes that had left her with a worse cough than any sailor's rolling tobacco might have done. Several ladies were seated in her shop surrounded by dusty jars and frightening hand-knitted clowns that no-one would ever buy, but Maria didn't care. She survived on the money her sons sent her, and the store was somewhere for the ladies to sit that wouldn't charge them. When they tired of Lola whisking their wineglasses away in the town square, they came here to complain about the world.

'*Hhhh*yperion *Hhhh*ouse,' said Maria, using far too many Hs before continuing in Spanish.

'She says she doesn't know why you didn't ask her about it in the first place,' Celestia translated.

'It didn't occur to me,' I replied.

'She says you didn't tell her you were writing a book. I told you, Maria, you don't remember anything.'

Maria said something and rasped with laughter again. 'She says she buried two husbands and she remembers every detail of their funerals,' explained Celestia.

'What do you know about the house?' I asked, but Maria was talking to another woman now who also only spoke Spanish, even though she seemed to understand questions in English. I was still at the stage where I could roughly follow conversations but not express myself.

'You remember Amancio Lueches?' said Maria in a sudden impassioned burst of heavily accented English. 'Healthy and happy one day, dead the next.'

The other woman replied in Spanish and they both laughed again. 'She says the Devil took him,' said Celestia, in some hilarity at the idea.

'This was the man who owned Hyperion House before we bought it?' I asked.

'The last of the Condemaine family,' Celestia confirmed. 'I think they were all either Condemaines or Lueches, the two sides of the family.'

'Did any of you ever go over there?'

'Oh no, we never went near the house. The Condemaines were private people,' said another of the women. 'They were better left alone. They didn't need anyone.'

'But I read that Senor Lueches was taken away suffering from dehydration…'

'After his wife died he stopped caring for himself,' she said. 'We thought the state would buy the house because it had once been an observatory. It should have gone to the state. But it didn't meet the requirements –'

Because it turned out not to be an observatory at all, I thought.

'– so it continued in private hands. Of course we're glad it did,' she added hastily. 'You are nice people, and the little girl –'

'*Una nina tan bonita,*' said Maria, and they all agreed.

Maria's friend added something in Spanish. 'She says they all avoided the house because of the *loco* old man,' Celestia told me.

'But you'd come back to the house now, all of you? If we held another party, for the adults this time?'

'*Ay, no!*' Maria and her friend threw up their hands. 'Ask Jerardo,' said Maria, continuing to Celestia in Spanish.

'She says Jerardo won't set foot inside the house itself, he says it has a history of madness,' said Celestia. 'The Condemaines, very nice people but all *loco*.' I wanted to tell her that I was sure Jerardo had been inside – he had helped Mateo move the chest of drawers – but I knew they wouldn't listen.

Maria leaned forward and waved a wrinkled finger at me. 'Ask your Rosita, she knows about *Hhhh*yperion. She knows everything. None of the older women will *ever* go there.'

'I'll come back anytime,' said Celestia brightly, 'if you're serving a decent drop of plonk.' We raised our glasses in a toast, touching them together.

'I was thinking of having a few people over for drinks on Friday, after my husband gets back from Madrid,' I said. 'The fiesta's on Saturday, isn't it? It would make a good start to the weekend.'

'There will be a *muy malo* storm on Saturday,' said Maria, squinting up at the clear azure sky.

'Really?' I had already checked Accuweather on my mobile; the weather was due to remain the same as always, hot and clear and fine. I didn't want to argue, but the prediction seemed typically doom-laden.

THE TREES WERE rattling in the swirling winds, the leaves spinning on their stems. Rain sluiced across the garden in a spectacular torrent, flooding sand from the paths and washing away the topsoil. At the cusp of the mountain ridge, lights flickered like poorly connected neon, but at this distance no thunder could be heard.

I pressed my hand against the glass and found it still warm – the sun had been on it until just a few minutes ago. Uncomfortable and overheated, I went to the drawing room and opened my laptop, trying the number again. This time it connected. Mateo appeared on the Skype screen, the airport shops at his back.

'Wow, looks like the storm has already hit there,' he said after a flash lit up the room. 'My flight just got pushed back, so go ahead and eat without me.'

'What's the problem? Did they say?'

'I guess the bad weather's having a knock-on effect, although it hasn't hit here yet.' He twisted the screen around to show me the view. The Madrid runways were still dry, but the sky was dark. 'How are you doing?'

'Okay, I guess. I was going to have some of the Gaucia ladies over for drinks but they already warned me about the rain. Actually I think they didn't want to come to the house. How late do you think you'll be?'

'I won't know until we get an announcement. The board says more information at six thirty. How's Bobbie?'

'She's with Rosita, learning how to make *empanadas*.'

'Maybe you should sit in with them and pick up some tips.' I knew he was gently chiding me for not being able to cook, but I had been too busy to start learning.

'I have a better idea. We nominate your daughter as the new house chef. Hurry home.'

'I'll be the first to board, don't worry.' He blew me a kiss and disconnected. I folded the laptop shut and tidied away my notes.

'Callie?'

I looked up to find Bobbie wiping flour from her hands onto the yellow flowered shift Rosita made her wear in the kitchen. 'What is it, sweetie? You all finished?'

'They're in the oven now,' she said. 'I don't like the storm.'

'There's nothing to be afraid of. It's just electricity moving about in the air. Do you want to come and sit with me?'

'The door.' She pointed across the drawing room, behind my head. The connecting door was ajar, revealing a sliver of darkness inside.

How did that happen? I thought, rising. I was sure I had locked it.

The storm clouds had dimmed all the rooms, but the lights weren't due on for a while yet; Rosita still had a specific routine she insisted on following. I decided that Mateo had probably gone into the other side for some wine and had forgotten to re-use the key on his way out. The door tended to pop open unless it was pushed shut hard and locked.

'Wait here.' I patted Bobbie on the head, then stepped inside and took a look around, feeling the familiar sense of tension rising in my chest. *You can control this. Whatever is here is inside you, not the house.*

'Are you all right?' Bobbie called.

'Fine, just stay where you are, honey.'

I took a further tentative step inside, past the sideboard lined with photographs, the overstuffed ottoman, the tasselled lampstand. Now that I was within the room, I had to stop and wait for my eyes to adjust to the shadowy gloom. Creeping forward, step by step, I was aware of every foot I moved further in, away from light and safety, but I was drawn by the need to understand.

The high-backed armchair ahead of me had been turned to face the wall and the dead fireplace. I assumed Mateo must have moved it, because it had always been facing the door. The floorboards creaked beneath my sneakers. I could hear the rain cascading onto the roof far above.

Beneath it was a faint but terrible sound, coming from somewhere close at hand.

A snuffling moan, so desperate and bitter that I could only imagine the person making it had sunk into the depths of despair.

As I drew closer, I saw that there was someone seated, or rather slumped, in the chair. I could see the top of a head, hair in tufted strands, matted and filthy. A thin arm rose and fell, hanging loose inside a dirty ragged shawl. There was the distinctive smell again, hard to place – not decay exactly, but neglect. The smell of dead flowers, unwashed skin, someone old who had been left alone for too long. This was surely a real person.

I moved closer. A sighing now, a sob forced from an old, dry throat. Slowly, as I crept forward, the being in the chair revealed itself. The skin was mottled blue and grey, a translucence revealing the aching arteries within.

The china mask turned to me, its pale ceramic features those of a young girl, but inside the eye-holes were filmy pupils rolling up at me in torment. The brown leather straps that held the mask in place appeared to be cutting into the poor creature's skin. The mask's carved lips were curled in happiness, but the effect was not joyful but horrific. Its hand reached out feebly, as if begging me to make contact and remove it.

Knowing that there were no lights on this side of the house I stood trapped amid the crowded Victoriana, trying to see the thing that was a part of the dark, its atoms coalescing from the very absence of light, and I knew that its fingers longed to dig into my wrist and draw me closer. I felt no fear now, just pity and revulsion.

But then, behind it, rising very slowly from behind the chair, came the malevolent creature I had first seen through the window. It rose with its chin on its chest, its hair forward over its features, and for the first time I knew who these terrible ruined beings were...

Bobbie's cry shattered the spell. I stumbled back toward the door, away from the chair. I could no longer see the older one at all. The air around the chair was thickening and growing dark, swarming over their forms and blurring them, as if a horde of flying insects had come to bear them away.

I ran back, catching my ankle on the dresser, bursting out of the door and slamming it to find Bobbie eyeing me in amazement.

'You *are* scared!' she said with a triumphant air.

CHAPTER TWENTY-FOUR

The Joke

I WATCHED AS Mateo devoured the cold plate left out by Rosita, forking rolls of *jamon* into his mouth. 'You should have seen her, screaming and whining about not being able to get on the flight, threatening to sue the counter staff. Man, there's nothing worse than a Bostonian with a sense of entitlement. It was as if she couldn't *imagine* that anyone else might want to catch the same plane, utterly incredible.' He stopped chewing and looked at her. 'Sorry, this is boring for you.'

'No, it's wonderful,' I said, relishing normality, the coffee cup pressed between my hands. 'Just keep talking.'

'So, after twenty minutes of being abused by this mad stick-insect of a woman, the counter girl beckons me on in her place, which only sets her off again, and worse this time, "Don't you know who I am" and all this shit, and I say "How do you stand it?" and the counter girl turns to me and says confidentially, "How do I stand it? I know that this bitch isn't getting on any flight while I'm on my shift, and that just about makes my day," and she waves me through with a cheery smile.'

'She was flirting with you,' I said distractedly, studying the spot where the dark hair of his wrists met the sharp white of his shirt cuffs. 'I bet they all do.'

He rounded up some salted *padron pimientos* on his fork. 'So how was your day? How's the book coming along? How many pages have you finished?'

'Mateo, do you believe in ghosts?'

'What do you mean?'

'Trapped spirits. Do you think a house can hold the soul of a dead person?'

He looked thrown by the sudden change in conversation. 'I don't know. No, I guess not. You're talking about – here?'

'I went into the other side today. The dark side.'

'*The dark side?* What is that?'

'The servants' quarters.'

'You don't like the dark. Why would you do that?'

'We live in part of a house, Mateo. Doesn't that strike you as odd?'

'The whole idea of living in an old observatory is odd, especially one with rooms for servants at the back, but you know why he did it, to study the sky and to spare his wife.'

'Don't you think there comes a time when fears have to be faced?'

'Well, it's an admirable idea, but if we're talking about you, perhaps you want to wait for a time when I can be here more and I'll help you. Once we're over the Christmas pre-orders –'

'This household has been invaded, Mateo. She's trying to get in. She wants the light. And I think there's more than one. I've counted two or maybe three so far.'

'Two or three what, ghosts?' He set down his wineglass and stared at me. 'You're saying you've seen *spirits*?'

'I don't know, not spirits, but not real people either, and they live in the dark rooms.'

'Have you told Bobbie about this –'

'No, I'm the only one who sees them. They've chosen me. I know how this sounds, God knows –'

'Why would they pick you?'

'Perhaps they need something, they're in pain and I don't think they realise it but they're going to cause terrible harm –'

'Oh, *man*.' Mateo passed a hand over his forehead. 'Is this why you're behaving so –'

'So what?'

'I don't know. You don't seem like yourself. Maybe you're tired.'

'I just want to know what she wants.'

'Who are we talking about, Callie? Who is "she"?'

'Elena Condemaine. She's just on the other side of that wall, biding her time. Her husband is with her, and maybe her children for all I know.'

'Wait, the architect and his wife are living with us? And maybe their kids too? You do realise he's been dead for almost a century?'

'I know that.'

'Why would she pick you? Why now? Are you going to tell me she's buried under the floorboards next? That her husband murdered her and she's chosen you to tell the world?'

'No, but her presence is tied to this house and those rooms.'

'If you're telling me that that our household has been invaded by the vengeful ghost of a woman who died nearly a century ago, I'd have to say she waited a long time to make her move. This is a joke, right? "You moved the cemetery but you left the bodies, didn't you?" Sorry, that was *Poltergeist*. "Go toward the light, Carol-Ann." Or was it stay away from the light? It's been years since I saw that movie.'

Something within me broke. I released the tension in my neck and gave in. He was never going to believe me. Who in their right mind would? 'Yes,' I said, 'it's a joke. Or maybe just a dream, a bad dream. I'm sorry, I'm really tired. I don't sleep well when you're not here.'

'Maybe you should try a glass of hot milk with a small brandy in it. It always works for me. I go out like a light.'

'Dear Mateo.' I wanted to stroke his face and feel the stubble on his chin. 'It's always so simple for you.'

'Really, you look kind of exhausted.' He smiled. 'Why don't you go and run yourself a hot bath, and I'll look in on Bobbie.'

I went and lay in the steamed-up bathroom, with the overhead lights ablaze. *It's me,* I decided. *For some reason Elena*

Condemaine has targeted me. No-one else can see her or be touched by her because no-one else can help her. If I can find out why it's happening I can put a stop to it, and everything will return to normal.

My first thought was that I should just tear down the shutters in the other rooms, clear out the furniture and paint everything white in a sort of exorcism rite. But the servants' quarters were buried deep in the shadow of the cliff where darkness naturally reigned, and I felt sure that something as simple as redecorating wouldn't solve the problem. If anything, it might drive her out into the house and make everything worse for us.

I needed to have all the facts at hand, I had to find out where Elena Condemaine had been incarcerated and how she had ended her life. Maybe Mateo's idea that she'd been buried in the room next door wasn't so crazy. In 1922 there was only one asylum within fifty miles of the house, on a private estate just outside of Marbella. It was now a state-owned hospital, and I was sure it wouldn't be hard to track down.

CHAPTER TWENTY-FIVE

The Asylum

THE FOLLOWING MORNING, Julieta handed in her notice. She told me she wanted to stay, but her mother had just undergone a hip replacement and was coming to live with her, as her own house had too many stairs. She insisted she would try to come back after the old lady had returned to her own home. It meant that I would have to pick up Bobbie's home-schooling until we could get her into the Christmas mid-term in Marbella. Bobbie was upset, but it couldn't be helped. I began to draw up a schedule for her, based on her curriculum requirements.

Meanwhile, I searched for the address of the Santa Isabel State Mental Hospital, the one that Elena's husband had originally been hired to redesign. It was easy to find, and I discovered I was able to fill in an online form requesting an interview with their head of records.

I arranged the appointment for Friday morning and booked out a taxi for half the day, extracting a discount from the driver on the condition that I took no longer than two hours before he brought me back to Hyperion House.

The building was set in sculpted parklands that must once have been beautiful. Now the watering systems had been removed in an economy drive, and the lawns had been scoured down to cracked earth. An avenue of brown, sickly trees had been partially replaced with a car park, the stumps left in place as a cruel reminder of more gracious times. The building's narrow perpendicular windows, chimneys and steep gabled roof looked out of place in the bare heat of late summer. There were cardboard boxes everywhere, evidence that the homeless had been granted a nightly refuge outside the centre.

I found Augusto Fernandez, a young intern who had inherited the additional post of being in charge of records, in the hospital's bright air-conditioned basement. Like so many other buildings that belonged to the state, the place seemed virtually derelict. 'I'm sorry about the walk,' he said, rising to shake my hand. 'The corridors were designed to be long so that they would exercise the patients. Are you writing a thesis?'

'An academic book about Spanish architecture,' I said, deciding not to go into too much detail. 'One of the architects I'm concerned with was employed by the hospital, and had a wife who was incarcerated here in May 1922. I'm just looking for some background information.'

'I can probably help you there. The old mental institution was closed in 1936, but the files are all intact. If any of the old patients are still alive, we certainly never hear from them. In 2006 the archive records became public, which means we're able to grant access. If you'd care to follow me?'

Senor Fernandez led the way to the rear of the building and down a concrete ramp. 'There were horses kept here once,' he explained. 'The stables were converted into records offices. There was talk of opening some kind of museum, but I'm afraid the economic downturn put an end to that idea.'

Ahead were tall grey metal stacks filled with boxes containing manila folders, labelled by year, then alphabetically. 'The years immediately following the Great War saw a massive influx of patients suffering from stress disorders,' Fernandez explained. 'Shell shock. Of course, nobody treated the women who were forced to bring up children alone without financial aid after their husbands were killed. In many cases it was simply assumed that they could cope.' He tapped a box. 'Here's your month and year.'

There were only half a dozen folders, and I quickly found what I was looking for. Attached inside one was a small sepia photograph similar to the pictures I had seen in the darkened rooms of the house. It showed a woman's thin tanned face tipped up at the sun, eyes narrowed in happiness, a broad rictus of a smile. I was immediately struck by the similarity between her smile and the one painted onto the creature's china mask, the mask she wore to prove that she was still happy, even though she was dying behind it. She wore the black high-collared shift of a widow, and no adornment save for a small pendant at her neck.

A date read; *May 16th 1922 Elena Mendez Condemaine.*

'She was Galician,' said Fernandez, translating for me. 'It was common practice to have two last names. The first was usually the father's first surname, and the second the mother's first surname. So presumably her husband had an English mother?'

'I know very little about her,' I admitted, turning the page. 'Could I get a photocopy of this?'

'*Seguro*.' He unclipped it and went off to make a duplicate. Bracketed into the next sheet was a formal family photograph, two boys and a small girl. I dug a fingernail under the picture and removed it, turning it over. The back read; *August 1913. Augustin, Farriol, 7 anos, Maria, 5 anos.*

So Augustin and Farriol were the twins. Francesco Condemaine was killed in battle four years later, and she would have raised the children by herself for the next five years, before being committed. I pocketed the tintype of her before Fernandez returned with the page.

On the next page were clipped some handwritten letters dated 1920 and 1921. 'Can you help me with these?' I asked.

Digging out his glasses, he read for a few minutes. 'These are from Senora Condemaine's sister-in-law in London, and from other members of her family,' he said. 'Mostly descriptions of family life. Her sister-in-law repeatedly offers her help. *You must accept my offer in good faith, for the Blessed Virgin cannot always be relied upon to provide for you.* Another from relatives proposing to take care of the children, but it sounds as if she turned down the suggestion. Descriptions of a picnic, a summer fiesta, hoping the children get over their colds – everyday life, all perfectly ordinary.'

'So there's nothing –'

'Wait, then there's this, later,' said Fernandez, 'a letter from the mayor of the region refusing financial assistance. He says that although he appreciates her husband put every penny he earned into their house, and that she has been left destitute, she must surely have relatives upon whom she can call.'

'Her husband was half-English. He volunteered to fight and it cost him his life. I'd have thought his widow would have got a war pension.'

'Perhaps not if he was registered as Spanish and living out of England. There would certainly have been a dispute over it.' He turned over a series of small printed slips and read them. 'Yes, these are formal requests for financial assistance, all denied. That's odd.'

'What?'

'There's no reason given. Usually there's a space – see? – in which the town clerk explains the reason for the council's response, but these have all been left blank. Then there's another reply to a request from Senora Condemaine, who has now declared that they have nothing left to live on. The note on the bottom looks like it's in her own hand. *No-one in the village will help us. It seems we must rely on providence.* She says this twice – *no-one will help us.* That is very surprising.'

'Why is it so surprising?'

'The village councils were usually good at looking after destitute residents.'

'Elena Condemaine lived out of town in a great house. Perhaps there was a feeling that she was too grand for them, or had ignored them in the past. Perhaps they thought she should sell up, or was being hysterical.'

Senor Fernandez shook his head. 'From the tone of these letters, there's no obvious indication of mental fragility. One normally finds something developing. Back in the years before Franco, the asylum was mainly used to house dangerous patients.'

'What about the servants? They must have noticed something.'

'There's no mention of servants. One housekeeper only. From these letters it doesn't sound as if they had any.'

'But Francesco Condemaine had servants.'

'How do you know that?'

'He must have done, he had the servants' quarters built into the house and furnished them,' I said finally. 'I think it was the estate agent who first mentioned it, but even she wasn't sure.'

On the following pages were handwritten medical reports. 'Can you give me some idea of what these notes say?' I asked, waiting with growing impatience while Fernandez read slowly through them.

Finally he removed his glasses and folded them away. 'Well, at least that explains why she was sent here,' he said with finality. 'Her admittance report has been included. Elena Condemaine either killed her three children or let them die. When the police arrived at Hyperion House, they found her happily living with the rotting corpses. It says; *con felicidas*. They had been dead for over two years – that's after she wrote some of these cheerful letters to her family, saying that everything was fine. A fairly clear indication of her mental state, I'd say.'

'That's awful – does it say how they died?'

'Only that all three children "departed life suddenly, at the same time, by intention." If they had died of neglect and malnutrition they would have passed away at different periods.'

'I read that Elena died a year after being admitted here. Is there anything more?'

'The diagnosis doesn't seem very exact. "Hereditary melancholy", "Disease of the soul", "Hysterical depravation", "Discomfiture of the womb". The latter state was supposedly connected to the states of menstruation and menopause. Elena Condemaine was given a variety of treatments but failed to respond.'

'What kind of treatments?'

'We still have a couple of the most widely used devices in our little museum,' Fernandez said. 'It's only open to the public through special request, but I think we can consider yours a request, if you'd like to see them.'

'Please.'

We left the archive and I followed him along a less well maintained corridor. A small square chamber had iron-barred slivers of window near its ceiling. Inside was a brown leather armchair that looked like an antique desk chair, except that it had wide leather belts attached to the arms and leg-rests.

'This is the Rotating Chair,' said Fernandez. 'The patient was tightly strapped in and blindfolded, and an iron handle was inserted in the side there, attached to a gear. The chair would then be spun on its axis at very high velocity, thereby building a centrifugal force that created extreme discomfort and terror from the intense pressure applied to the brain. It caused nausea and a sensation of suffocation. The idea was that the treatment could be used to reset the patient's equilibrium and brain.'

'But that's barbaric.'

'Unfortunately it was a time when doctors were prone to experimentation on the most vulnerable.'

He walked over to what I now realised was another device, a large box made of sheets of iron, painted black. 'This is the Belgian Box. It's padded on the inside, and there was just enough room for the patient to sit in it with their legs folded up. The hatch would then be sealed and they would be left in the dark for up to twenty-four hours at a time. There are some tiny airholes, but not enough to admit any light. Again, the idea was to "clean" the brain and reset it, allowing the patient to emerge and start afresh. Thankfully the use of both devices was discontinued in the 1920s in favour of more humane methods of rehabilitation.'

'I think I have quite a human story for my project,' I said. 'Elena Condemaine suffered from stress because her husband went to war, presumably against her wishes, and when he was killed she struggled to raise three children alone. At first she was too proud to accept outside help, then was turned down when she finally did so, and it all got too much for her to bear.'

'It certainly sounds that way. Apparently she committed suicide on the first anniversary of her admission. It doesn't say how but I imagine she would have hanged herself. It wasn't uncommon then.'

'Is she buried here?'

'There's no mention of it, and I doubt she would have been.'

'Why not?'

'The asylum was a Catholic institution run by nuns,' Fernandez explained. 'Patients who died by their own hand could not be buried within the grounds.'

'Where would they have gone?'

'I daresay their relatives took them back to their own churchyards or non-consecrated burial grounds. Senora Condemaine was probably taken to your nearest town. I don't know what happened to the children. It would have been a matter for the police, but pre-Franco police records are very hard to come by.'

I thanked Augusto Fernandez and left. As I walked down the drive, I thought of the appalling cruelties inflicted on Elena Condemaine. Her nyctophobia had not been diagnosed by the doctors. Only her loving husband knew about it, and had even built her a house to banish the darkness from her life.

Instead, when she arrived here she had been blindfolded, spun around and shut in darkness, subjected to remedies that mockingly subverted the means of her salvation.

If any woman had reason to return from the dead and demand wrongs to be righted, it was Elena Condemaine. And I was sure that the means to do so was hidden somewhere in the house.

CHAPTER TWENTY-SIX

The Graves

'WHAT DO YOU think happened to the original floor plans?' I casually asked Mateo over dinner that night. Bobbie was battling with a bowl of short noodles – Rosita had taught her how to make *fideua* earlier, and I was showing her how to pile the unfamiliar food onto her fork. 'I tried the land registry office in Gaucia but they had nothing on file. Weren't you given anything from the vendor?'

'You saw the only file they handed over to us,' he said, peering into a bowl of grey-green mush. 'What is this?'

'Aubergines. Our housekeeper has some help in the kitchen,' I explained, 'and your daughter has been watching *Masterchef* again. The technical drawing in the file was little more than a sketch. I've got all I need from my present measurements, it would just be helpful to compare them to the originals. The estate agent told me that the last owner left all his belongings here. He was sole surviving member of the family, wasn't he? It seems as if Francesco Condemaine made sure that everyone would keep the house private.'

'He was building it for his wife, not for public acclaim,' said Mateo. 'He wasn't interested in becoming famous, he only wanted to make her happy.'

I stopped eating and looked at him. 'Tell me, do I still make you happy?'

'Of course you do. What a question.'

'I know I'm not the maternal type, but –'

'What are you talking about? Bobbie adores you. She'll miss you when she goes to high school. Bobbie, tell your stepmother you love her.'

'I *lurve* you,' said Bobbie obediently, flicking tomato sauce everywhere.

'When you go off to your glamorous boarding school overlooking the sea, Callie will be left all alone here with Rosita and the gardener,' said Mateo, 'so you'd better remember to Skype her when I'm away.'

'Thanks for reminding me,' I said with a shiver, thinking of what might happen if I was alone and one of the connecting doors came open at night.

'If I can find someone to handle the longer trips, I can probably get away with just doing Madrid and Jerez.'

'I'd like that.'

'And then perhaps we should start thinking about a baby.'

I froze.

I had been dreading this moment, and now that it was here I was too dry-mouthed to answer. 'Yes,' I replied, 'but my main concern at the moment is to finish the first draft of the book.' We ended the meal with awkward silences settling between us, silting the air with unspoken doubts.

I sat on the floor of the reading room with my sketches unfolded on the rug. Mateo had driven Bobbie into Gaucia for the evening. As the hours of light shortened, Eduardo's café showed films in the square, and tonight they were running one of Bobbie's favourites, *Close Encounters of the Third Kind*. It seemed like a good idea to let father and daughter spend some time together without me for a change, especially as she would soon be going away. Rosita had the night off, so the house was quiet but for the ever-present ticking of the clocks.

This is what it will be like when Bobbie has gone, I thought morosely.

Marcos Condemaine's drawings from his monograph on Hyperion House covered the light parts only, and made little sense. Parts of them were faded and scribbled over in indecipherable Spanish. There were peculiarities I didn't understand; the passage of the sun was detailed, with pencil lines indicating where light would fall at different times of the year. The only thing you could discern from this was that the so-called servants' quarters remained in perpetual night. Also, the positions of all of the larger clocks in the house were already marked on the plan. Why would you work out where the furniture was going to be placed when the house was still at the building stage?

I sat back on my haunches and thought about Hyperion. He was supposedly the first god to understand the movement of the sun and the moon, and their relation to the other stars, which made him a perfect symbol for the house, and explained his presence on the sundial in the garden. But was it a sundial? The drawing on the plan read; *compass*. I checked the position of the clocks again and looked around for a black felt-tip marker.

Carefully, I drew a line between the seven largest clocks and found myself looking at the constellation of Ursa Major. One of its key components was Mizar, the double star twinned with Alcor.

Francesco, you trickster, I thought. *What were you up to?*

A telescope that wasn't a telescope.

The brass brackets around the edge of the atrium.

Clocks that reflected the constellations.

And then I knew.

He hadn't built a telescope at all, but a *camera obscura*. They looked very similar, but the camera obscura was much lighter and projected the constellations onto an octagonal table, so that the stars could be easily plotted and traced. It was an ancient instrument; the first had been built four hundred years before Christ. That was why Condemaine had needed to build his house here; the equipment required light to operate, and this had probably been the brightest spot for stargazing within a thousand miles.

Heading out into the garden, I looked up into the darkening sky and followed the constellation's faint tracery through the indigo hemisphere. Beneath it stood the bronze boy-god.

It's not just a sundial, I thought, *it's a compass.*

I made my way to the statue that stood in the centre of the lawn. I studied the disc in the boy's hands; perhaps the two halves represented night and day. At first it was hard to see any other correlation, but as I ran my hands over the statue's base I felt the fine grooves cut into its foundation.

There it was, the same pattern of Ursa Major, transcribed from the rotating heavens and set in stone to form the pedestal for a god. The disc which Hyperion held in his hands trembled a little, and I realized that it was not fixed in place but balanced perfectly, an engineering grace-note that was admirable but seemed to serve no real purpose.

And yet when I touched it, it tilted imperceptibly away from the house.

I wondered if this, together with the pattern of stars, might be some kind of marker. The constellation's tail pointed to the rear of the garden, the untamed area ruled by Jerardo. I knew I should wait for the return of daylight, but the house was empty and my impatience overcame my fear. Walking back from the statue in the indicated direction, I reached a thicket of dark bushes, and pushed between them into the wilder grass and rocks.

Even though the light was low, it was hard to imagine what I might find here. At first I'd thought that because Francesco Condemaine had built his baroque home in a spot where few would ever see it, he could afford to have a little fun with the design. Architects often included design gestures to amuse themselves. But the *camera obscura* gave him an accurate reading of the universe, and he used the stars to plan the house. Why? The trees were probably planted later – what else was back here?

Dry bracken covered the area that the watering system could not reach. Past rainstorms had cut gullies through the rock, washing the topsoil out into the barren land beyond the property, making the ground hard to negotiate. I was about to turn back when I saw them, the faint outlines of regular stones, set in a familiar pattern.

The constellation of the Great Bear. It seemed Francesco had not only planned for this life but the next.

I had found the Condemaines' burial ground. Here were small weathered stones roughly conforming to the pattern of the stars, seven of them, all with markings cut into their faces, all rendered unreadable by the elements, their engravings etched away by diurnal bouts of wind, rain and scorching sun.

I felt vaguely disappointed by the discovery, as if I had uncovered a treasure chest only to find it empty. A family graveyard, most likely a cremation site given the resistance of the ground – it was hardly a surprise. After all, unless Francesco Condemaine's body had been shipped home from the battleground at Passchendaele, his children would have been the next to be interred, then his wife, and given the disturbing circumstances of their deaths it was hardly likely that they would have been granted Catholic burials.

Beneath the dry branches and dead leaves I found one of the stones marked by a thin bronze plaque, free of any verdigris. I was still carrying Bobbie's pencil and paper, and knelt down to make a rubbing of the lettering, to translate later. There was also a small white ceramic pot with holes in the top for mourning flowers, badly cracked, its pattern erased long ago. Carefully digging it out from the dirt, I pulled it free and turned it in my hands. As I did so it sifted dust from its fissures and fell apart, and something metal fell out.

When I bent down to retrieve it, I saw that it was a tiny brass key. I felt sure I had seen something similar before somewhere, but where?

Back at the house I took out the tintype of Elena Condemaine that I had taken from the hospital file.

I was right. The key had been attached to a chain to form a pendant. Elena had worn it around her neck in life, and it had been set beside her in death. I wondered if it fitted something in the house, something on the dark side that I had yet to discover.

My heart thumping in my chest, I ran upstairs to try and find what it might open, feeling as if I was about to commit a terrible act of treason.

CHAPTER TWENTY-SEVEN

The Family

When I reached the connecting door on the landing, I baulked at the thought of opening it again. *What the hell are you doing?* I asked myself. *Why would you put yourself through another fright? You've wasted too much time chasing around after phantoms. Too much imagination, that's what Anne always says. You need to put all of this behind you.*

And then I heard Bobbie running in excitedly, followed by the deep bass tones of my laughing husband, and my secrets were tucked away as normal life returned. I slipped the key into my pocket and tried very hard to forget about it.

That evening we were completely at peace with one another. I committed every tiny detail to memory, because it was one of the last times we were all happy together. We played an old-fashioned board game Bobbie had found in one of the bedrooms, a silly thing involving animals and their noises, but it made us all laugh, and Rosita returned to bake a rich, soft *Bica Gallega*, and we ate the whole thing with gallons of buttery cream. Mateo fetched a bottle of Amontillado from his wine rack and we celebrated, and I got a little tipsy. In my London days I'd been able to slam back a bottle of vodka without discernible effect. Now I was drinking like a maiden aunt and loving it.

As we readied ourselves for bed, I made the suggestion that had been rattling in my brain for days, 'Why don't we open up the remaining rooms, Mateo? It seems such a shame to leave them stuffy and closed just because the house keeps them in darkness.'

'You know why,' said Mateo, struggling to undo his shirt buttons. 'I don't want you becoming frightened of the shadows.'

'I'm learning to deal with it, honestly I am. Today I –' I had been about to say *Today I found the Condemaine's family cemetery*, but I realised how that would sound in the wrong context.

'What if you had a panic attack and I was miles away? Worse still, out of the country?'

'I would have to handle it,' I said defiantly. 'I would be fine.'

'I wasn't thinking of you. I was thinking of Bobbie.'

'Bobbie will be going to boarding school soon. Anyway, we have Mrs Delgadillo with us.'

'She's old, Callie. Have you noticed how slow she's getting on the stairs lately? I couldn't take the risk.' He got into bed and turned out all the lights except the little nightlight I kept on my side of the bed, and held me lightly until I fell asleep.

The weather was changing. I checked the forecast and found nothing but storms ahead. 'That's the summer over,' said Rosita with grim finality, passing me on the landing, her ruddy arms loaded with soap-fresh laundry.

Mateo had already left for five days in Madrid. Bobbie was fractious and fidgety. If Julieta had been here, she would have known how to calm the girl with lessons that looked like games, but I was at a loss.

The damp heat rose throughout the morning, making me nervous and uncomfortable. Sweat trickled down the back of my neck, and I spoke sharply to Bobbie, who was aimlessly running about in the hall. Nothing seemed to be in its rightful place.

'What are you doing?' I asked Bobbie. 'Can't you just play quietly somewhere? Those are your best white socks.'

'There's no-one to play with, unless you count *them*,' said the girl, sliding off along the freshly polished hall and colliding with a grandfather clock so that it chimed dully in its case.

'Count who?' I asked, following. 'Stop doing that.'

'The people who live in the back rooms,' she said matter-of-factly.

'What are you talking about?'

'I've seen them.' Bobbie concentrated on her sliding. 'I didn't before, I thought you were imagining things. But I see them now. I see more of them every day.'

'Wait, where do you see them?' I asked. 'The doors are locked.'

'Outside of course. Through the windows of the closed parts, if you look hard enough. You can see them too, I know you can. You told me you could. They hate us.'

'Even if there were such people,' I said carefully, 'why would they hate us?'

'Because we're living, and we're happy. They want us to be like them. Sad and dead.'

'How do you know this? Who are they, Bobbie?'

'Don't you know?' She slid back and forth, teasing me, getting on my nerves.

'I just wondered who you think they are. Stand still for a minute. What do they look like?'

'There's an old, old woman who's gone mad. And there's her child who's rotting to bits. And there's a man who looks like he's been blown up, and another one that looks like –'

'Stop it,' I said. 'There's no-one there and you know it. You're just being naughty because you're bored today –'

Bobbie finally stopped sliding. 'I'll show you if you like. If you really can't see them for yourself. But I know you can. And Rosita can see them too. And Jerardo.'

I knelt and held her shoulders. 'How do you know all this?'

'I don't for sure because she never talks about them, but I've seen Rosita looking toward the dark parts. I follow her when she winds the clocks. She's frightened of the other people. She stays away from the doors.' Thunder rumbled distantly. 'And Jerardo won't come inside the house. He's frightened too.'

'Now you're frightening me,' I said. 'Let's just stop all this nonsense.'

'Don't you want to see them?' Bobbie teased. 'Are you really scared?'

'I can't see them because there's no-one there.'

'Isn't there? Then you must come with me.' Bobbie grabbed her hand and pulled me toward the front door, yanking it open. Outside the first fat drops of rain had begun to fall from the blackening sky.

'Bobbie, let go,' I said, trying to free my hand, worrying that I might hurt the girl if I tugged too hard.

'It's alright, they can't get you so long as you stay on this side of the house.' She ran along the sandy path in her socks as it began to turn to mud, and I was forced to follow.

Finally Bobbie stopped in the lee of the cliff wall. 'Here,' she said. 'We have to go down the back of the house.' And she ran into the narrow corridor between cliff and brick, forcing me to follow. 'They won't be able to see you because the sky is dark, so you won't stand out. It's the best time to see them.' She stopped before the window at the rear. 'Look through the crack in the shutters and stay very still,' she instructed.

Slowly, I brought my face to the glass and waited for my eyes to adjust. I saw the familiar wing-backed chairs, the pine dresser, the framed photographs on the sideboard, the brown rugs and brown paintings.

And then I saw her, forming very gradually from the thickening darkness. That pitiful creature with the white china mask and a body that had seen no sunlight for so long, and the straggly unclean hair that she pulled at in misery, tearing it out one strand at a time. The back of her head and her bare shoulders were covered in livid dry patches and sores. The dusty black material of her dress had worn through and was barely hanging on her thin frame. Even though no sound came through the wood and the glass, I could imagine her ulcerated mouth opening and closing in a series of pitiful sobs. Every now and again she pulled feebly at the frayed leather straps of the mask.

Another creature scampered past, something filthy and feral that ran on all fours, circling around her, shoving at her. It twitched and twisted like a trapped animal, then darted behind the dresser.

'Come on,' said Bobbie excitedly. 'There are others. The worst one is in the room next door.' As the rain began to torrent into the chasm she pulled me along to the adjoining window. 'Get close,' she said excitedly. 'The shutters are tighter in this room. You can't see so much.'

I felt unable to think for myself, and could only do as I was instructed. 'Do you see?' Bobbie kept saying. 'Do you see it now?'

I peered through the narrow crack but could just make out the dim shape of the fireplace and one of the armchairs. There was nothing else. The room was empty. 'There's nothing here,' I said uncertainly.

'You have to be patient,' warned Bobbie. 'He's trying to trick you but he's there all right, he's always there.'

'No, there's nobody...'

And then he was there. A terrible staring eye occupied the gap between the shutters, first one then the other, bobbing back and forth. An occluded eye blotched with some terrible sickness. It pulled back sharply, the better to judge me. This creature was different from the others, angrier and more aware of its cage, twitchy and furious in its desire to get free.

Five members of the same family. Francesco, Elena, Augustin and Farriol and Maria.

An entire history of lives tragically diverted from light into darkness. First Francesco had been killed, then the children's lives were stolen away by someone or something, and the distraught Elena lost her wits, finally taking her own life. Death, murder, madness. Wrongs unrighted, harms unhealed.

Elena had been promised a life of light and happiness. Instead she had lost everything. No wonder the Condemaines wanted to reclaim what was rightfully theirs. But how could they do it, when they were unable to leave the sunless rooms of the house? All they could do was make themselves known to us and what – try to drive us out?

I was filled with a terrible feeling of sadness for the unfinished lives of those left behind in old houses. The Condemaines had not meant to hurt with their clutching and scratching but had been trying to reach us. I knew that we had to do something that would reach out to them.

'You see?' said Bobbie with an air of triumph. 'We can both see them now. Something else is going to happen. We must run away with Daddy and never come back.'

'This is our home,' I cried. 'We can't –'

Bobbie's shriek cut me off. As the rain sluiced down in the chasm between the house and the cliff, there was the sound of a window being pushed open. Raising my eyes, I saw to my horror that he had shoved the window up on its sash and was climbing out like some monstrous spider, his arms angled sharply, his head low, pulling himself through the space toward us.

I grabbed Bobbie's hand and we ran as fast as we dared, the brickwork and the wet wall of the cliff catching at our clothes. I didn't dare to see how close he was behind us.

And then we were back out and sliding, slipping across the lawn to the entrance with its open door, still in the downpour but out of the shadows, running toward the safety of the house.

CHAPTER TWENTY-EIGHT

The Confrontation

IT WAS MY fault, I knew.

The one phobia that could be transmitted to others was my fear of the dark, and now I was sure I had infected Bobbie. Elena Condemaine had revived it in me and I had passed it on to Mateo's daughter like a virus. Wracked with guilt and shame, I dragged the girl back into the bright rooms and took her upstairs to run a bath for her, forcing her to wash even though she complained in confused defiance.

It was my fault that Bobbie had been unwittingly placed in danger. The phobia had become a contagion. Why else did the girl believe she could see things that couldn't possibly be there?

Even though the situation seemed absurd, I tried to think it through with some sense of logic. If the house was haunted by the ghosts of that tragedy of nearly a century ago, were those poor creatures doomed to stay in the shadows until something could liberate them? What if I tore down the shutters and tried to get some light in there, no matter how faint, would it despatch them to another place or merely draw them into our world? Would we have to die first, so that they could take our places?

I didn't understand why the events of the distant past should continue to afflict those living in the present. The ghosts of the Condemaine family only stayed in the darkened areas. Were they somehow connected to the construction of the *camera obscura*?

Maria had been right about one thing: our housekeeper had to know more than she was letting on.

In the back of my mind was one abiding thought; that Mateo must know nothing of this. If he knew, all of my mother's predictions would come to pass. Anne had been a force of disruption and damage before, and might become so again. That could not be allowed to happen. I had finally made a happy life for myself and them. We were happy as a family, and nothing could be allowed to jeopardise that state.

I had to solve the problem alone, and the first step toward doing that was by making some assumptions. The fact that the Condemaine family had allowed themselves to appear to the living was an indication that something was still terribly wrong and needed to be put right. I *knew* this stuff, I knew how hauntings worked.

The key held the answer. Elena Condemaine had worn it around her neck while she was alive, and had been buried with it. But it was too small to fit any of the connecting doors. It had to belong to something inside one of the shadow-rooms. There was something in Elena's mirror-bedroom which she alone could access.

I went to the summer house and found a hammer and chisel.

'What are you doing?' Bobbie called from the bathroom.

'Nothing. Dry yourself and stay there. I have to make some noise but it's nothing.'

Heading for the upper hallway, I approached the connecting door at the end and unlocked it, crossing swiftly inside to the bedroom. I had brought the torch with me. Flicking it on, I moved the beam around the dusty still air, highlighting a bed similar to our own, but much smaller and lower, covered with an ancient floral spread. The dressing table mirror had clouded with age. It was just another room, another minor reflection of our own, trapped in the period of its creation, with ugly old furniture and depressing half-tiled, half-papered walls. But if it truly matched, there would be a small room beyond it, the equivalent of my dressing room, little more than a cupboard. I'd known it was there but had never considered it important.

It was there, and it was locked. The key didn't fit, either.

The noise of the hammerhead hitting the chisel could be heard throughout the house, but it couldn't be helped. I punched at the brass ferrule on the dressing room door again and again until I could feel it tearing loose. The wood started to splinter, covering the floor with slivers of brown paintwork. With one final blow the lock broke away from the door. I threw the chisel aside and pulled it open.

All I could see was blackness.

Barely able to control my panicked breathing, I prepared to cross the threshold. It was silent and dead inside. I took a careful step forward, feeling a familiar terror rising in my heart.

I edged further in and listened. Nothing. A few clothes still hung in an open-fronted cupboard. Everything was so small. People had been shorter and thinner then. The plain black-buttoned dresses smelled of mothballs and rot. I reached in and touched a yellowed gown, only to find that the material crumbled beneath my touch, sifting to the floor.

I was out of ideas. The only other room was the bathroom, its gangrenous copper boiler dead and decayed, the bath stained brown. Remembering the leeches stretching their grey bodies out of the standing water toward a source of fresh blood, I hastily moved away. Behind me, some dresses slid from their hangers and fell in a powdery heap, making me start.

On the other side of the bedroom, the door through which I had entered quietly closed.

I turned slowly, sensing a presence. The torch beam wandered across peeling wallpaper, some fallen plaster. I stepped out of the bathroom, back into the dressing room, and felt a breath of air passing me. More dark clothes had drifted down from their hangers.

This is my fear made real, I thought. *If I fail now, everything comes apart.*

The dressing room was still and silent. No clocks could be heard ticking in the rest of the house. My torch picked up nothing but motes of dust in the necrophile atmosphere. I stepped over the fallen clothes and back into the bedroom.

She was here again, and had moved to the dressing table.

I could see her masked face clearly in the mottled mirror, her neck bony and green-tinged. Her matted hair had a shimmering surface that appeared to move back and forth in the penumbral gloom, as if she was covered in a fine web of spiders. There was nothing threatening about her, just a sense of bitter distress, as though she had been creeping back and forth here all through the years, wondering what she had done to deserve her fate.

She tugged a blackened silver brush at her tangled locks, tearing out the knots as if deliberately trying to hurt herself. The feral child-creature crept out from beneath the dressing table, scuttling on all fours. It watched me from behind its mother's frayed black dress. I needed to speak to her, but did not want the husband to hear and find me – I knew that he was the dangerous one.

'Senora Condemaine,' I began. 'What can I do? What do I need to do to set you free?'

The brush fell to the floor with a clatter. The poor creature turned and its eyes widened inside the mask as it stared past me. She raised her hand to her china smile as I turned.

I could smell his musky stink and felt sure that here was someone to be truly feared. I stepped back and stumbled, regained my footing but found I was cornered beside the windowless bathroom where I would end up being imprisoned if I didn't make my move.

The buzzing of hornets filled my ears as a black and yellow cloud dropped down from the corner of the ceiling behind us. The noise seemed to cause him intense pain, and as he bellowed I ran for the door, dropping the torch, slamming into the furniture, shifting chairs, rucking the carpets, knocking the photographs from their place on the sideboard.

Throwing open the door and slamming it behind me, I passed through to the other side and into the safety of the light.

I knew then that this was a war between two families – one living, and one dead.

CHAPTER TWENTY-NINE

The Confession

THE CEILING FAN.

I could hear it cutting through the air above me. I was in my bedroom, lying on my own bed looking up at the ceiling, and there was someone sitting with me.

'You're awake,' said Bobbie. 'I tried to wake you up but I couldn't do it.' She gave a tentative smile.

I tried to speak but my mouth was too dry. I fumbled for the decanter of water on the bedside table, and spilled some into my mouth. 'What happened?'

'You got out.' Bobbie pointed back out to the hallway. 'It was lighting up time. Getting dark. I knew they'd be awake. I heard the clocks strike.'

'Is Rosita back?'

Bobbie nodded. 'She saw the open door. She's gone down to the kitchen now. I think she's scared.'

I pushed myself up onto one arm and found it ringed with a yellowish bruise. 'I bet she's not as scared as I was.' I tried to make light of it.

'We have to tell Daddy,' said Bobbie.

'We can't,' I replied. 'He'll blame me. He'll think I've got you to believe my crazy stories.'

'You should rest.' She could be very grown-up and serious. I knew one day she would be loved very deeply by her partner.

'I've done enough resting.' I climbed off the bed but the room swam. Getting out into the corridor was like crossing an ocean deck, but I made it to the landing and swayed down the staircase.

Senora Delgadillo was in the kitchen, taking a tray of cooked pork from the oven. The smell made me feel sick. 'Rosita, I want you to come with me,' I instructed.

'I am preparing supper,' she said.

'Just leave it.'

'But it will be spoiled –'

'Now!' I pointed toward the stairs. 'I want you to see this and explain it to me.' Rosita followed me in silence. She had seen the opened connecting door and knew exactly where I was taking her.

We reached the upper hallway. Bobbie had run off, not wishing to witness what would follow. I pushed open the door and placed my hand firmly on her back. 'I want you to look in there and tell me what you see.'

She stalled. 'I can't.'

'You can do it.'

'I mean I can't see. There's no light.'

I searched the floor for the torch I had dropped and found it, switching it on, running the beam around the walls. Everything was as it had been. There was not a piece of furniture out of place. They had put it all back.

'What do you expect me to see?' Rosita asked.

'You know the Condemaines are here with us. You know they live on in this side of the house.'

'The family has gone, Senora Torres. They are no longer here.'

'They are here,' I said doggedly. 'Their bodies are buried in our garden, and their spirits are here. They want to take over our lives. This is a terrible, dangerous place and you know all about it – you've always known about it. Francesco's wife always had to look happy for him – why? What was wrong with her? Why is there so much sadness on this side?'

'This is *not* an unhappy house!' cried the housekeeper, affronted but plainly upset. 'I have never suffered any bad experiences here.'

'You're lying.'

Rosita twisted free. 'I think perhaps you are unwell, Senora. You should allow me to call your husband.'

I knew she was trying to hide the truth from me. 'All I want you to do,' I said, trying to stay calm, 'is to admit what you can see. What the rest of us can now see.'

'But I don't see anything. I don't know why you're behaving like this.'

'How could you have been here for so long and *not* notice? All those years, sometimes entirely alone? You didn't hear or see anything at all? I don't believe you.'

I no longer cared what Rosita thought of me, or whether I had to bully the truth out of her. The first step to ending the situation was to make her admit that it was real. 'Maybe you see something different when you look at them,' I said, 'but you know they're there. What do you see?'

'I see only happiness in this house,' Rosita replied stubbornly, 'so long as we all stay in the light.'

'Why? What if we don't? What happens in the darkness?'

'You can see for yourself. You know what happens. Don't ask any more of me – I can tell you nothing more.' It was tantamount to a confession, but of what? That she knew something she could never speak of?

I didn't understand. Releasing the housekeeper's hand, I sent her from the room as the strain broke over me and I fought back tears. Was that it? Did the Condemaines need me to be unhappy before they could take over my life, take my husband and his child, steal back the lives that had been cruelly snatched from them?

I felt on the verge of understanding it all – the key, the stars, the house, the Condemaines, everything – but still the last part eluded me. If only I had realised then and stopped. But of course, it was already too late to stop what had been set in motion so long ago.

CHAPTER THIRTY

The Artist

'WELL, HELLO STRANGER!' said Celestia, folding away her copy of The Times. 'My dear, do pull up a chair. We haven't seen you in weeks.'

The square was all but deserted now. Even though the temperatures were still fairly high, the season had ended and the last tourists had gone home, leaving the former artists' agent by herself outside the café. 'Lola told me they're planning to shut this place next month for the whole of the winter,' she confided. 'Apparently there aren't enough of us left to warrant keeping it open anymore. I think that old bastard Eduardo wants to skip off to his winter bolt-hole with his ugly little mistress. What are we poor ex-pats expected to do in the meantime? Cook for ourselves?' She donned the glasses she kept hooked on a chain around her neck and peered at me. 'My dear, you look absolutely awful. What on earth have you done to yourself?'

'I had a go at trimming my hair,' I said apologetically, touching the ends. 'I didn't like the cut I had here, and don't want to go all the way into Marbella. But it didn't take very well.'

'You look very tired.'

'I haven't been sleeping –'

'But everything's all right? I mean, you and Mateo, you're getting along? In my experience couples always lose weight just before they announce they're getting divorced, and you've shed loads, not that there was much of you to begin with.'

'No, we're fine. It's just – Rosita's meals are too big and they put me off eating. But really, we've never been happier. Bobbie's studying hard, getting ready for her move to boarding school. Mateo's going to spend less time travelling so that he can be at home with me more often.'

'I heard you lost Julieta. That's a shame. She's having to look after her ghastly old mother. How's Rosita?'

'She's – well, exactly the same.'

'Then whatever could be wrong?' Celestia poured a hefty measure of wine into a clean glass and slid it across the table to me. 'And don't say there's nothing because I can see it. You look positively drawn with worry.'

'There are some things –' I dropped my head, trying to work out how much I could reveal. 'Mateo wants us to try for a baby.'

'That's wonderful.'

'No, it's not. I underwent a very difficult termination when I was seventeen. It's doubtful I'll ever be able to go full term.'

'That's not the end of the world these days.'

'He's passionately against abortion. I never told him.'

'Oh. Now that *can* be a bit of a stumbling block when it comes to the older Spanish male. He'll just have to understand that times have changed. We're not living in the dark ages anymore.'

'I don't want to fight with him. He's away so much, I get frightened he'll stop caring for me.'

'You need to have more confidence.' Celestia looked shrewdly at me. 'What happened to you?' she asked. 'When you arrived here you were so feisty and emancipated and full of beans. It's like something has knocked all the stuffing out of you.'

'I've had trouble adjusting to life here. The house –'

'Ah, the *house*.' She lit a fresh cigarillo. 'I wondered if that was the problem. I was talking to Jordi the other day and he said you'd had trouble finding out anything more about its rather chequered history.'

'Yes, there were some missing pages in the only reference volume, and nobody here was able to help me. I don't think I'll be able to finish the book without more information. It crossed my mind that perhaps some of Francesco Condemaine's more important private papers never left the house, although I've searched everywhere and found nothing. And there's something else.'

Celestia jetted smoke into the air, and waited for me to form my thoughts.

'Do you believe in ghosts?' I said finally, realising how stupid the G word sounded when spoken aloud.

'That rather depends on what you mean by ghosts. If you're talking about hidden things that resurface, then there are phantoms here, certainly. Ghosts of old treacheries, ghosts of dead family members, ghosts of the Civil War. They leave long shadows. There was an old man in this village, a Nationalist who raped his daughter for years and beat his sons half to death. Now his penniless great-grandchildren are fighting not to let that awful past return. There are those who say his spirit is trying to break through once more, into the next generation. There's such a thing as ghosts in the blood.'

'But real ones,' I said. 'Physical manifestations that look and feel like real people?'

'Spain has a great many ghosts,' she said evasively, waving away smoke. 'Some are real, some imagined. Of course, people have seen phantom versions of the dead in every age. The phenomenon isn't always associated with the illiterate and ignorant. And they're not always ghosts as you or I would imagine them. They've been called other things: *larvae, umbrae mortuorum, lemures*.'

'So what are they?'

'I tend to think of them as shadow people. They're a mirror, an inverse of the living, that's all. They don't necessarily want to hurt anyone, just to be left alone. You can think of them as animals that scratch because they don't like to be touched. And perhaps your house really is haunted. You say there are clocks everywhere. A clock is a familiar *memento mori*, symbolising the flight of time, a funerary motif. You said you heard breathing, another common phenomenon. These days all sorts of personal items are pronounced haunted in order to shove up their resale value on eBay.'

'Am I supposed to take that seriously?'

'Darling, you're the one who raised the subject. But you know, the oddest thing is that there are no *actual* haunted houses, by which I mean there are no apparitional buildings, just ghostly projections inside them. Perhaps you have the only one in the world. Wouldn't that be something? Then the sightseers would really come!'

'You seem to know an awful lot about it.'

'I do, so it's just as well you came to me. Why, have you seen an actual ghost?'

'Not one – several. They live in what I thought were the servants' quarters. I've seen them. I've felt them.' I held up the underside of my arm, which was spotted with black bruises.

She was taken aback. 'What the hell are those?'

'Sometimes I go into the other half and look for them,' I explained quietly. 'I have to be sure that what I'm seeing is real, that it's not just me. I went in again last night and one of them grabbed me and threw me across the room.'

'But that's a hand print,' said Celestia, examining my arm with care. She took my right hand and placed it over the bruises. The shape of my thumb and fingers matched perfectly. 'Are you sure you didn't do this to yourself? In your sleep, perhaps?'

'That's what I thought at first, that I was imagining them, but now Bobbie sees them too. Yet she seems utterly unperturbed, as if it's to be expected. She's a child of course and is quite happy believing in such things. But I'm frightened for her safety.'

'You really believe what you're telling me?'

'I've seen Elena Condemaine. I know she's real, and that she's responsible for everything I've seen happening. I saw my husband die, and I think she'll try to take him from me because she lost her own husband so tragically.'

'Have you told anyone else about this?'

'I tried to tell Rosita, but you know how she is. She puts the house before everything.'

'Oh dear.' For once Celestia seemed at a loss for words, and I was wondering if she was trying to find a way to humour me.

'What is it?'

'There are people here who could tell you stories, but I didn't want them to upset you. Certain people in the village envy your husband's wealth. They resent the intrusion of outsiders. So far, Maria and I have managed to keep them away from you. Perhaps there's someone you should meet. Alfonse may not be able to tell you what you want to hear, but he might just help. He's an artist, he's been here longer than any of us. Let me make a call.' She dug out her ancient mobile.

A few minutes later, Celestia took my arm and led me across the square to the higher reaches of the village, where the last remaining streets overlooked the green plains and the glittering ocean far below. The end house we reached was, by Gaucia's standards at least, grand and old.

Celestia knocked on the door and stood back. 'I'd watch yourself around him,' she warned. 'He's a randy old goat.'

The door was opened by a sun-wizened old man in a straw hat and shorts who stood not much more than four and a half feet high. 'So this is the girl,' he said, openly staring at my bare legs. 'I suppose you'd better come in.'

He set out sherry and trays of almonds on the veranda. We sat facing the distant band of silver sea. 'I knew them all except the first – Francesco was before even my time – but I knew them from Marcos Condemaine to Amancio Lueches. They weren't like Francesco at all.'

'What do you mean?' I asked.

'They were weak,' said Alfonse. 'Marcos was a mechanic who failed at everything he touched. Amancio – who even knows what he was? I don't think he ever held down a proper job in his life. But Francesco, by all accounts he was a man of vision, a genius. And despite what you may have read he was more astrologer than astronomer. He built the house for her, to make sure she would always be happy. And she was.'

'Alfonse, we all know what happened to Elena,' said Celestia impatiently. 'She went mad trying to keep her children alive without a father. She couldn't have been that bloody happy.'

'She wrote letters to her family,' I said. 'She told them that she could manage by herself and that she was fine, but she wasn't.'

'My grandfather adored her,' said Alfonse. 'But nobody would help her.'

'What do you mean?'

'Have you heard of the Hyperion Society?'

'Yes – but I couldn't find out what it was.'

'Francesco Condemaine was an occultist. There was a crippled boy who worked on the building of the house, and it was said that in order to consecrate Hyperion he carved the pattern of the sun into the lad's back with a razor. Oh, don't look so shocked. He and the Society were rumoured to have done far worse than that. The upper classes treated the uneducated with terrible cruelty in those days. Many so-called intellectuals thought themselves occultists back then. For a time it was fashionable among a certain class. It was an era of table rappers and séances, and reading fortunes from the stars, a time of seers and spiritualists. Every small town had a crazy old woman who mixed love potions for lonely girls and then dispensed herbal remedies when they got themselves pregnant. And they're still around. It's just their methods that have changed. Look at Maria Gonzales and her shop full of shit. A hundred years ago she'd have been branded a witch. Amancio told me that Francesco was on a higher plane. He trusted in the sun, the moon and the stars. He worshipped Hyperion. And he knew that the heavens governed the actions of man. That's why he built the house.'

'Alfonse, Callie thinks she's seen Elena Condemaine and her husband in the house,' Celestia explained.

The old man spluttered out a chuckle. 'She's long dead and gone. I imagine her ashes are buried in your garden with the rest of them.'

'But I saw her for myself, living in the rooms we don't use.'

'There are no ghosts,' said the old man adamantly. 'There's only guilt, which lasts longer than memory itself, and evil, which always overcomes goodness. But you're far too young and pretty to know about things like that. The Condemaines were too high-born for us. They kept to themselves, and there was resentment. After news reached us that Francesco had been killed fighting on the side of the English, while Spain maintained its neutrality, the villagers demanded that his house be given up to the state. The people here were simple folk. Most of them had hardly ever even been to the coast. They heard about the architect and his belief in astrology, and probably misread something more exotic into that. They took a vote to refuse Elena help, and punished anyone who tried to break ranks. Elena killed her children to stop them from starving to death. In the process, she went mad.'

I could suddenly imagine it all, the wealthy Condemaines who never visited the village, the stupid gossip about secret cabals and strange rites, a workman who had seen the stone lettering and planet-studded friezes, the patterns of the heavens cut into the doors, the story of a boy tortured by the cruel builder, all of it feeding into their fearful ignorance. A vow of silence against Elena Condemaine, even when she desperately needed their help.

'So they shut her out and left her to die.'

'Oh, I don't suppose it was as dramatic as that. They turned a blind eye and got on with their own lives. By all accounts she was too proud a woman to persist in asking the villagers for aid.'

'But they must have known that her children were suffering.'

Alfonse sighed and sipped his sherry. 'A lot of people went through terrible hardships back then. It was all a long time ago. Who knows what really happened? Stories get embellished with the retelling. Everyone likes to write themselves into a tragedy.'

'Well, now they're trying to get out,' I said miserably. 'They're in terrible pain. I don't know what to do.'

'Perhaps you read something, heard about them, and it played on your imagination. You fell asleep,' said Celestia kindly.

'No, what I saw – what I can see – is very real. There's not just one of them anymore. I can see the whole family. And it keeps happening. Every time I go into the dark.'

'You may really think you can see these people, my dear, but you know what I think?' said Alfonse. 'It's a trick. And if it isn't, what could such trapped souls possibly want?'

'Isn't it obvious?' I said. 'They want me to take their place. So that they can have the lives they were promised. Don't ghosts always need something?'

'In my experience it's the seers who need something, not the spectres.' Alfonse drained his glass and set it down. 'Such visitations are more about the living than the dead. You must ask yourself not what they did wrong, but what you have done.'

CHAPTER THIRTY-ONE

The Car

THE FOLLOWING AFTERNOON, Jerardo had a hospital appointment for an injection that would ease his arthritis, and as it was hurting him too badly to drive, Rosita accompanied him to the Santa Theresa Hospital in Estepona. It was Mateo's last day at home before his bi-monthly New York trip, and he took Bobbie into Marbella so that she could have lunch with her mother, who was staying there overnight, attending some kind of fashion show.

The skies were cooler today, and grey cloud had locked itself in, screening out the sun all the way from the cliffs to the coast. I told myself that the light was nowhere near as low as it would be under similar circumstances in London, but even so I warily skirted the shadow of the trees as I headed for the property border to collect the mail.

I arrived just as the yellow postal van was pulling away. Bobbie had asked her father to send her a postcard from wherever his trips took him, but they turned up with hopeless irregularity. I found a pair inside the box, one with an out-of-date photograph of the *feria* at Jerez and one of the Sherlock Holmes pub in London. The wind had been ever-present for the last few days, and had battered the loose leaves from the trees. I stopped and looked at the altered view, the bushes and rocks of the lower road exposed for the first time since I had arrived.

I could see something yellow angled between the branches.

The wind caught the leaves again and shifted them, removing the view. Frowning to myself, I set off down the hill. As I drew close, an uncomfortable feeling began to settle in the pit of my stomach. I stepped up onto the empty roadway and followed its curve, waiting for the object to reveal itself. When I drew level with the site, there was nothing to be seen. I turned about. The blacktop ran around an outcrop of boulders that shielded passing drivers from a series of indentations in the landscape, where the runoff came down from the mountains. Sometimes eagles and vultures swooped and wheeled above this spot, searching for prey. I cautiously approached the edge and looked down.

There, almost completely buried by broken branches, was a canary-coloured Seat.

The vehicle lay tipped on its side, its offside wheel badly twisted. It appeared to have been there for some while. It was hardly surprising that no-one had noticed it; very few cars passed this way, and if they did it was usually because they were returning from the hills above, which meant that they coasted down on the other side of the road.

Puzzled, I clambered down the scree-covered slope. There was no-one inside the vehicle. The passenger-side window had shattered, so I peered in. A red Avis folder lay on the floor of the car. The door wouldn't open, but I was able to reach inside and grab it.

The vehicle had been registered to Anne Constance Shaw. A London address had been hand-printed underneath in blue biro. My mother's car. I tried to fit the pieces together, but drew a blank. What the hell was it doing here? I had watched Anne leave the house nearly six weeks ago, and had spoken to her twice on the phone since, but she hadn't mentioned having an accident. Why would she hide such a thing?

I tried the boot. It opened easily but was empty, as was the glove compartment. The only thing that identified the car as the one hired by my mother was the rental agreement.

I tried to think what could have happened. Anne never did anything without a carefully reasoned plan. Her trip to visit me had been far from accidental. I wanted to call her, but I had left my mobile back in the kitchen.

As I headed back to the house, the familiar distant sound of thunder trundled over the cliffs.

I kept Anne's number on speed-dial, not that I used it much. Too often our conversations had turned into arguments, and after the last time –

'Hi, I can't get to the phone right now, but leave a number and I'll get back to you.' Anne was never around to take calls in the day, and hadn't a clue how to pick up her messages, so the process was always hit and miss. I left a short message and rang off. I waited, thinking, listening to the ticking in the rooms and halls, the endless counting down of time.

I tried to recreate events in my head. Anne said she had been visiting a friend of Sandy's, but I had no idea who that might be. After our argument, she had left without waiting for her alcohol-high anger to subside, and must have driven off the road. But if she had deliberately chosen to abandon the car, how did she get to the coast? And if she'd had an accident, why didn't she come back up to the house? Admittedly, it would have been difficult for her to swallow her pride and return, but the day had been scorching and she was half-cut. She wouldn't have got far on foot.

I heard the key in the front door, and Bobbie came running in. I rose and handed her the postcards, trying not to show concern. 'Look, two more for your collection. They arrived after Daddy came back from his last trip.'

Mateo was wearing his first sweater of the year. Like all people of Spanish descent, he started layering up the moment the thermometer fell below twenty five degrees Centigrade. 'That's because the cards go to the post office at Gaucia. I'm amazed anything gets delivered here at all.' He kissed my cheek. 'How are you doing? You look a little tired. Is Rosita back yet?'

'No, she has to wait with Jerardo until he's had his X-ray,' I said. 'I can make you a toasted sandwich.'

'No, it's fine, I'll get something at the airport later. But you might be required to feed missy here, she's not stopped eating all afternoon. I still haven't packed.'

'Mateo...'

He turned on the stairs to look at me; never more handsome, never more trusting. 'Yup?'

I had been about to tell him, but the words fell away. He was leaving in a little over an hour's time. What could he do if I told him about the car? It would only make him worry more, and he had enough on his mind. Right now it seemed that our love for each other was the only thing that made any sense. 'It's nothing,' I said. 'You need to get packed. Rosita insisted on folding your shirts.'

I sat in the drawing room and watched the view, the green gardens, the statue, the amber mountain edge, the dip of the coastline beyond. The shadows never changed. The effect was so subtle that I only noticed it when I went elsewhere, to the café in Gaucia, where Celestia constantly moved her table to stay out of the sun's glare, or to Jordi's library, where slivers of sunlight crept over the untouched shelves. Everyone else had to move to accommodate the sunlight except us.

And the Condemaines.

While Mateo was packing I rang my mother again, but as usual the call went straight through to her voicemail. When Mateo came back down with his bag I made him drink a cup of coffee, and sat watching him. 'What?' he asked, amused.

'Do you have any idea how beautiful you are?' I asked.

'As long as I make you smile,' he said. 'I've been leaving you alone too much. After this trip things will be easier. I'm dreading it. Do you have any idea what the immigration lines are like at

JFK? A nightmare. And when I get there I have to fire someone. I've seen enough of the unemployment crisis here to know how that feels. You will be okay, won't you?'

'If you remember to Skype me.'

'I just don't like to wake you.'

I smiled. 'Wake me, whenever, wherever.'

He rose and came over to me, lifting me from my seat to take me in his arms. 'My last big trip,' he promised. 'After that it will just be about the three of us.'

I kissed his chin, his lips. I touched his neck, his hairline. 'Do you ever feel that maybe we don't deserve our happiness?' I asked.

'That's a strange thing to say.'

'It's just that when I'm with you I'm so content, I start to think it's too good to last.'

'If you want to feel guilty about being happy, you should convert to being a Catholic,' he said. 'Anyway, you deserve happiness.'

'Why?' I asked. 'I've done nothing for you.'

He studied my eyes. 'You really don't see it? You've given me the world. After my marriage failed, I buried myself in work. I might never have been able to break out of that if I hadn't met you.' He brushed my cheek with the back of his hand and picked up his bag. Bobbie was dancing ahead to open the front door and ask questions about his return.

The feeling of foreboding would not leave me, as if this might be the last time I would ever see him.

CHAPTER THIRTY-TWO

The Letters

I WAS AWOKEN by the sound of falling rain. My head was full of clouds, and would not be shaken back to life. Rising, I wrapped myself in my grey silk dressing gown and went to check on Bobbie, but found her room empty, her bed a mess. According to the clock it was nearly nine. That meant I had overslept. I had taken two Zimovanes the previous night.

I stood at the head of the stairs and called, but heard nothing. The house was empty and silent but for the ticking of clocks. In the kitchen I found a piece of cardboard propped against the olive oil bottle on the table; 'Gone shopping with Rosita, we're buying you a SURPRISE! xx B'.

I showered and made the beds, thinking that it would make a change not to leave all the clearing up to the housekeeper. I was putting away the bottle of Zimovane tablets when I saw the little brass key on my bedside table, and once again wondered why it didn't fit any of the doors.

Because it opens something precious, I realised, *not a door at all.* No woman would choose to wear a key on her bosom unless it unlocked something close to her heart.

I thought of love letters, and then I knew. The first time I had gone beneath the building to look at the old telescopic mechanism with Mateo, I had seen an ornate French *bonheur du jour* writing desk in the corner and had assumed it belonged to Francesco Condemaine. But it was too elaborate and delicate for a man. And I was now sure that whatever was inside it belonged to his wife.

Going to the staircase, I opened the door to the basement. The writing desk still stood there untouched. Its lid was down as before, but I could tell that the little brass key was at least the right size. It fitted smoothly, and unlocked the wooden panel on the front.

Inside, it was clear that nothing had been disturbed for the best part of a century. An old fountain pen lay on a blotter, next to a dried-out inkwell and a wooden rocker covered in peeling green felt, used for pressing letters. Several small sepia photographs in tarnished silver frames held portraits so small and faded as to be unidentifiable. A drawer stood on either side of the *escritoire*. One held a folded sheet of draughtsman paper, which I carefully opened out.

It was Francesco Condemaine's missing sketch of the house, each room and passage carefully labelled. Everything was so tiny, precise and delicate. But I could see at once that there was something different about it. There were no servants' quarters marked out at all. Instead there was just a gap between the rear wall of the house and the cliff. All I could think was that he must have changed his mind and added the rooms after finishing his design.

In the other drawer I found a bundle of letters tied with fine blue ribbon that proved surprisingly tough to break apart. Knowing that they would be in Spanish, I needed to show them to Jordi.

I found Jerardo in the garden, digging out the dried stump of a rose bush. 'Could you take me into Gaucia?' I asked.

He gave me a look that explained with perfect eloquence that he was not my taxi service, but finally creaked to his feet and dusted down his jeans, beckoning me to follow him.

He took the bends in the road with such ferocity that I was thrown against the door of the truck, but at least I was able to keep my window open and breathe fresh air. Depositing me in the town square, he barely stayed long enough to allow me to climb out.

I found Jordi in the library, half-asleep. He sat up sharply when I entered, smoothing down his hair and cleaning his glasses. 'Senora Torres, it's good to see you. I hope you are well.'

'It seems I'm always asking for your help,' I apologised. 'I wondered if you would mind taking a look at these.' I opened my bag and removed the letters and the floor plan, placing them before him. 'And this is a rubbing I made from a headstone in the garden. I tried to translate it but some of the letters are faded. Let me at least make you some coffee while you take a look.'

'The inscription is easy,' he said. 'It's a famous passage from Miguel de Cervantes Saavedra;

"Here lies a gentleman bold
Who was so very brave
He went to lengths untold,
And on the brink of the grave
Death had on him no hold.
By the world he set small store–
He frightened it to the core–
Yet somehow, by Fate's plan,
Though he'd lived a crazy man,
When he died he was sane once more."

Jordi gave me an odd look. 'Who did the headstone belong to?'

'I think it's the marker to the cemetery. It wasn't attached to any particular plot, but then it was hard to tell if anyone was even buried there. It's all so overgrown.'

'I think you're right – this would have been a general inscription for the family. An interesting choice. Let me have a look at the other stuff.'

While I waited for the water to boil, I glanced back and saw him poring over the pages in puzzlement. 'What is it?'

'The floorplan of the house,' he replied absently. 'I thought you said the servants' quarters were sealed off.' Setting down the coffee mugs, I came around his side to see what he was looking at. He tapped his finger on the plan. 'There aren't any servants' quarters marked here. But there's handwriting in the space, see?'

'I couldn't decipher it.'

'It says, "Where they shall live for our freedom." It sounds like a quote, but I don't think it's Cervantes. Of course, you can study him all your life and still find new things you've never noticed before. His writing is as astonishing as Shakespeare's, as you'd know if your English language wasn't so dominant. Let's have a look at these –' He picked up the letter packet tied with ribbon.

'I think they're from Francesco Condemaine to his wife,' I explained. 'It was said that he wrote her a love letter every day. She kept them in a bureau and always carried the key with her.'

'Well, that's romantic.' He cut the rest of the ribbons and sifted through the envelopes checking the dates. 'Perhaps not one a day but there are quite a few here. Do you mind if I open them? They're not very fragile – they had good quality paper back then.'

'No, of course not.'

Jordi cleaned his glasses. 'It's very florid styling, a formal technique. Typical of traditional Spanish petitions of love for that period.' He peered more closely. '"*When you gave me the fortudinous honour of becoming your enamoured*", and so on... This is interesting: "*For neither good nor evil can last forever, and so it follows that as evil has lasted a long time, good must now be close at hand.*" That's definitely a quotation from *Don Quixote*. And this –' he held up a single page with just one line written across its centre. '"*Demasiada cordura puede ser la peor de las locuras, ver la vida como es y no como debería de ser.*"'

'Can you translate?'

'"Too much sanity may be madness. And maddest of all, to see life as it is and not as it should be."'

'That's what he wanted for her. He built the house to protect her.'

'So it appears. "*My rituals, which must seem absurd to you, can only ensure your lasting happiness.*" I wonder what rituals he's talking about?'

'God, please don't let there be Satanic rituals involved,' I said. 'That'd be the last thing I need, on top of everything else that's happened.'

'Why, what else has happened?'

I was surprised that Celestia hadn't confided in him. 'I've been seeing them in the house.'

'Who?'

'The Condemaines. The whole family. They live in this part, the part that doesn't seem to exist.'

'Okaaaay,' said Jordi slowly, giving me a very strange look. 'You've actually seen them?'

'I've been attacked by them.'

'Why? What do "they" want?'

'Fine, you're humouring me, I shouldn't have said anything,' I replied with more anger than I'd intended. 'The Condemaines – their spirits, their souls or whatever you want to call them, they're still in the house. Trust me, Jordi, I'm the last person who'd ever believe in this sort of thing but I've seen them, felt them.'

'Has anyone else? What about your husband?'

'No, he's so wrapped up in his work at the moment that he doesn't have time to think about anything else. Bobbie believes me – she's seen them too.'

'She's a child.'

'I didn't coerce her. She came to the conclusion herself.'

Jordi set aside the letters and looked at me. 'It strikes me you've gone a little off-subject. Weren't you meant to be working on your architectural book? And here you are exploring ghosts? This is very Spanish behaviour. Are you sure you're not a Catholic?'

In answer, I rolled up my sleeve and showed him the marks on my arm, which still had not fully healed. 'What do you think these are, stigmata? I was attacked in the rooms that don't appear to exist.'

He was silent for a long time. 'Okay,' he said finally. 'I think you need to take a break from this. Maybe you should just put the writing aside for a while. You don't look –'

'I know, everyone keeps telling me how terrible I look.'

'It's just – maybe you should spend some quality time with your husband.'

'How can I? I hardly ever see him anymore.'

'It'd be good if the two of you came into the village one evening and just had dinner together, away from the house. Get to know some of the residents here, not just on a superficial level but so that you can properly understand them. So few foreigners bother, and it would be to the benefit of both sides.'

Jordi made sense. Just like Mateo, he had that forthright manner I had come to identify as typically Spanish, honesty without insult, a quality I greatly admired. Chastened, I started to gather the letters up.

He appeared embarrassed, as if he had overstepped the mark. 'Look,' he said, 'why don't you leave the letters here and I'll go over them in my spare time? Perhaps there's something else I can find out that might explain what's happening to you –'

I could have kissed him.

CHAPTER THIRTY-THREE

The Doubt

THE MANIFESTATIONS – I had come to think of them as that – suddenly stopped. Sometimes I listened at the connecting doors, or stood outside at the windows trying to see through the gaps in the shutters, and was relieved when I saw and heard nothing.

But new fears surfaced. Four days after Mateo had left I found a postcard in the mailbox. On the front was a monochrome photograph of Greenwich Village in the 1920s.

It read: *Hola Cachonda – I always send Bobbie a card so I thought you should get one too. Working hard here, no time for fun, NYC exactly the same as London, overcrowded, same people, same shops, movies and shows but longer working days. Miss you horribly. Probably back B4 you get this! XXX M*

There were two cards for Bobbie: one from Julieta, who had set her study schedule up to the Christmas season, the other from Mateo. I found I had little of the teacher's patience. Bobbie would focus on one element and keep asking questions about it until I had no answers left. Lessons were exhausting.

My mind kept drifting to the abandoned car, and the fact that I had still not been able to get hold of Anne. I tried again when I returned to the house with the card, and miracle of miracles, she answered.

'I was starting to think that something had happened to you,' I said, relieved to hear her voice.

'Don't be silly, darling,' said Anne, 'I'm sure I told you I was going to stay with Sandy for a few days? My phone doesn't seem to work down there. She lives in a sort of hollow and makes most of her calls through her computer, which I don't understand because how can a computer get through when a phone can't? It's simply absurd. And there's no television reception so I'm missing my favourite soaps.'

For once it was a pleasure to hear her prattle on. 'What happened to your hire car?' I asked, cutting across her complaints about the general uselessness of phone companies.

'You mean after I left you?'

'Yes, I found it off the side of the road.'

'Oh, I meant to tell you about that, it was just so embarrassing. I was feeling a little the worse for wear when I left your lovely house and pulled over to take an analgesic, but somehow it was still in gear and I went off into some bushes. Well, obviously I couldn't come back up to you after we'd parted on such bad terms, so I called a cab company. When I got to Malaga I told Avis that their car had broken down, but I don't understand why they haven't come to collect it.'

'It gave me a fright finding it down there.'

'I imagine it would have done. Listen, I know I rarely admit such things, but perhaps I was wrong to say what I did that day. I just get so – frustrated – with you sometimes. You know I don't mean half of what I say, don't you?'

'I suppose I do, but you do hurt me.'

'Well, I shall try to make it up to you, darling, I promise.'

My mother had no intermediate modes of expression; either everything was wonderful and I was a darling, or the world had gone to Hell and I was a bitch. She displayed all the symptoms of maternal bipolarity. I rang off, not entirely surprised by her explanation for abandoning the car.

With Bobbie busy taking a home tutor course on my laptop, bemusedly supervised by Rosita, I got a taxi into Gaucia. Jordi was at his usual place in the library, stacking trashy paperbacks for the few tourists who passed this way in the off-season.

'I went through the rest of the letters and made some notes,' he said. 'The Condemaines had no servants beyond a housekeeper, Senora Delgadillo's great-grandmother.'

'So the dark rooms weren't servants' quarters.'

'I guess he left them off the floor-plan because back then, in this area, you were taxed by the number of rooms you had. They don't appear until the next owner's survey.'

'That would have been Marcos Condemaine,' I suggested. 'He stayed there until the outbreak of the Civil War. After that it fell to Amancio Lueches.'

'Obviously the letters don't cover later events, but there are a few references to Senor Condemaine's occultism. Let me see.' He ran down his notes. 'Yes, he refers to the house as "a psychic conduit of the eternal soul" – more flowery language. He created this conduit "by the practice and ordinance of sacred ritual." Unfortunately he does not say what these rituals were, but they seem to have involved the worship of Hyperion. There are references to the performance of them in the back of the house.'

'Thanks, Jordi, but you're right,' I said. 'I shouldn't have sent you off on a wild goose chase. I'm meant to be producing an architectural work, not a folklore history.'

Jordi shrugged. 'I think the beliefs of people are tied to the houses they build, don't you? Look around the houses in Gaucia, and the smart rooms for receiving guests that always have a crucifix or a statue of the Virgin, just to prove how pious they are. I think your architect did not believe in God – but he did have faith in the power of the sun and moon.'

'It would explain why he incorporated so many planetary symbols in the decoration,' I agreed. 'But I don't understand why he believed they had the power to make his wife happy, or what it has to do with me.'

'Our surroundings can have a powerful effect on us,' Jordi said. 'Look at the height of our cathedrals, designed to encourage prayer by instilling a sense of fear and awe at the power of God. Maybe the small rooms were built to remind them of what they had.'

'You're a smart lad,' I said. 'You're wasted here.'

'I know.' He lifted his feet off the desk and grinned at me. 'But I'll get away. I've had enough. I want to find a nice girl of my age. Do you think if in another life you hadn't been married, you would have gone for me? I'm closer to your age than your husband.'

'Jordi, that's inappropriate,' I told him, but felt secretly flattered, even though it explained why he had been so keen to help me.

'WELL *OF COURSE* he's in love with you,' said Celestia when I found her in Eduardo's café. 'If you'd arrived here single, you could have done a lot worse for yourself.'

'I'm not sure I enjoy seeing the life I didn't have,' I said, accepting a glass of coffee. 'Besides, I wouldn't be here if it wasn't for Mateo.'

'At least Jordi's around all the time.' She set aside her newspaper. 'We hardly ever see that husband of yours.'

'You saw him last Saturday,' I said. 'He came in to get some paintbrushes.'

'Perhaps he did,' said Celestia, 'but I never saw him.'

'But he told me he had a drink with you.'

'He may well have had a drink with someone but it wasn't me, I can assure you. I was here all afternoon with Maria, and we didn't set eyes on him.'

I was positive I had not made a mistake. I distinctly remembered Mateo saying that he had shared a bottle of wine with Celestia, which was why he had got back so late.

'He came in on the evening of the Wednesday before, as well,' I said. 'He had a drink with you then, didn't he?'

'I know my memory's going but believe me, I'd definitely recall sharing a table with your husband.'

'He said he was here with you.'

'Callie, I hate to say this but, well, he's away a lot –'

'Many people are,' I said, instantly defensive. 'It's the way the business world works now.'

'Perhaps he just needs some time for himself occasionally.'

'He gets that when he travels.'

'I mean proper time. He obviously loves you but maybe he needs something else.'

'Are you suggesting that he's having an affair?'

'No, of course not, but men respond differently. Most of them find us tiring to be around all the time. My husband left because he said I was too needy.'

'That's just an excuse – I'm sure it's the house, it's doing something to him.'

'The house? What could it be doing?'

'I don't know. They want to destroy us.'

'Who are you talking about?'

'The Condemaines, of course! They want what we have, and I won't let them have it.' I pushed my coffee aside and rose. 'I have to go.'

I heard Celestia calling after me, but I ignored her.

As I arrived back at the house, the postman was just arriving. He handed me an envelope which I recognised as being from Bobbie's new school; details of her uniform requirements and where to buy them. 'Two deliveries in one day, that's unusual,' I said.

He leaned out of the van window with a look of apology on his face. 'I only just got here.'

'Yes, but you came earlier.'

'No, you're my first stop today.'

'No, you delivered two postcards this morning.'

'Not me, Senora.' He turned the van around and pulled away. It made no sense. If he hadn't put the postcards in our box, who had?

I returned to the house and put in a Skype call to Mateo. It would be early in New York but I needed to hear his voice. I clearly pulled him from the depths of sleep; as he sat up in the hotel room bed I could see that his eyes were barely unglued and his hair was a rats' nest. 'Honey, I was out with clients until late last night. Isn't it a little early?'

'I'm sorry, I'm just feeling a little weirded out here.'

'I told you there'd be times like this after the summer was over, didn't I? How are you going to be through the winter months?'

'I know I shouldn't pester you, but there are odd things happening that I can't explain.'

'Christ, Callie. I need you to hold it together for me.' He rubbed a hand over his face and tried to concentrate while he threw a capsule in a coffee machine. 'Come on then, what is it, hit me. What's happened?'

'Why did you say you had a drink with Celestia on Saturday? She says she never saw you.'

'What?' He scratched at his hair, trying to think, or perhaps trying to come up with a fast excuse. 'She's going crazy. I was walking across the square with the paintbrushes and she called me over.'

'Who was she with?'

'Nobody – she was by herself at that table, where she always sits, and she had half a bottle of wine left and poured me a glass –'

'What was it?'

'What, the wine? It was a good Rioja, a *Sierra Cantabria*.'

'Okay, now I believe you – you never forget a wine label.'

'You know she's a drunk, don't you? She's been frying in the sun drinking for the last twenty years. I'm surprised she can remember where she lives. Is that all? Can I go back to sleep for a while now?'

'Yes – I'm sorry – things have been strange around here since you left. You sent postcards.'

'Yeah – you already got them? My God, the Gaucia postal service is finally improving. Honey, I'm going now, say *bye bye Mateo.*' He timbered back onto the bed with his coffee and the picture vanished.

But the feeling that I was being lied to by everyone wouldn't be shaken. Mateo, Celestia, Jordi, the postman, even Bobbie for all I knew – it felt as if they were trying to humour me. But the more they wanted to hide the truth, the more I needed to know.

CHAPTER THIRTY-FOUR

The Opening

CELESTIA STOOD IN the porch rattling the rain from her umbrella. I had invited her over, and arranged for Rosita to bake some cod with *mojama* for our evening meal. 'I shouldn't use this, we get the most dreadful lightning sometimes,' she said. 'I've seen it scorch great patches on the ground at this time of year. I got a taxi here. If I stay too long and get too pissed you can put me up, can't you?'

'Of course,' I told her. 'Come in and get dry.'

That afternoon, Bobbie had been taken to Marbella to be measured for her school uniform by the mother of Yolanda, one of the girls who had already started at the school the previous term. Yolanda's mother said that Bobbie could have a sleepover and that she would return her first thing the following morning, so we had the evening to ourselves.

I had looked in on Rosita while she was preparing the meal, but she had been even more morose than usual, and eventually explained that she did not care for Celestia, who had apparently said bad things about her in the village. She asked if she could take the evening off, and as the meal was already prepared I agreed.

I had decorated the dining room table with olive leaves and candles, and the cod was laid out on a bed of tomatoes and onions, with tortilla and a salad. I had even found one of the few bottles of Manzanilla that hadn't been tucked away in Mateo's wine racks.

'Well, this is nice,' said Celestia, taking off her maroon cardigan to reveal a green dress, rather old-fashioned and floaty, with a matching scarf thrown around her throat. 'I so rarely get a chance to dress up.'

'It's very pretty,' I said.

'I didn't get to see much of the inside of the house last time I was here, what with all the fuss about that little girl getting shut in one of the rooms. The village ladies still talk about it, you know.'

'I think it was my fault,' I admitted. 'I can't be sure if I locked the door behind me or not. It's dark in there and I don't suppose she could reach the handle. You thought she'd got in from outside but I think she went to the bathroom and tried the wrong door coming out.'

'So you don't believe the house is haunted anymore?' Celestia asked, tucking in. 'The cod's amazing, by the way.'

'Perhaps not haunted in the traditional sense, but there are people here with us.' I tried to sound casual but it came out strangely.

'You really believe that?'

'I think after the Condemaines died in such tragic circumstances that their spirits lived on. Francesco planned a series of little rooms where they would be able to live after death.'

'But I presume these spirits could get out whenever they opened the doors, if they really wanted to. I mean, you must go in there from time to time –'

'Yes, Mateo keeps his wine in there.'

'So why don't they escape?'

'I don't know. They want something more. They have another agenda.'

Celestia stopped eating. 'Which is?'

'To take over from us. To shut us in there and live their lives out here in the side that gets the sun.'

'You mean they want to *possess* you?'

'Yes – no – I don't know.'

'Because spiritual possession is supposedly a phenomenon in which some stray, damaged being from the other side takes over a living person and exerts a negative influence on them. And I know you can be a little strange, but honey, I don't see your head spinning.'

'Do you have a faith?'

'Yes, I'm a Catholic. My mother was Irish – that's my excuse, anyway.'

I looked at her in the light of the guttering candles and thought uncharitably, *You only have a few years left, you need something to believe in.*

'I take it you're an atheist?' Celestia asked, not unkindly.

'I have good reason to be. The problems I had when I was younger were caused by my father. He desired me. I wasn't being punished or tested by some higher power. And I suppose I know in my heart that whatever I'm seeing in those rooms is because of me, not some wandering lost soul looking for peace or revenge. But it still doesn't explain –'

Celestia pointed. 'Darling, your hands are shaking.'

'I'm sorry,' I said, 'something is happening here, something very bad. And I don't know what to do or who to turn to –' I didn't mean to cry, but once I started I found that I couldn't stop. Celestia came over and put her arm around me, waiting until I could regain my composure.

'Listen, why don't we test your theory?' she said gently. 'I never told you the real reason why I left London, did I?'

'No,' I sniffed, looking up at her, 'I'm not sure you did.'

'I used to help people.'

'What do you mean?'

'People who were in spiritual need. I've always had – well, let's not call it a gift. Let's say an ability to see things a little more clearly. You've seen those incredible digital photographs they can take now, where you can zoom in to see details that aren't apparent at first? I've always felt as if I could do that. It's almost embarrassing to talk about.'

'No, please,' I said.

'Well, people would come to me with problems and I was able to sort them out. Sometimes I took a little money from them, just to cover travel expenses and to get a meal. This was back when times were hard for me. I was young and naïve. I thought I was helping. But taking money, well that was defined as something else by the police. It was suggested that I intentionally set out to mislead. Nothing could have been further from the truth.'

'So you left the country.'

'I was advised to leave. I stayed on for years, but when I started to try and help people again, I was issued with an ultimatum. What I did wasn't illegal, but there was a troubled young woman I tried to help. Of course, I should never have got involved. She had made a terrible choice in life, marrying a man who had no respect for her. Within minutes of meeting him I knew he was having an affair.'

'You just – intuited – it?'

'I suppose so, at first. I saw a dishonest aura about him –' She fluttered her hand around her face in vague indication. 'It's hard to explain and makes one sound so foolish, but there was something physically there. I did a little checking and found the address of his girlfriend. He lodged a formal complaint, and in order to avoid court procedure the officer in charge of our statements suggested a solution. That's really why I came here. I don't use my ability anymore – there's not much call for it in a country that has so many Catholic solutions. But perhaps I can help you.'

She's bats, I thought, but by now I was ready to try anything. 'Okay, what do I have to do?'

'A little ceremony, not exactly a séance, just an opener of the way. I'll need a few things, one of these candles, a little snip of your hair – really, anything with your DNA in it will do, an item strongly associated with the person we want to talk about – and some water that's been standing here for a while.'

'One of the upstairs bathrooms has a leak. I put a coffee mug underneath it, just until Mateo gets back and can change the washer. Will that do?'

'How long has it been standing?'

'Probably over a week.'

'Then that will perfect. And I need you to open the front window a crack, to get some air through.'

I returned with the water and the key Elena had worn around her neck. 'Just tip a little very slowly into that saucer,' Celestia said, removing her teacup and pushing the saucer toward me. I did as I was instructed. 'There's really no science to this. Over the years I've just sort of worked out what gets the best results.'

'How much hair do you need?'

'Only the tiniest amount. I have some scissors in my bag.' She reached over and took a small snip from the back of my head. Dangling it over the flame of the candle, she then dropped it in and poured the molten wax into the water, adding the key. It all seemed utterly ridiculous, but then I supposed that my experiences were just as absurd when described in the cold light of day.

'Sometimes it seems possible to bring things into the light,' Celestia said, 'and people do seem to expect some sort of a formality at the start. A ritual just cuts the ribbon to allow progress, that's all, like the opening of a new highway.'

A ritual – an opening – something stirred in the back of my mind but vanished when I tried to look at it. 'What happens now?' I asked.

'Let's just be quiet for a while.'

We sat there in silence, she and I, for nigh on twenty minutes, breathing in unison, listening to the ticking in the hallways and the wind rising in the trees. Finally, though, I was ready call a stop to the whole thing. When Celestia cleared her throat and spoke, I was relieved to hear that it was in her own deep tones, not in some high-pitched strangled voice from beyond.

'I can't tell you what you need to know,' she said briskly, as if having struggled with some decision. 'I can only show you what you already understand. No-one ever told you lies to hurt you, Callie. Take my hand, we have to go and find her. Come with me.'

I placed my right hand in hers and we left the room. She led the way to the front door. 'Open it, please. I'm not allowed to touch it.'

The rain was torrential and obscuring. She stepped into it without flinching, pulling me behind her. 'This way. We should have done this earlier.'

We crossed the lawn, now slippery with pooling water. Celestia's ballet shoes, which she wore for her bunions, raised splashes as she slid onwards. Her green dress darkened and stuck to her. 'Over there, I see her now!'

I knew at once where we were heading; to the Condemaine cemetery behind the trees. 'Hurry,' she called back, 'or we'll miss her!'

Lightning flared over the cliffs behind the house, and for a brief moment I saw her hunched shape between the bare bushes, so thin and tiny that she hardly seemed capable of pulling the thing at her feet.

'There, you see?'

The branches were springy and wet, and fought back, whipping as Celestia released them. I could only follow. Just as we reached the clearing she stopped, holding me back. I followed her outstretched arm and pointing finger. The spindly ravaged creature with the smiling face was barely more than a rain-drenched bundle of rags. She suddenly stopped pulling the bundle and fell to her knees. I knew that poor Elena was dragging the remains of her husband, returned to her after his death at Passchendaele.

'She can't hurt us, nor we her,' whispered Celestia. 'She's in a different time. You're seeing something that happened in the past. We can't cross the gulf, but if she sees us there could be terrible consequences. Come back now.'

'Wait,' I said. 'I have to see, I have to know what she did.'

'You can't be here, she'll return to the house shortly, but we can go ahead of her.'

Back we went, fighting through the leaves once more, wet thorns clawing and dragging at our clothes, then across the waterlogged lawn, the paths turning to sandy rivers, and into the house at last.

'She'll try to get back to the other side, won't she?' I said.

'Yes, I imagine so.'

'Then we need to confront her.'

CHAPTER THIRTY-FIVE

The Fire

'WE'LL GO INTO the other side together,' said Celestia, pulling off her shoes in the hall and shaking away as much rainwater as she could. The hall lights flickered, then glowed bright once more. 'How do we get in?

I had the keys on me. Perhaps I had always known we would pass into the darkness tonight. 'Follow me,' I instructed, leading the way to the connecting door in the drawing room. Celestia peered inside. Her clothes were weighted down with water, her hair plastered across her face. She looked more than a little mad. 'Can you put a light on?'

'There aren't any in here. I have a torch or candles, but they won't be enough to deter her. She was burying someone, wasn't she?'

'It would seem so, yes.' She didn't sound too certain. 'I imagine she's doomed to repeat her actions over and over again.'

Emboldened by Celestia's presence, I flicked on the LED torch and led the way. 'Mateo and I have talked about tearing the rooms out, but it wouldn't make any difference,' I explained. 'The cliff face is right behind us, so there could never be any natural light.'

'Then why build rooms here at all?'

We edged into the mirror-drawing room like children, the torch beam scanning the walls. Outside, I could hear the rain spattering against the windows. Celestia saw the framed photographs on the sideboard, then reached the seven ugly dolls dressed in adult clothes. 'Are these meant to be the Condemaines?' she asked. 'It's as if they always lived on this side, not the other.' I realized she was right; that was exactly how it appeared.

'Callie, are you going to be all right?'

Shivering and soaked in the dark, I realized I must have looked more frightened than even I supposed. 'It's something Senora Condemaine and I share,' I explained. I pointed to the high-backed chair by the fireplace. 'That's where I first saw her. He was behind her, and one of the children was running around on all fours – he or she, it was impossible to tell – seemed to have become feral. It was as if they were all in the most terrible torment.'

'Well, wouldn't they have been?' said Celestia. 'Elena Condemaine lost her husband in a devastating battle. She tried to feed her children alone and failed. Did you even know she buried them in the garden?'

'The grave markers are all eroded. It's impossible to tell what's really there.'

'I imagine all Francesco's money was tied up in this monstrous overwrought house, so when her pride finally crumbled she threw herself on the mercy of the villagers. But they had always treated her with hatred and suspicion, and she was rebuffed. Her children were starving, so she took their lives in an act of mercy.'

'My God,' I cried, 'To reach the point whereby killing your children was the only alternative to watching them starve to death – weren't they all in Hell?'

The idea struck me just as lightning sharded the room, but even as it crackled and burned away the thought was lost. For the briefest moment I had understood, and now it was gone.

But the lightning was still here. The room was shining with electrical energy. As I watched, the rugs burst into vivid blue-edged colours, the wood renewed itself and appeared brand new, the dolls regained their lustre, their hair and clothes shining. The dust was falling from the glittering crystal chandelier, and there was even a fire burning in the grate.

Everything was as it had once been. The searing light blurred my vision, the roar of the storm filled my ears, and I saw...

'Don't you understand,' Celestia was saying, 'don't you see what happened here, what's still happening?' Her mouth continued to move but I could no longer understand the words, and then she was hurling the dolls into the fire and moving to the mantelpiece, sweeping the glass and china from it, shouting and gesticulating wildly as I tried to understand what she was telling me.

'The Society,' she was saying, 'they blinded you to the truth. It was for your protection!'

And as she stood beside the fire shouting at me, it suddenly popped and belched, the flames enveloping the hem of her dress, flickering over it to catch a light to the end of the scarf. The material was wet but that didn't stop it from burning; it caught immediately, and her shouts turned to screams as she tried in vain to slap away the flames. I did nothing because after all there could be no fire there, so what I was experiencing was merely what I had seen so often before, some kind of synaptic overload, a parlour trick of bright colours and frightening noises, a short-circuit of my faculties, and all I could do was push back and away from the absurd spectacle of Celestia engulfed in some kind of spectral inferno, rushing out of the room, closing the door behind me and locking it, and covering my eyes and ears with my hands until it had gone away, all gone away, and there was nothing more that could deceive my senses.

I stayed against the door until all the noise and light had gone, and only then, when my racing heart had returned to something like its normal pace, did I allow myself to open the door again.

Nothing on earth would make me go all the way back inside, but I had to make sure I had not shut her in. I thought of Liana, the little girl who had become trapped in the room, and wondered for one awful moment if I had somehow done the same to her, but remembered that I couldn't have because I'd been outside on the lawn, and we had both entered together.

I pushed the door wide and looked in dread. The room was still exactly as I had left it. Even the dust appeared to have settled over our footprints once more. Then where was she? Everything was dark and faded again, just as it had always been, the cobwebs on the chandelier, the dolls in their places, the china and glass all in place, the grate cold and empty.

And there was no sign of Celestia anywhere.

CHAPTER THIRTY-SIX

The Screen

THE DINNER TABLE lay as it had before, set with two places, the cod and tortilla eaten, knives and forks set aside, the wine glasses half-emptied. Celestia had carefully moved her chair back and there it stood accusingly, turned slightly, her maroon cardigan draped over one arm as proof that she had been there.

My head throbbed. The power appeared to have been cut off, but as the table had been lit with several fat white church candles the ambient light remained. I returned to the connecting door and listened, my hands shaking, but there was only silence.

I rang Celestia's mobile, but the line was filled with electronic scratches and clicks. Although I hated doing so, I ending up Skyping Mateo again. The six hour time difference meant that he was still probably at the New York office, and I knew he'd be working on his laptop. This time he answered at once. He was wearing his smartest blue suit and tie.

'Hey, I was about to call you,' he said, tearing himself away from his spreadsheets. 'How's it going?'

'We're having a storm,' I said, trying to work out what on earth I was going to say without alarming him.

'Too bad, it's a beautiful autumn day here.' He panned the screen around and I realised his window was high above the Manhattan streets. 'Noisy, though. Police cars, taxis, the usual. After Spain it just seems so damned intense. I can't wait to get back.'

'I was having dinner with Celestia and I've lost her,' I said lamely, as if she were a hat or a pair of glasses I'd absently set aside.

'What do you mean?'

'She was here and now she's gone – it's as if the house swallowed her up.'

'Hon, I'm having trouble hearing you. Is that rain?'

'Sorry, it's really coming down now.'

'You mean she went home in that weather?'

'I don't think so. She just – disappeared.'

'You know she's a little on the crazy side, don't you?'

'I know, but she was fine. We went into the other drawing room –'

'Why would you do that when you know it freaks you out?'

'I just wanted Celestia to see it for herself. She's only been here once before and didn't get a good look. Nothing strange had really had happened before then.'

'Nothing strange has happened now, Callie. It's all in your imagination.' His impatience was starting to show. 'Listen, I can't stay on long, I'm running late for a meeting and I have to get this done before I go in. How's Bobbie?'

'Fine. She's on a sleepover with her friend Yolanda. She'll be back first thing in the morning.'

'Cool – listen, is Rosita there with you?'

'No, she's taken the night off. '

'Then I guess you found Celestia.'

'Why?'

'Honey, there's someone standing behind you.'

My skin prickled with needles of ice. 'What are you talking about?'

'Right behind you, over your left shoulder.'

I slowly turned, and saw her.

Lank hair hung over her downturned face. She wore the ragged shift covered in the dirt of a century, which her withered body barely inhabited. I couldn't bring myself to seek out her eyes, and jumped away, knocking the laptop from the table. It crashed to the floor as she moved toward me, her fingers connecting with my arm, the clutch not of a corpse or a phantom, not connected to anything in the volumes of ghost stories I'd read as a child, but a physical entity of cold flesh, sinew and bone, somehow both alive and dead at once.

I screamed and shoved my way aside, slamming back against the table, filled more with revulsion than fear, my hands before my face as if trying to beat away invasion. I know I fell over the chair leg and landed heavily, heard thunder and breaking plates, Rosita's best china, and I remember that when I looked up the creature had gone, because lightning was flooding the room with such brilliance that it could not survive, only retreat to the dark.

The storm had freed it, but had also prevented it from fulfilling its intention.

I lay on the floor, terrified, not prepared to move until I was sure it had vanished. The silence was broken by Mateo's voice. Turning, I saw him on the laptop screen.

'Callie, what's happening? What the hell is going on? Are you all right? Darling, for God's sake talk to me!'

The laptop's screen had snapped clean away from the keyboard. Its cable had come out of the wall. There was nothing left that could possibly make it work, but there it was, the glowing screen with Mateo still talking, unconnected. As I picked up the screen, it fuzzed and fragmented, turning black, the sound phasing and echoing away, leaving only the light of the guttering candles and the patter of falling rain.

CHAPTER THIRTY-SEVEN

The Disappearance

THREE WEEKS AGO I would have found a way to justify the events of that night, to write off Celestia's sudden departure as a quirk of her impulsive nature, to put the computer screen's activity down to some anomaly caused by the storm's electrical charge, to dismiss the poor creature's reappearance due to my heightened imagination.

But now I could no longer do any of these things. A few minutes later the power was restored and I was able to move once more, freed from the restraining terror of the dark. I cleared away the shattered plates, loaded the dishwasher, tidied the room, made everything normal, then tried Celestia's mobile again, only to find it still out of order. Eventually I went to bed.

In the morning I made sure that there was no sign of disturbance left in the house. I called once more, knowing that it would be too early to get an answer from her anyway, and got the broken line, as if the mobile was ringing somewhere beyond time and space.

I composed myself as best as I could and waited for Bobbie's return, listening to her excited account of the sleepover when she came charging in.

'Where's Yolanda's mother?' I asked. 'Didn't she drop you off?'

'She just brought me to the gates. Jerardo didn't come and open them, so I had to walk up the drive. Where is he?'

'Where is anyone?' I muttered.

A few minutes later Jerardo appeared with an apologetic look on his wizened face, and offered to drive us into Gaucia. In the village, Bobbie sat on the wall reading while I attempted to find Celestia. Nobody had seen her. For want of something else to do, I tried to get my laptop repaired. The man who ran the hardware shop doubled as Gaucia's IT engineer, and told me it would have to be sent away to the Apple concession in Marbella.

We walked back through the square, but found Celestia's usual table empty. Lola was nowhere to be found. The village seemed unusually quiet, as if everyone had been instructed to stay indoors and keep away from us. I thought of looking in on Jordi, but the library doors were locked shut.

The strange part was that I was desperate to get back to the house again, to stay there in the warm autumn sunlight where I knew I would be safe. By the time we returned Rosita was back, and I had never been so pleased to see her. As she cleaned the kitchen and tutted over the broken plates I thought I had successfully hidden in the bin, she kept glancing over as if wondering what on earth had got into me.

With my work on the book abandoned, I sat in the atrium with Bobbie and we played silly word games until it was time for lunch, and nothing could dent my feeling of euphoria. I no longer cared what had happened the night before, or where Celestia might have gone. I only knew that I belonged here. Mateo was due back from New York in two days' time, and I decided to tell him that I was setting the book aside. There was too much to do now, and anyway, the house would always be here. I could tackle the project once Bobbie had started boarding school.

Just before sunset I walked down to the little cemetery. Flowers of sunlight patched the grass, giving the glade a magical appearance. The ground had dried and there was no sign of the previous night's disturbance, not so much as a broken twig. I tried to recall the exact spot where we had seen Elena dragging the body, but the evidence had, as usual, been erased. I supposed

Jerardo and I could dig up the ground, but what would it reveal after a hundred years, a bone or two? And what was there to gain from such an action?

Celestia was not to be found.

Two days later we had a visit from the Gaucia police, who were looking into her disappearance. They had received contradictory reports; she had either been seen or not been seen at the café in the square. She had bought provisions from Maria's store, but no-one could actually remember when. One of the women swore she had passed her pulling a wheeled suitcase, looking as if she was going to the airport, but perhaps that was just wishful thinking. Lola thought she had seen her on the afternoon after she visited me, but couldn't be sure. There was no clue as to her whereabouts, and as nobody had any idea of her movements on Saturday night, I decided not to tell them that she had come to me for dinner, knowing that it would only complicate matters. She had not used the only local taxi, because the driver had been at his step-brother's wedding. The police were checking car services in Marbella, without much luck.

I tried to understand what could have happened, but drew a blank. I remembered the storm, the lightning putting out the local power grid, my panic in the dark causing me to hallucinate, but that was all.

Celestia had definitely been seen in the town square shortly after lunchtime on the day she came over to visit, because she had told Eduardo that she was not feeling very well and was going to go for a walk. The assumption was now that she had headed off to the cliff path, the only area near the village that had any shade, and had collapsed somewhere. The walking routes had all been thoroughly searched, but no body had been found. The problem was that a river ran in the ravine below, and at this time of the year its swollen waters and fierce current flushed freshwater out on the coast somewhere east of Marbella. It was therefore assumed that she might have drunkenly fallen in and been lost to the sea. It had happened a number of times in the past, most recently in 1997, when a tourist from Dortmund had alighted to take a photograph of the eagles and his feet had slipped on the scree, sending him tumbling into the gorge. The other accepted idea was that she had taken off without telling anyone – so unreliable, the English – and would turn up in a week or so.

I had a different theory; that something had terrified her and she had run out into the night, where she had met with an accident. I walked the roads around the house, checking all of the goat-paths, the sudden drops and gullies, but found no sign of her.

I couldn't shake the feeling that I had somehow caused her death, that if she had not come to the house that night and insisted on contacting the Condemaines, she would still be alive.

CHAPTER THIRTY-EIGHT

The Acceptance

IT WAS SHOCKING how quickly everyone came to accept that she was gone. The townsfolk had regarded her as imperious and something of an annoyance, but Eduardo felt the loss in his till receipts, and Lola crossed herself whenever Celestia's name was mentioned.

Acceptance. It's a hard state to achieve, but if the residents of Gaucia managed it, the house made it easier for me. If I didn't fully understand the forces at work in Hyperion, I at least came to terms with them.

As far as I was concerned, there was nothing left to discover. I didn't need to decipher any more of the monograph to understand what Francesco Condemaine had done. He had built a *camera obscura* and mapped the heavens, using the clocks to calculate the most propitious time for his society and its rituals. He had performed them, either alone or with his acolytes, and with the protection of his family set firmly in place he went off to fight for the British. But his plan failed... he was killed in action, setting off a chain of terrible tragedies. As a result, the Condemaines became victims of an experiment gone wrong, and lived on in the rooms mirroring the ones they had inhabited in life.

Why did we always find so many reasons not to believe? Why could we not learn to accept things for what they were? The only obstacle to my happiness lay in my refusal to admit that the world held unfathomable mysteries.

I went to find Rosita.

The housekeeper was scrubbing down the cooker, where I had made a mess serving up the previous night's meal. 'It's alright, Rosita,' I told her, 'I understand now. About the house. Remember you said what a happy place it has always been?'

'Yes, Senora.'

'I know why. Your employers are still here with us, in those other rooms we don't use.'

She did not look up, but scrubbed hard at a spot on the enamel. 'My employers are all dead.'

'Do you know what I believe? That Francesco Condemaine conducted a ritual to ensure that his family's spirits could live on here. Even though it meant that they would have to remain in darkness.'

Rosita stopped working and looked at me. 'No, Senora. That is what the women of Gaucia believe. It is not what I know to be true.'

'But I've seen them, and I fought against believing in them, don't you see? If I don't let them out, if I just keep them where they belong, then there's nothing they can do, and there can only be happiness here. That's why Elena Condemaine appeared to me, to let me see the truth.'

'The house puts things right,' said Rosita stubbornly, scrubbing away once more. 'It can only help those who stay in the light.'

'Yes, and that's why we need the clocks, isn't it, to work out where the stars are and to warn us about the hours of darkness. You always knew that the Condemaines were still here – you never go in the other rooms.'

'You are angry with me.'

'No, of course I'm not angry with you. I just need to understand the rules by which I'm meant to live. Rosita, I tried to kill myself in London, I tried because I was so desperately unhappy, and this house has given me everything. But it also terrified me because I didn't understand! Please, if you have it within your power to help me, do so now!'

'Then you must know that there are no ghosts here,' said Rosita, her face grimly set. 'I'm an old woman, my time has passed. There is no happiness without loss. And there is nothing I can do to change things.'

'I'm not asking you to change anything, just to acknowledge it! If I have that, then none of this is in my head. Knowing that I'm sane will allow me to cope with almost anything else.'

'But the house –'

I raised my hand. I needed her to understand how I felt. 'No more. The house has made a believer of me. Do you know how momentous that is? To realise that there's more to the world than we ever dreamed? All my life I've felt shut outside, lost somehow, as if I was just looking in on other people's lives, missing some kind of – survival map – that they were in possession of and I had never been given, and for the first time I've been granted access to their world. I can live like this, with them, and still be happy. Of course I won't say anything to Mateo, or to Bobbie, they needn't have to suffer what I've been through. I can even protect them in the future. Everything is going to be fine from now on, you wait and see. I feel truly well again, for the first time in years.'

I saw the doubt in Rosita's eyes, watched as she almost spoke but changed her mind, but it didn't matter whether or not she believed me. I had discovered a kind of faith, and it was all I needed to put my mind at rest.

I simply had to follow the rules of Hyperion. And by taking this course, I ignored all the warning signs.

CHAPTER THIRTY-NINE

The Confession

Of course Mateo returned laden with chocolates and gifts, a silver Tiffany bracelet for me, a rather creepy gothic doll for Bobbie, and a promise for both of us; that he only had to make one more trip before passing over the international side of the business to one of his colleagues. He would exclusively handle the exportation of Riojas and sherries within the EU. It meant that his longest trips would now be the overnights to Madrid or Jerez, and the rest of the time he would be home with us. There would be no more empty nights filled with wild imaginings. Our world would slowly shift back into balance once more.

I set aside the study of Hyperion House telling myself that I would return to it, but I wasn't so sure that I could. The only person who seemed genuinely disappointed by my abandonment of the project was Jordi.

'I couldn't see any point in continuing it,' I said. 'There are too many other things taking up my time.'

'I don't like to see people waste their energy,' he replied, clearly annoyed with me. 'Remember what Celestia always used to say about people who came here with good intentions, and how they ended up drinking and reading?'

'Has nobody heard from her?' I asked, remembering that I had to have seen her after everyone else.

'Not a thing,' said Jordi. 'Eduardo has the keys to her house, and has been over there to check on it several times, but it is empty. He says some of her things are missing, and her handbag and purse, so the thinking is that she went to England to see friends and didn't tell anyone. She'd done it before.'

I was still sure that she had left at the height of the storm, and had suffered some kind of an accident, but it seemed utterly bizarre that there was no trace of her. She'd told me she had no surviving relatives in England, and some years before had signed over her power of attorney to her neighbour. I didn't remember seeing her purse or her handbag, and it seemed more likely that he had nipped in and stolen them. I imagined he and his family were hoping that everyone would quietly forget about her. But an Englishwoman abroad, albeit one as vague and hippyish as Celestia, surely couldn't vanish without investigation?

'I'm certain she'll reappear in the square any day now,' said Jordi, uncertainly. 'I like her. I like you, and it seems a shame that you're going to give up the book. You were so excited about it.'

'What about you?' I said defensively. 'You're the custodian of a library nobody ever uses. Why would you stay here?'

'I'm not,' he replied. 'I've been offered a job as an archivist in Cadiz.'

'Are you going to take it?'

'I think I will, now.' When he said this, I realised something that should have been blindingly obvious, that he had actually been holding out some hope for the two of us.

'I think that's a good idea,' I said stiffly. 'You'll be able to make something of yourself.'

'Very well. I have something for you.' He dug in the drawer of his desk and pulled out an envelope. 'I thought it might be useful for your book, but you won't need it now.'

'What is it?' I asked, accepting the gift.

'I took the shelves down to clean them and found a letter that must have fallen from your monograph. I made a translation of it for you. I think you should still read it.'

I didn't like to tell him that I could have easily run it through a translation app, so I thanked him and took my leave. As I walked away, I glanced back and saw him standing at the library door, pretending not to watch me go. When he saw me looking he stepped swiftly back inside and was lost in the shadows.

As Mateo prepared to start his new domestic-trip-only schedule, I reached a decision. Toward the end of October, I sat with my husband in the glass atrium and we talked until late into the velvet night, beneath a star-spattered sky.

I told him the truth about me; that it was unlikely that I would ever be able to have a child, but that there were methods we might try. I talked about my father, how I had been forced to lock my bedroom door against him at night, and why I had tried to 'make myself ugly' as Anne had euphemistically described my cutting and anorexia. I made no excuses for my plunge into the hedonistic lifestyle that had finally resulted in my unwanted pregnancy. I held nothing back. Nothing at all.

At the end of this protracted bout in the confessional booth, Mateo told me that he had definitely suspected something along these lines, and that yes he carried his Catholic baggage, but it made no difference to how he felt about me. I was the love of his life and would always remain so, and we would try to have children of our own, but if we failed that didn't matter either because there was wonderful Bobbie, who if truth be told, had come to love me as much as she did her natural mother.

It felt as if he was telling me what I wanted to hear, as if it was all too good to be true. But that night, as we made love, I realised that he meant every word.

As I had decided for now that I would not continue with the book, which would only concentrate interest on a house we both wished to keep private, I decided to take over Mateo's accounts. I sent away for a Sage Accounting software package, and taught myself how to use it. The Apple laptop proved irreparable, but Mateo bought me another and I set to work. Rosita seemed pleased that I had decided to give up the idea of gainful employment, as if it was not the sort of thing a lady of Hyperion House should ever consider. She offered to teach me the principles of rustic Spanish cookery by way of compensation, and dear God, I accepted. Although I was still convinced that it was basically about sticking things in tomato sauce.

CHAPTER FORTY

The Children

I HAD BROUGHT up the *bonheur du jour* writing desk and made it my own, and put Jordi's envelope in a drawer, fully intending not to bother with it. Meanwhile, I concentrated on Mateo's accounts. He was hopeless at keeping receipts, and some of the discrepancies in his files were impossible to reconcile. For a start I could find no records of his recent flights to London, Madrid or JFK, even though he said he had booked the trips online and printed out receipts. Worse was Mateo's habit of keeping unopened mail, which he told me he'd intended to get around to but had somehow forgotten about. A stack of it had mounted up and I hardly knew how to begin to sort out the bills and queries, most of which had now become urgent.

After working my way through the pile for a day, I took a break and decided to open the envelope Jordi had given me. The letter had been chewed by mice and soaked in some kind of brown liquid, but he had included a translation on a fresh sheet. Attached to it was a note.

I thought you should have this. I think it must have fallen from the part of the monograph that had come loose from its binding. It's from Amancio Lueches to his wife Nina and is dated February 2009, six months before he was removed from Hyperion House to the Santa Theresa hospital. I couldn't read all of it, as his handwriting was very hard to decipher and the paper is badly damaged, but I have copied out the passages that I thought might be relevant to your studies. Your friend, Jordi.

I folded the translation flat on the desk and began to read.

Marcos Condemaine was, of course, a fool. Foolish to have supported the Republicans and to have defied the Movimiento Nacionale. The Civil War had its deepest roots in the battle of ownership for the land, so what did he, a Republican landowner, expect would happen? If it had not been for my government connections we would never have returned the house to its original family! And please by God's will we will live in it until we die, and that will be the end of us.

But what a strange dwelling Francesco built for his timid little Elena. A home without darkness! An unparalleled achievement! Of course, bricks and wood cannot build happiness by themselves, and I am sure Francesco filled Hyperion House with the power of God's almighty love.

Of course there was a price to pay for so much happiness. For you know there must be harmonious balance in all things. There can be no happiness without loss.

No happiness without loss. The phrase resonated.

Francesco conducted a rite of consecration on the darkened grounds behind the house where no shaft of sunlight would ever touch. It was said that by the time he finished, the soil was so soaked in blood that no blade of grass could ever take root on it.

Acts that seem necessary to one generation appear barbarous to the next, but there is little justification for my ancestor's behaviour. When the people of Gaucia discovered what had happened, did they try to have him arrested and tried? Of course not! They bowed low as the landowner passed by in his carriage, averting their eyes, and muttered darkly to themselves behind closed shutters about revenge.

This is why Marcos built those other strange rooms which are denied the sunlight, to complete his cousin's plans for the house and to cover over the evidence of his sins, so that he could say, see, this house is complete – how could such a thing have happened upon this spot when you know my ancestral home stands upon it!

But that, of course, was not the only reason, I know that now. It was for the family.

The question that most vexes me is this: of what practical purpose was that ritual? How was it intended to ensure lasting happiness for those of us living in this house? The answer continues to elude me. Francesco Condemaine remains an enigma; a man of faith and science, the two held in equal balance, what did he achieve? It is certain that our lives here have been happy beyond imagining, and continue to be so, but at what cost? It seems certain now that we owe this state to my ancestor, but at what expense to our own lives?

The passage raised more questions than it answered. Could Marcos Condemaine have added the rooms to hide his ancestor's sin, whatever it was, only to accidentally create a haven for them? There was one fact of which I was sure: Amancio Lueches had never posted the letter to his wife. He couldn't, because he had written it twenty-two years after she had died.

I was about to throw away the envelope when I realised that there was something else in it, and shook out a small sepia photograph of three children. On the back of the picture was handwritten: *Las Niñas, 1911*.

I had already placed the silver-framed photograph of Francesco Condemaine's offspring inside the writing desk and didn't need another, but I idly put the two pictures side by side for comparison.

They weren't the same children. *Las Niñas*. The three in the photograph Jordi had found were all girls, slender and darker, dressed in little more than rags, and the date, 1911, was the year before Hyperion House was completed.

A sickening feeling crept over me as I began to suspect the truth about the nature of Francesco Condemaine's happiness ritual.

'Why else do you think the people of Gaucia shunned the owner of Hyperion House?' said Alfonse, as if it should have been obvious to me from the outset. I had come to ask the only person I still knew who might be able to throw some light on the matter.

'Why on earth didn't you tell me?'

'I didn't think it would help you to know – and it doesn't, does it?' He sat back in his rattan chair and considered the view from his chaotic studio. 'The story is that Francesco and two other members of his society stole the children away one night and slaughtered them on the site of the house. It was all to fit some crack-brained theory about there having to be a balance between joy and misery. He believed there was no other way of guaranteeing his family's future happiness.'

'How do you know about this?'

The old artist's eyes lost focus. 'How does anyone know anything? Stories, rumours, gossip passed off as the gospel truth. Apparently Condemaine said that he and his pals had legitimately "purchased" the girls from a destitute family in order to give them better lives. Like all these stories, the reality was obviously somewhere in between.'

'What about the parents? They allowed this?'

'Who can say now? The mother was either a widow, a whore or married to a drunk.'

I could see it now. A virtually destitute woman coming home from long, backbreaking hours in the fields, only to find that her daughters' beds were empty. Running into the street she sees a cabriolet, a landau or even perhaps a motor vehicle heading away into the night, and there is nothing she can do, no-one she can turn to.

And the fact that the men of the Hyperion Society had chosen little girls for their purpose suggested much worse –

'You have to let go of all of these dusty old stories,' said Alfonse, reaching out to place a hand on my knee. 'None of it matters now.'

'It matters to me,' I said, rising and leaving.

CHAPTER FORTY-ONE

The Condition

I'D THOUGHT THAT the anomalies in my new life were not intended to be understood, that they were the price of my choice to remain here and be happy. Now I knew that wasn't true; it was all just another trick of the house. It was embarrassing how easily and willingly I had been seduced. For all its sunlight and beauty, this was a tainted place that tainted others.

While I tried to work out what to do, I busied myself by turning to Mateo's unopened mail. I was surprised to note that the top envelope was from the Santa Theresa hospital in Estepona. It took a few minutes to load the contents of the letter into iTranslate, but the gist was immediately clear.

Dear Senor Torres,

I am concerned that you missed your follow-up appointments with our therapist to discuss the management of your condition. If you remember, at the end of our last session you agreed to the drawing-up of a ***possibly timetable*** *(calendario) when we would resolve the outstanding issues and implications for your family.*

Please get in touch with either myself or Senora Pachas at the earliest opportunity.

Sincerely,

Dr Javier Areces

I found Mateo in the garden, talking to Jerardo about one of the cork trees that had been damaged in the most recent storm. The gardener was angrily stoking a bonfire of dead branches. Mateo looked up, clearly taken aback by the look on my face.

'Why did you stop seeing your doctor?' I asked, cutting across him.

He seemed genuinely puzzled. 'What are you talking about?'

I held up the letter. 'This. You've been for hospital tests three times in the last year.' I turned over the page. 'It doesn't say why. You were supposed to see a therapist to talk through "the implications"? What implications?'

Mateo excused himself and took me to one side. 'I didn't want to alarm you. I was getting short of breath, particularly when I lifted heavy luggage at the airport. Areces took some scans and ran lots of tests. They decided I had something called acute unstable angina. It's caused by a restriction in the supply of oxygenated blood to the heart. The symptoms develop rapidly and last up to about half an hour. He put me on glyceryl trinitrate, but I developed a resistance to it.'

'Well, what does that mean? What are the implications?'

'They offered me an arterial bypass graft.' He pressed his finger over his heart. 'You take a section of blood vessel from another part of the body and use it to re-route the flow of blood past the narrow section that's in here.'

'And what – you said no?'

'I said I'd think about it and get back to them, and I didn't.'

'Why not?'

'Partly because of where it is – there's some risk involved. But it's okay, I'm giving up the international flights. And I'm being careful – I always get a porter to take my case now, and I stay well away from hornets.'

'Why hornets?'

'Anaphylactic shock exacerbates the condition. I'd die within seconds if I was badly stung.'

I felt sick at the memory of him lying on the path, but was thankful that the nest had been destroyed. 'You were supposed to attend further appointments.'

'What's the point? I know what they're going to say – don't exert yourself or suffer undue stress. I'm fine, really.'

'Mateo, if the doctors think the operation could be a success, you should do it. I don't know what Bobbie and I would do without you. I get frightened just thinking about it.'

'That's exactly why I didn't tell you, Callie. I knew how you'd react!' He held out his hand. 'Please, let me have the letter.'

I resisted feebly, then finally handed him the page. He screwed it up and dropped it into the bonfire. 'There, now. Don't look at any more of the unanswered mail, okay? There's a reason why I don't answer them. I don't want you to upset yourself. I want you to be happy.'

'But what if you – ?'

'What if I *what*? Drop dead in JFK airport? What do you want from me, Callie, certainty? Our lives have no certainty. You can't quantify and predict everything, you can't know which of the choices we make will turn out to be right or wrong, all you can do is make intelligent guesses and enjoy what there is. What if you had gone to the police about your father? What if you hadn't had an abortion? What if we hadn't met and moved here? Who knows what the shape of your life would be? We all make mistakes, we can't do everything right.'

'Don't you see, Mateo, I never thought I would find any happiness, and then I met you and Bobbie and came to this house, and even with everything that's happened since then I'm still here, because I know this is my only chance to be happy.'

'Then you must know that nothing lasts forever, my love.'

There was a forlorn expression on his face that I had never seen before. Unable to bear looking in his eyes for a moment longer, I ran back to the house.

CHAPTER FORTY-TWO

The Ghosts

THE BRANCHES HAD elongated their shadows across the ceiling, and juddered back and forth in the wind. The rains were coming again.

When the storm hit, the ceiling turned into a glittering waterfall. I rose and watched the reflection of the rain sluicing down the windows. There was no point in trying to get to sleep. Even though Mateo had acted for my sake, I was unable to shake off the conviction that I had been repeatedly and deliberately lied to. It was as if I had been watching a play in which everyone had a carefully rehearsed part, performed for an audience of one.

When I was nine years old, my mother had told me that the world was not waiting to see what I did. That it would go on around me, without me, and nobody would care if I was there or not. After that I put it to the test a few times and thought that she was right – no matter how I behaved, nothing changed. Puberty altered all that. Suddenly everything had a consequence. I saw that life was a domino pattern waiting to be tumbled, one piece hitting the next, and that once it was set in motion there was no way to put the parts back in place.

I went down and boiled hot milk for cocoa, then sat drinking it in the kitchen that smelled of lavender and warm bread, watching the pair of them: Mateo sitting at the table, tapping at his iPad and frowning, Bobbie playing some kind of complicated card game that required her to lay out the pack according to the constellations. I listened to the wind and rain, and said nothing. Rosita came in and went out with some plates, a walk-on part in the unfolding dumb-play around me.

At one point the power glitched and the lights flickered out. Neither Mateo nor Bobbie even flinched. When the power came back they were in exactly the same positions, Mateo tapping away, Bobbie carefully laying down cards, as if they hadn't noticed a thing.

'Did you see that?' I asked.

'Hmm?' Mateo looked up and studied me, then smiled vaguely. 'No, what?'

Later he stayed downstairs watching a loud science fiction movie with Bobbie. I let him put her to bed, heard him turn off the TV, heard him head for the distant kitchen where I knew he would make one last *cortado*, heard his creak on the stairs and his clothes falling to the floor, felt his warm hands close over mine in bed.

And still I knew I had been lied to.

The next morning began with one of those glorious skies that set a blue luminescence over the world. By 8:00am it was already too hot for an autumn day, and the wind had fallen away, allowing the heat to settle across the landscape.

I sat at breakfast while Rosita served eggs, *tostadas* and coffee, as she always did on a Saturday, and I could feel the conspiracy of their smugness. I would do as I was told, and I could be kept in the dark just as much as those poor dead creatures in the other rooms. They would stay there, and we would stay here, and so long as nobody upset the order of things we'd just go on as before, as people always had in this house. This damned house.

I silently watched Bobbie engrossed in the buttering of her toast, carefully taking the butter all the way to the corners, something Rosita usually scolded her about because the Spanish never seemed to put butter on their bread while tomatoes were available. Mateo was in faded blue jeans, an Ajaxx T-shirt and

Adidas trainers, his weekend uniform, every bit as graceful as his weekday suit. Bobbie had tied her hair in perfect braids.

'Are you okay?' Mateo asked solicitously. 'You're very quiet this morning.'

'I'm fine,' I lied. 'I thought we'd all go into Gaucia today. To go as a family for a change.'

Mateo looked pained. 'Oh honey, can't you go? I promised Jerardo I'd give him a hand. Some more branches came down in the night and we need to get them clear of the paths. To be honest, I think the garden is getting a little too much for him.'

'Then we should let him go and bring in some new help. He's far past retirement age.'

'We couldn't do that, he's always been here with the house. He's spent most of his life here.'

'I *forgot*, the house must come first. Well, he can carry on living here on the premises, like Senora Delgadillo.'

He gave me a strange look. 'What's got into you this morning?'

'Forget it,' I said, rubbing a patch of dry skin on my forehead. 'I didn't sleep well.'

'I need to finish my essay,' said Bobbie. 'It has to be posted on Monday morning, remember?'

'So it has,' I said. 'Well, there's always something.'

Bobbie's new school was giving her assignments that would bring her up to speed for the new term. I hadn't been to the school and met the governors; Mateo had taken care of that. At least, that was what he had told me.

'So, are you okay to go into Gaucia with Rosita?' It felt as if Mateo was pushing me.

'You never come with me anymore. I can't remember the last time we all went together.'

'I know I've been away a lot, but that's finished now.'

'What do you mean?'

'Well,' he turned and sent a secret smile to Bobbie, 'I thought about what you said and you're right, there's no point in making myself sick. I cancelled my final New York trip. The new guy's already started in Madrid, so he can take my place. I emailed him this morning and he agreed to take over.'

'You mean it?'

'Sure I mean it. Work-life balance, right? We sort that out and everything else falls into place.'

I was so surprised that I could find no voice. I cleared my throat. 'Okay. If you're sure. If it doesn't get you into trouble or anything.'

He ruffled Bobbie's hair. 'Of course I'm sure.'

I glanced over and noticed that Rosita was listening. 'Maybe we could go somewhere, just for a few days, the three of us. We haven't been away together for ages. It'll be our last chance before Bobbie starts her new school.'

Mateo hesitated for a split second, just long enough for me to notice. 'Yes, sure. As soon as we've got this place straight. And I'd have to give head office a month's warning notice.'

'But she starts school in two week's time, how can we go anywhere?'

'Oh, we'll figure something out, I'm sure.' He grinned at Bobbie and she lowered her fork long enough to grin back, the *tostada* packed in between her teeth. It was as if they were sharing some private joke at my expense. Behind them, Rosita bustled out triumphantly with the dishes.

I grew increasingly angry. I'd had enough of the house, and them. I pushed away from the table and booked a taxi into Gaucia.

As I made my way up the hill, I could see Alfonse on his terrace, painting. Hearing the taxi turn he looked over the rail and gave me a wave. 'My dear, this is a nice surprise. I thought I'd scared you off for good. Come on up.'

He was smearing thick cyan onto a canvas with a palette knife, and kept comparing the results to the view. If the picture was a landscape, it was an extremely abstracted one. Beside his spattered paint-stand stood a coffee pot and a brandy bottle.

'Which is it to be?' he asked. 'Let's start with coffee. You look done in – are you alright?'

'I keep asking myself that,' I replied. 'Has anyone heard from Celestia?'

'Not a word, it's all very peculiar.' He poured thick *cortados,* adding milk from a sun-warmed steel jug. 'The police don't seem to care. They're used to ex-pats behaving strangely. Her neighbour's family have taken over her house. I see them sitting on the porch and they wave to me as I pass, quite brazenly.'

'What do you think happened to her?'

'She didn't take off for London, that's for sure. She hated the place.'

'Alfonse, if I tell you something, can you make sure it goes no further?'

'Honestly, Callie, who am I going to tell? Apparently I'm a recluse.'

I sipped my coffee and looked out over the landscape. 'Celestia came to the house the night before she went missing. She wanted to try and "read" the place – she said she had a gift for understanding such things.'

'Oh God, why is it that old women always go loopy? I suppose she told you about her run-in with the law back in Blighty. Maria's just as bad, forever sloshing holy water about and seeing omens in flocks of birds. What happened?'

'If I tell you, promise you won't think me crazy?'

'Go on, then.'

'She saw the ghost of Elena Condemaine dragging her husband's remains – we both saw her. The storm put the lights out, and when they came back on, she'd gone.'

'Dear God. Was she driving?'

'No, she came in a taxi, but no-one's ever traced it. The distance is just about walkable – but not for her, and not in the rain.'

'The cops think she missed the edge of the ridge somewhere around here, and ended up in the drink.' Alfonse set aside his brush and smeared a dab of paint with his thumb. 'If they're right, she'll never be found. Not that anyone wants to find her. It suits them all that she's gone missing. Of course, Maria and her coven think she was snatched by the Devil for saying rude things about the church. They presume she was an atheist.'

'She told me she was raised as a Catholic.'

'Because you can't believe in the supernatural without faith? Well of course women can believe any bloody thing. They rewrite the world to suit themselves. I don't suppose we'll ever get to the truth of it.'

'I did see someone,' I insisted. 'We both saw her.'

'And I suppose when you looked again in the morning, there was nothing.'

'I'm trying to make sense of it all. It's there, right in front of me, but every time I concentrate it vanishes. '

Alfonse laid a paint-crusted hand on my wrist. 'I'm sorry, my dear, I'm not poking fun at you. Tell me, how are you keeping?'

'I suppose it appears we're all well,' I said. 'Bobbie's about to start boarding school in Marbella.'

'Then I hope we'll see a little more of you. Your visits are most welcome. I suppose you heard that Jordi left town.'

'No, I was about to look in on him. Did he go to Cadiz?'

'No, in the end he decided to take a position in the library of the *Universidad Complutense de Madrid.* He assured us he would be in touch once he'd settled into his apartment, but I don't suppose we'll ever hear from him again.'

'It seems like everyone is going,' I said, unnerved.

'It always feels like that in small villages,' said Alfonse. 'Eventually you just get left with the ghosts.'

CHAPTER FORTY-THREE

The Grave

I HAD TAKEN to sitting in the little glade of the Condemaine cemetery. It was one of the few spots where the bleaching rays of the sun were diluted by the overhead fronds, and I could be left alone with only a few birds for company. More and more often I needed to get away from the overwhelming *niceness* of everyone.

When I returned from Gaucia, I found Mateo in the drawing room helping Bobbie with her essay. They were laughing together at some private joke, so I decided not to interrupt them. Instead, I lugged a wicker chair from the atrium down the garden, and filled my bag with the remains of the unopened correspondence from Mateo's desk, together with a letter opener.

Settling myself between the worn-away headstones, I sat back in the chair and watched midges glittering like flakes of gold in the shifting light. The letters lay on my lap, in danger of slipping off, so I began to sort through them. There's something permanent about written correspondence, the date-stamps placing markers in time that make you recall what else you were doing on the day the letter arrived.

Which was why I noticed that the first letter, from Mateo's company, had arrived on the Thursday after I dreamed he had collapsed in the garden. Its tone was formal and polite. In it, someone called Senor Alex Mendoza was enquiring frostily (as far as I could tell) when Mateo might be expected in Jerez to discuss their distribution problem.

I opened the next letter, dated a week later, this time from someone billed as a Senior Production Manager. This one was in English. He was disappointed that the meeting had not taken place in Jerez, and promised to catch up with Mateo in New York.

One after another, they said the same thing. When are you coming back, why aren't you answering your phone, why couldn't you make the meeting in Jerez and finally, why did you not come to the convention in New York?

But he had been in New York. I had seen him on Skype, the Manhattan skyline clearly delineated in the background. I had always seen him and spoken to him wherever he went. I tore open the rest of the letters to find more complaints, more requests, more threats, including two from Bobbie's school concerning the non-arrival of his promised cheque.

It made no sense; what could possibly be gained by lying to me? If he was in financial trouble, why not tell me? But of course Mateo was an old-school gentleman. If he was in difficulty at work, I would be the last to know. What if it was worse than that? What if he had lost his job? What if he was having some kind of mental breakdown?

I had read of a Swiss banker who had carried on going to work for full two years after losing his job. Eventually the strain of pretending that he was still employed, coupled with the mounting debts he had incurred, caused him to go crazy and slaughter his entire family before killing himself.

I stacked the letters and returned them to my bag, trying to work out what I should do. Confront him? Or pretend, like he always did, that nothing was wrong?

I sat back and looked up through the branches of the cork trees at Hyperion House, remembering something that Celestia had said: that houses weren't haunted, people were.

For no particular reason I dug out my mobile and called her.

It heard it start to ring. Then I realised I could hear it twice.

Once on the phone at my ear, and once from somewhere else below my chair. I climbed off the seat and searched the unruly grass. Nothing. I remembered she'd told me that she had never got around to setting her voicemail. Taking the mobile away from my ear, I listened, and could still hear the ringtone. I lay flat on the grass and heard it more clearly, coming from under the ground.

I needed something to dig with.

Sticking the brass letter opener into the grass, I twisted it and pulled out a chunk of earth. I punched the letter opener into a rough circle, removing the dirt with my hands, working as quickly as I could.

The ringing became clearer.

I didn't have to dig very far. Moments later, the letter opener stuck fast, and I realised it was caught in something that felt fleshy and human.

As I scrabbled away at the patch of dirt, something began to appear. I saw dark skin, grey lips and white teeth, the mouth filled with soil and ants. Frantic, I tore away at the softly packed earth until Celestia's dead eyes were exposed, staring up past me at the hard blue sky.

CHAPTER FORTY-FOUR

The Light

As I RAN into the house I shed everything I was holding, the letters, the opener, my bag. Dirt from my shoes and my bleeding hands scattered across the polished floor. Rosita was coming down the stairs, and looked at me in astonishment.

On the way I had collected a hammer from Jerardo's shed, and was holding it in my right hand. I drew several deep breaths and tried to calm myself.

'Where is Mateo?' I asked. She dumbly pointed at the drawing room.

My husband was kneeling on the floor beside Bobbie, helping her draw a huge map of the area on cardboard. I waited for him to look up and acknowledge me. His shirt was so white that it seemed to shine in the sunlight. He slowly raised his eyes and a smile formed.

'Is everything all right?' I asked.

'We're making a 3D picture of the whole area,' said Bobbie. 'It's going to be so beautiful.'

'I thought you were working on your essay.'

'I'm going to do that later.'

'But it's why you said you couldn't come in to Gaucia with me.'

'Daddy said we could do this.' She looked to Mateo for approval.

'That's okay, honey, it's fine isn't it?' Mateo asked.

'There were people hoping to talk to you,' I replied. 'They say they never see you anymore.'

'They'll only start inviting us to their festival planning committees,' said Mateo. 'You know how many Saints' days they have, and there are still so many things we need to sort out at the house.'

'You're right,' I said, looking about. 'I should do more around here. Perhaps I can help.'

'Sure. It would be great to have a hand.'

'Oh, by the way, I thought you'd be interested to know that I've found Celestia. She's buried in our garden, in the Condemaine cemetery. But I suppose you know that already.'

I turned on my heel and went upstairs to the bedroom. Digging into the second drawer of the clothes chest, I found the ring of keys and ran back downstairs, my heart thumping. I walked into the drawing room and headed for the connecting door, my fingers feeling for the right key in my pocket.

Mateo looked up. 'Wait, hon, what are you going to do?'

'Something I should have done a long time ago,' I said, unlocking the door to the dark side. 'I'm going to let some light into this place. I know the windows back onto the cliff but if we take down the shutters and open all the connecting doors, maybe take them off their hinges, we must be able to at least get some brightness into the rooms. Wouldn't that be nice?'

'But Rosita will be devastated,' said Mateo, rising. 'The house has never been altered.'

'Then I think now's the time to alter it,' I said, throwing open the door. A broad panel of sunlight sliced across the floor of the darkness beyond.

'Callie, you mustn't!' cried Bobbie, rising.

I brandished the hammer with menace. 'Don't worry about it, either of you. Get on with your fucking drawings and let me sort this out.'

The first shaft of light from our drawing room allowed me to head deeper into its mirror image and reach the shutters. I unbolted them as far as I could, then used the hammer to bash back the bolts and break the slats free of their swollen frames. There was a shower of dust as the shutters unpinned themselves and folded back, letting in at least some light reflected from the cliff wall. Chunks of wood split apart and fell.

Mateo and Bobbie were shouting behind me, but I ignored them as I headed for the next window. The shutters here were stiffer, painted over so that they stuck in their frames, but I could use the hammer to smash out the slats. Once I realised how flimsily they'd been made, I punched more of them out. Shafts of dust-filled light began to criss-cross the room. As more shutters came down beneath the weight of the hammer, more sun was reflected in. It wasn't dark at all. The light was bouncing off the amber cliff face.

Bobbie and Mateo were still yelling at me but they remained outside as I pushed past them and worked my way upstairs. Unlocking the mirror-bedroom and throwing the sun-side doors wide, I ran into the room in time to see *her* rise from the safety of her high-backed chair and flit through the shadows, as startled as a fox.

It was no time to commune with ghosts. Grabbing the tall maroon velour curtains with both hands, I pulled as hard as I could. The ancient fabric tore, but most of it came down from the poles in cascades of dust. Behind them, the shutters opened easily. I moved onto the next window, tearing down the filthy curtains, attacking the wooden blinds and punching out the windows, until only one more room was left.

I looked about for the phantoms of the Condemaine family, but they were nowhere to be seen. I could only think that the light was driving them from the room.

Up here it was possible to let in more light because the cliff started to slope a little further away from the house, but I couldn't loosen the shutters. Dragging a chair over to the window I pulled down one of the metal curtain rods and thrust it into the slats, cracking them apart. First a single ray of light angled across the wall, then another and another, driving out darkness in a matrix of luminescence.

I went back to the others and used the rod again, smashing the remaining slats away from the frames, completely flooding the room with afternoon sun. How shabby and faded everything looked in the dusty maelstrom, how desperate and impoverished! Coughing, my eyes streaming, covered in cobwebs and grime, I threw the curtain rod onto the floor and made my way back out.

Bobbie was standing on the landing with tears running down her face. I could see Senora Degadillo at the foot of the stairs, her whitened hands knotted together, her face unreadable.

'You've ruined everything,' Bobbie cried. 'Don't you see? You've ruined *everything*.'

'What are you talking about? Where's your father?' I asked. She pointed back downstairs between sobs.

I ran down and all but slid into the drawing room, swinging on the door jamb, only to find myself in eclipsing light. Mateo was patiently and methodically closing our shutters, drawing our blinds.

'Why are you doing that?' I asked.

'One side has to stay dark,' he said, as if explaining something to a child. 'Otherwise we'll be destroyed.'

'What are you talking about?' His words made no sense. I started to back away as Bobbie arrived behind me.

'You've broken the shutters,' said Bobbie. 'Where are they going to go?'

'Well, they'll have to come into this side.' Mateo calmly pointed into the shadows, as if the answer was obvious.

'Then you believe me?' I asked. 'Mateo, we can't let them come in here, they can't just take over our lives!'

Mateo remained surprisingly calm. 'Darling, we have no choice in the matter,' he said quietly.

'No? You're just going to let that poor diseased thing stay here with us?' I said, pointing to the corner of the drawing room beside the high-backed chair, *our* drawing room, the chair on *our* side. Now I could see Elena Condemaine cowering behind it, her frail form half-bent in terror, like a cat that had been driven from one hiding place to another.

'Don't, Callie,' said Mateo. 'Please, you're not thinking rationally. Just come back here and forget about all this. Let me finish making everything okay in here and we can go back to –'

'To what, Mateo? No-one's seen you at work. You didn't go to Jerez. You didn't go to New York. You didn't see the doctor. You don't go into town. Nor does Bobbie.'

'No – no, of course we don't,' he replied, sounding confused. 'How could we?'

'But you can see her, can't you? All of you?' I jabbed my finger at Elena again. 'You can all see Francesco's wife right there, trying to hide in the shadows!'

'I think you're overwrought,' said Mateo. 'Let Rosita take you to the kitchen while Bobbie and I finish up here.'

Rosita tried to take my arm. 'Please come, Senora Torres,' she said. 'I'll boil some hot milk and make cinnamon chocolate.'

'I'm not a fucking invalid,' I shouted at her, 'let go of me!'

Pulling free, I ran to the fireplace and the high-backed chair where Elena still cowered, turned aside in shame, her withered features hidden by the smiling china mask she was always forced to wear. I reached out and grabbed at her tattered grey dress, turning her around to face me.

I looked deep into her dark eyes.

And I saw.

CHAPTER FORTY-FIVE

The Past

I SAW THE horse and cart that the young man drove through the whitewashed streets, rattling over the cobbled lanes under the cover of darkness. It was a Saint's day, the festival of San Isidro, May the 15th, and the roads were hung with bright cloth flags. In the square there was a bonfire and a platform for dancing, and around the edges were tables of food. Children ran everywhere, chasing after dogs and cats with fireworks, stamping on them to cause explosions.

I saw Francesco Condemaine speak with his cart-driver, Jerardo's great-grandfather. The pair of them left the horse and slipped around the corner of the square, to where the smallest children ran with hoops. I saw the ragged little girls, three of them, not invited to join the others because their mother was a *puta*, their father a drunk.

I saw the men return with the wriggling hemp sack, tying it at their feet and placing it in the cart, the children's screams lost under the deafening rounds of *fuegos artificiales*, the rockets and jumping jacks and Roman candles spitting tongues of flame over the squealing children and the parents who were watching the band.

I saw the wooden scaffolds of the nascent Hyperion House, the dusty piles of bricks, the workers' dying bonfires, the uprooted rocks and stacks of planks. It was late now, and everyone else was at the fiesta. I watched as Francesco and the cart-driver carried the wriggling sack to the foundation pit and slit open the canvas, tipping its contents into the darkness.

I saw what they did to them.

I heard the clatter of their shovels as they later filled in the pit, working fast and without taking a breath, until rocks and soil replaced the hole and they could tamp the ground flat. I saw them carry the stones and drop them onto the earth, the start of Hyperion's foundation.

I RELEASED MY hand in horror and she fell back. But she clutched at me once again...

I SAW THAT the whitewashed walls of the village were dirty now, the painted doors peeling and faded. Gaucia had fallen on hard times. Litter swilled through the rain-flooded streets. Two starving dogs were fighting at the corner, one tearing mouthfuls of flesh from the other's hindquarters until it squealed and limped away, trailing spurts of blood.

I saw Elena Condemaine trudging through the closed-up town in the downpour, banging on each of the doors in turn, working her way along the street. As she approached, shutters closed and curtains were drawn. A small child watched from an attic until she was torn away by her mother and slapped, and the window bolted shut.

Elena dropped to her haunches in the gutter and cried bitter tears, but no-one dared to look out until she had moved on. At the edge of the square one shopkeeper threw her a hardened heel of bread, but she was not quick enough to catch it and it broke apart in the gutter, to be snatched away by the dogs.

She gathered the remaining scraps in the pockets of her skirt and continued blindly on, praying she might find something that would keep her children alive for just a few more days.

When she slipped inside the church of the Blessed Holy Virgin, she sought only to rest, but the priest twisted her arm behind her back and forced her outside, hurling her onto the steps and slamming the door behind her. She lay in the inundated gutter sobbing, knowing now that the lives of her children were beyond redemption.

They wanted nothing to do with her. Three children had been taken, three would now starve to death. God had answered their prayers and allowed their revenge.

I saw her forced attempts at gaiety, and the handfuls of sugar Elena used as a bribe to lure her three listless, sickly children into a merry game. She brought them to the back of the house, to the small patch of stones and rubble under which Gaucia's own lost children lay ravaged and buried.

Here, she bade them kneel, demonstrating first how they should hold their positions. She blindfolded each in turn, whispering words of comfort, speaking of meeting with God's good grace, and if the children suspected anything they did not cry out, because even now they trusted their mother.

When the three were lined up facing the cliff wall, she rose and walked behind them, taking the carving knife from her pocket. She started with one of the twins. Gently, lovingly, she tipping back his head, exposing his white throat, and swiftly drew the blade across it, curtaining blood onto his chest. He fell forward as gently as a sapling falls, with the faintest rustle, and lay still.

She moved onto the next and performed the same simple movement, sliding the knife over his exposed skin, parting the flesh so quickly that he had no time to cry. He, too, fell with the grace of a dying bird.

She was brought to her favourite, her youngest, her beautiful dark daughter Maria, and for the first time her nerve failed, and the knife stayed at her side. The girl waited, motionless, trusting. When nothing happened, she reached up and raised the blindfold from one eye, and saw what her mother was about to do.

With her eyes crushed shut, Elena had raised the knife above her daughter's throat. When Maria saw the blade, she released a cry that cut into Elena's very soul.

But it was too late to stop. Elena brought down her arm and did the deed, turning aside with a sob as her beloved, wasted little girl was released from the misery of existence.

She would have joined them, had planned it that way, but now the weight of her actions overtook her with the speed of a hurtling train and she howled to the sky, and her wits departed, never to return.

Soon she would gather up the bodies and take them inside, to be with her forever. To live with the worst sin any mother could commit.

I saw all this, and more.

My sight was marred by a shimmering veil of tears. The world rained. The ragged grey figure before me gently unclenched her bony fingers from around my wrist and turned her cruelly perfect face aside.

CHAPTER FORTY-SIX

The Decision

I AWOKE ON the striped sofa, under a blanket. It was dark. Candles guttered at either end of the darkened drawing room. The candlesticks had come from the other side, I was sure of that. Mateo and Bobbie sat solicitously, awaiting my return to consciousness.

I tried to raise my head but it ached so badly that I had to put it down again. I tried to speak, failed and tried again.

'Do you want some water?' Mateo asked gently.

I nodded. He went off and returned with a crystal carafe, holding my head up with one hand while he raised the glass to my lips with the other.

'What happened?' I asked.

'Well, that's kind of hard to say. You passed out and banged your head on the corner of the table. There didn't appear to be any real damage but you concussed yourself. You've got a nasty bump there.'

I caught a glimpse of myself with the curtain rod, prising off the slats from the shutters. 'Oh God, I smashed up the windows, didn't I?'

Mateo gave a small laugh. 'That you did, babe. Nothing we can't get repaired. But you know something – first I think we should have a talk. Bobbie, why don't you go to the kitchen and see how long dinner's going to be?'

'Okey doke.' Bobbie rose and scampered off. It didn't make sense. Everyone was being so pragmatic and unemotional.

'I must have made a lot of noise,' I said. 'How come Rosita didn't go crazy? She's still here, isn't she?'

'Sure. She came running when she heard you but what could she do? Even I wasn't about to stop you, not with that thing in your hands. You went a little whacko there for a while. Don't worry about it. Jerardo and I will put everything back together. Soon you won't be able to tell that there was ever any damage done to the house. It will be just like it always was.'

'But I don't want it to be like it always was, Mateo. I want to get rid of the other rooms.'

He sat on the edge of the sofa, lovingly massaging my knuckles with his fingers, clearly uncomfortable with what he was about to say.

'That's what I wanted to talk to you about, honey. You see, there have to be a few changes, just until we can get the place fixed up.'

'What kind of changes?' I pushed myself up on my left elbow and saw something that made no sense. There were no overhead lights on. Instead, clusters of candles sat on every flat surface. The room had shrunk, and the furniture was faded and dusty. The ceiling was too low.

'Callie, listen to me –'

'We're in the wrong side! What have you done?'

'They have to stay somewhere dark,' said Mateo reasonably. 'You broke the shutters in here, so we've shut out all the light in the other side. They'll just stay there until we've done the repairs.'

'Listen to what you're saying, Mateo, this is madness.' I threw off the blanket and climbed up from the sofa, fighting nausea. 'I have to get out of here.'

'All right, if that's what you want.'

'And I want you and Bobbie to come with me. We need to get away from this house. Can't you see what it's done to us? We can go to Marbella, just rent a room for the night while we figure out what to do. We can sell the place. I can get in touch with Julia and put it back on the market –'

'I wish we could, but it's not that simple.'

'It is, Mateo. Bobbie can still start school on time and you can commute from the coast.'

'We can't come with you. We belong here now.'

'You don't know what you're saying.' I looked about the drawing room. Mateo had stacked the broken shutters neatly against the wall. Moonlight shone through the tops of the windows above the cliff edge. 'I feel sick, I need some air,' I said, heading for the door. He didn't try to stop me.

I stood in my moon-shadow at the centre of the lawn, and breathed deep. I could smell pine, lavender, night-scented stock. The night sky was sprinkled with sharp spikes of cold starlight. Out here it felt as if normal life could be continued. I didn't understand how or why, but my nyctophobia had lifted.

I slowly turned and looked back at the house, glimmers of candlelight showing from the rear rooms through the open front door. The main windows – *our* windows - were heavily draped now. At the top of the house Rosita's bedroom light was on.

So we were to hand the house over to the tragedy-haunted Condemaines and live in their home like tenants. Even Mateo was no longer denying that we had been trapped here by the house's ancestors. The living and the dead existing side by side… it was as if some kind of collective madness had fallen upon us.

Looking back at the house once more, I reached a decision. I took one final deep breath of the cool night air and headed back inside, where I found my husband still seated on the striped sofa.

'We can't stay here any longer, Mateo,' I said, sitting beside him and taking his hand. Bobbie was perched primly on her chair, watching me. 'I won't be lied to anymore. I'm not giving up either of you and I'm not giving up the light. Mateo, you must be honest and explain to me exactly what's been going on. Then we'll sell up and go somewhere else, for the sake of our sanity and our family.'

Mateo's face fell. 'The house has done everything it can to bring you joy, Callie. Why can't you just accept that? Out there the world is unknowable. There's no way of guaranteeing your happiness. In here, your life is always good.'

'Why would I want that? Happiness lies in overcoming your problems, not pretending they don't exist. So I can stay here and never feel pain again, is that it, so long as I share my world with the dead?'

'We're always linked to the dead, right from the moment we're born. The link should be respected. Why can't you just accept that this is how things are, and make the best of it?'

'Because I'm not like you, Mateo. You're so kind and gentle. You never seem to have a bad word for anyone. I spent years hating my life. Then you came along, and all that bitterness drained away. You saved my life, baby.'

'Don't say that, please,' he begged. 'Please, Callie.'

I took his face in mine. 'Why not? It's true. I'm alive because of you.'

'You are alive,' he said, a tear sliding down his cheek. 'And I want you to have a long and happy life.'

'Then let me do this one thing,' I said, rising. 'I have to know the truth.'

'Please – don't.'

'I want to see Elena one last time.'

'No, darling, I beg you.'

Bobbie rose and went to her father, to be at his side, and the pair of them watched me leave the room. I was struck with a terrible moment of *déjà vu*, from a time soon after we had moved into Hyperion House, when the pair of them had studied me carefully to see what I would do. Back then, my only intention had been to please them. Now, I was acting against their wishes.

I walked away, then stepped into the mirror-drawing room and looked for Elena Condemaine. I knew exactly where I would find her; where she always sat, in the high-backed chair beside the empty fireplace. *Our* chair this time.

As I approached, she slowly came into view; the bony fingers resting on the arm, the unkempt hair, the ragged clothes.

Once again, I found myself looking at someone who was not a ghost but flesh and blood, although grey and wasted and reeking with the terrible sickness of neglect. As always, her head was lowered so that her dank grey locks hung over the straps of the smiling china face.

'Don't be frightened, Elena,' I said. 'I just want to talk to you. I need to understand. Is that alright?'

A faint gasp of breath came from her, starting deep inside her infected chest.

I moved closer. 'Why are you still here?'

There was still no answer, just a terrible wheeze of air as she fought to speak.

'What is it that keeps you in this house?'

Slowly, she raised her right hand and pointed at me.

'*I* keep you here? But how is that possible?'

She lifted both hands and fumbled with the leather straps that held the doll mask in place, trying to loosen them. Anxious to help her, I reached around her thin neck and unclasped the buckles, trying not to let the leather bite any deeper into her damaged flesh. 'Why must you always wear this?' I asked – but then I realised that I already knew the answer.

She wears it from choice. She wears it to look happy even when she is heartbroken. She wears it to look like me, the woman she envies so desperately.

I took the edge of the unbuckled mask in my grip and slowly lifted it aside. And for the first time, I truly saw her.

No-one had lied.

There were no ghosts here at Hyperion House. Francesco and Elena Condemaine, Augustin, Farriol and Maria were all long dead and gone.

Instead I found myself looking into the heart of Hyperion, and the truth.

She tried to speak.

'I am not Elena Condemaine,' she said. 'I am you.'

I looked, knowing that I had seen her ravaged face before and would see it again, or at least a version of it, every time I stared into a mirror.

CHAPTER FORTY-SEVEN

The Two Sides

MATEO TOOK MY hand and led me to the kitchen where Bobbie and Rosita sat waiting patiently, with a great tray of *jamon* and tomato bread between them. The room was filled with warm candlelight. Mateo held out my chair, and waited until I was seated before sitting down, always the perfect gentleman.

'Here,' he said, pouring me a brandy. 'You're shaking like a leaf. Try and drink it straight down.'

I did as I was told, and coughed violently.

'Part of you always knew,' he said. 'It was the one thing none of us ever lied about. Francesco got what he wanted, at a price.'

'What do you mean?'

'Hyperion House creates – shadows.'

'Mateo, I don't understand.'

'A mirror-family that lives in the dark side of the house. When anything bad happens, it happens to them. They take all the pain. That's what the shadows are for.'

'I don't – I can't –'

'When Francesco was killed, his image lived on in the sunlit side. His children stayed healthy and Elena remained in perfect bliss, while the real tragedy was lived out by their counterparts.'

'Something made her suspicious –'

'She disobeyed her husband's instructions. She entered the other side of the house and saw the truth. In the dark, that was where the real tragedy of her life continued. That's when she became afraid, after she realised how her life had turned out. Her husband dead, her children brought to starvation and murdered out of mercy – her own descent into insanity. What she'd believed was true was just a sunlit dream. If she hadn't doubted her happiness and questioned it, she'd have remained here peacefully until she died.'

'Living inside a dream version of her life,' I said angrily.

'No, her life as it *should* have been, as it deserved to be. If her husband hadn't gone to fight for another country, leaving her destitute. If her children hadn't faced starvation. Every day we make decisions that alter our destiny, Callie. The house gave her the best possible future, the way things should have turned out.'

'People take drugs to wipe out the tragedy of their daily lives, Mateo. Is that what you wanted for me, to live in a state of ignorance for the rest of *my* life?'

'If that's what it took to make you happy, yes,' said Mateo.

'My God – you knew about Hyperion House.'

'I'd heard stories about it when I was a child. We all had. And I knew about the difficulties you'd had in the past. Your mother made sure of that.'

'Does she have to hear the rest?' asked Bobbie gently, touching Mateo's arm.

'Listen to me, Callie. What you saw in the garden that day was real. You tried to save my life, but I died. You moved my body into the shadows, and Jerardo buried it. But I lived on for you, so long as you stayed in the light. What you saw in the darkened rooms was *us*. It was better for you to believe it was the Condemaines.'

'No,' I said, 'That's not possible, there were too many of them –'

'No, Callie, think about it. You never saw more than three at one time. You wanted so badly to believe they were the Condemaines that you allowed yourself to be fooled.'

'I won't hear any more of this.'

'Your mother – Anne – she came to break us apart, so we took her away to the cemetery in the garden. We took her life as gently as we could. Celestia got even closer to the truth, so we had to act again.'

'We did it all for you, Mummy,' said Bobbie.

She had never called me that before. I looked over at Mateo's daughter, sitting there quite unconcerned, carefully separating pieces of scarlet *jamon* with her fork.

'After my death you lost your senses and neglected her,' said Mateo. 'She wasted away, and fell into a sleep from which she never awoke. She felt no pain. Did you, love?'

'Nope.' Bobbie kept her eyes on her plate.

'But then you started to neglect yourself. And that shows. Which is why we want you to eat.'

The revelation overwhelmed me. I started to shake, fighting back the sourness rising in my stomach. 'I failed to save you and I let Bobbie starve, and you took care of anyone who could have hurt me,' I whispered. 'What's next? Am I destined to go mad and kill myself, just like my predecessor?'

'Don't you see, it wouldn't happen to you,' said Mateo, 'it would happen to *her*. The other Callie the house created for you. We couldn't come with you to town because we no longer exist outside of this house. And we didn't want you spending too much time away because when you're away from Hyperion its power starts to fade.'

'So the phone calls, the flights, the "meetings" in other towns, none of them ever happened? They couldn't, because you couldn't be there, could you? Once you died, you were tied to the house. It was you who put the postcards in the mailbox. Bobbie could never really go to school somewhere else because she doesn't exist outside of Hyperion.' I shook my head at him. 'You're a fool. Francesco Condemaine was wrong. Tragedy always finds a way out. Did you honestly think you could keep hiding the truth forever?'

Mateo and Bobbie looked at each other and then at me. They had no easy answers, and nothing more to say.

'I have one question,' I said, trying to sound in control of my emotions. 'This feels real. *I* feel real. Which side is real and which is the dream? Does the true world belong to those things in there, or to us, in here?'

Bobby put down her fork and raised her index finger, slowly pointing back through the wall behind her, to the dark side where there was only insanity and death.

'To them,' she said.

CHAPTER FORTY-EIGHT

The End

I STOOD ON the balls of my bare feet, balancing in the doorway that connected two worlds; living and dead, real and false, sane and mad, light and dark. In one side my husband and step-daughter sat quietly and happily at a table, finishing their dinner, thinking of dessert and games to play, discussing the next day, and the day after that. In the other there was nothing but loss and sickness and insanity. Francesco had known that the two worlds would have to be kept separate. And he knew they could only exist here in the house. It was the flaw in his plan, and he had no way of resolving it.

But the worst part of all was knowing which side was real.

Rosita stepped forward and tugged at the hem of my T-shirt. 'Please, Senora, you must forget all of this. You can live as before, like the others. You can still be happy here.'

I turned to her. 'You knew, Rosita. You always knew, just as your mother and grandmother did before you. Just as Jerardo knew. Someone had to take care of the house.'

'You must see it as we see it,' she said, 'as a force for good. I was always honest with you. I always told you there were no ghosts here. There is only what happens in life, to everyone.'

'And what happens to most of us is tragedy, is that it? Well I don't believe you. I don't believe that we must always lose more than we gain. If we thought that there would be no point in going on, would there?'

'Tell me, Senora, is it better to know everything, or to be happy?'

I had no answer for that. All I knew was that it could not continue.

I balanced in the doorway and raised the yellow canister, and unscrewed the lid, filling the house with the scent of kerosene.

'Listen to me, Callie,' Mateo pleaded. 'If you do this, you'll lose me forever.'

'I already lost you,' I replied, and began to pour.

CHAPTER FORTY-NINE

The Beginning

THE ROOM IS blessedly cold. The icy air pumps through the slotted steel ventilation panel in the ceiling. I hate air-conditioned rooms. It's very white. I must still be in Spain; the light outside is dazzling. There is a huge picture window and the blind is half down, diagonally dividing the room into light and shade. How appropriate. The bed is sliced into two equal pieces.

I'm not sure which half I'm in.

I hear the squeak of trainers on rubber tiles and turn my head to see a nurse, overweight and jolly enough to quickly become annoying. She moves to the side of the bed and adjusts something – a saline drip. The tube goes into the back of my right hand, held in place with a rectangle of pink tape. My other arm is sore with what feels like a bad burn, and is bandaged from the wrist to just above the elbow.

'Well now, look who's awake. I bet you're ready for your din-dins.'

Fucking hell, she's from Kent. What's she doing here? That awful Estuarine accent, smug and condescending. I decide not to answer her.

'You've been asleep for a very long time, sweetheart. Did you have lovely dreams? How are you feeling? Dry mouth, I imagine. There's some water by your pillow, love, whenever you're ready.'

I point to the end of the bed.

'What do you want? Oh, the mirror? Hang on a mo.' She presses the button that adjusts the bed, and it slowly rises so that I can see myself.

Jesus Christ, I look awful, like I've lost half my body weight. I haven't been this bad since I made myself anorexic. I try to speak. She gets the message and tips some water into my mouth, then waits patiently while I smack my lips and move my tongue.

'What happened?' I manage to croak. 'Where is my husband?'

For the first time, she looks uncomfortable. 'I'll just go and get someone for you.'

'Where is Mateo?' I shout, and a black spear of pain shoots through my temples, and I fall back on the freshly laundered pillow.

As consciousness starts to seep away, I catch myself wondering; which side am I in? My real life or my dream life?

I sleep like the dead.

From time to time I awake. Sometimes the sun is too high to be seen, sometimes it's low in a blue and orange sky. Nobody visits.

Gradually I stay awake for longer and longer periods. Gradually my memory returns. The smell of kerosene, the heat of the flames, the crack and roar as the ceiling falls in.

I stand in the garden watching it burn, knowing that I have freed them, and in doing so, I have damned myself.

Above the cliffs, high in the night sky, the constellation of Ursa Major shines down mockingly, the stars in alignment at the end of Hyperion's life, just as they were at the beginning.

Nobody will answer my question, no matter how many times I repeat it. *The doctor will talk to you about that,* they say. *Someone will come to see you shortly.* But no-one ever comes. Who is there left who could help me?

Gradually I reach the understanding that Mateo and Bobbie have gone. I receive no visitors. No-one talks to me about what happened.

I find that strange, and start to wonder once again which life I'm in. I want an answer.

One morning the overweight nurse enters with a great smile on her smug face and tells me that the doctor is on his way. When he arrives – Indian, serious and impossibly young – he tells me my left arm will always be scarred, then pronounces me well enough to go home. Even though I have no home.

I get my clothes back. The old blue Nike T-shirt and my faded jeans and trainers. There's money and credit cards in my wallet still. I sign the release forms. The nurse asks if anyone is coming to pick me up, and I shake my head. They're not happy about letting me go without an escort – something to do with insurance. But they can't make me stay.

I sit in the ground floor reception area of the Santa Theresa hospital, next to a ridiculous stone statue of a dancing rabbit that's presumably meant to make patients feel better, and I wait for my taxi to arrive.

I get into the back of the bright yellow cab and keep my hand on the warm leather arm rest, watching the empty streets of Estepona slide past. Soon we climb, leaving the town behind, heading into the bare hills. The driver has no English, and does not speak. On his dashboard, the address I had written down for him is sliding about every time he hits a curve. My right hand has a yellow bruise on it from the drip. It'll be gone in a day or two. My left arm is still lightly bandaged. I find myself sweating with nervous tension, terrified by what I'll find.

There are no houses now, only some thin horses and the occasional burned-out barn. We climb toward the cliffs, making our way through the meandering roads toward Gaucia.

From time to time the driver checks me out in the mirror, as if to make sure that I'm not going to do anything crazy. I open the window. The air feels November-warm on my arms and neck. The bushes and fields fly past, and we reach the turn-off.

I look out and see the road, rocks shimmering in the heat haze, a dense dry row of gnarled olive trees. It still looks like we've driven into the middle of a Spaghetti Western.

And there, over to the left, the familiar amber cliffs.

The sunlight is punching down through a sea-blue sky. There's the break in the dense tree-line. I hold my breath and close my eyes, hardly daring to open them again. Knowing that when I do, my question will be answered.

'Just here,' I tell him.

He shrugs at me. *Are you sure?*

'*Seguro.*' Of course I'm sure.

I give him far too much money and quickly get out, waiting until he drives off uncertainly. Then I make my way over to the iron gates as the sound of crickets fill my ears. The sound reminds me of the ticking clocks.

There's no lock on the gate anymore, so it's easy to open. I step inside.

The statue of Hyperion is still there but he has lost his left arm, and the centre of his disc has fallen out, the black and white halves lying shattered in the brown, dead grass. The honeysuckle, campion and lavender have all dried out and gone to seed. There are leaves everywhere like upturned hands. It's amazing how quickly everything reverts from its groomed state.

I'm frightened of looking up. Either I'll be faced with shattered brick and charcoal rafters, little more than a blackened cavity in the cliff, the home of rats and lizards now.

Or they'll be there, the high stone walls inset with glittering windows, the house never looking better, aglow with colour and light. It will still look incorrect, though, an Alice in Wonderland building that might suddenly play tricks on me, closing its doors, turning its walls and twisting its corridors until I can never find my way out again.

Perhaps I'll head up the path and stop before the studded

front door, wondering what to do when, before I can reach a decision, one side of it swings inwards, and there they are.

Mateo will be sporting his sharp blue suit with his whiter-than-white shirt and gold cufflinks. Bobbie will be in bloom, even though she wears the old-fashioned outfit her mother bought for her, the clothes she wore the day she came to the house, the round straw hat, the skirt of tiny brown flowers with a shapeless grey-green top.

'We were beginning to think you'd never get here,' she'll say. 'Daddy said we had to wait to eat. I'm starving.'

Mateo will be so pleased that all he'll be able to do is flash his killer smile. They'll place their arms around me and hold me tight. Nothing will have prepared me for the warmth and light that surrounds me once more. In the hall of midnight blue Castilian tiles, sunlight will bounce off every surface.

'Rosita is preparing something extra special for you,' Mateo will whisper in my ear. 'Welcome home, darling. I'm so very happy you found your way back to us.'

I will go into the house with them, safe in the knowledge that nothing can ever destroy my serenity again.

I stand there just inside the gate with my head bowed down, then slowly walk forward, moving to the statue and its shattered halves of dark and light. I pick up the white half, the sunlit half, and hold onto it tightly as I head in the direction of the house, knowing that when I look up the answer will be before me, and my life will have ended, or just begun.

I see my place in all of this, the place of everyone who stands upon the spinning earth in their lonely havens, pinned between hope and loss, love and desperation. All around me the shadows fly, hands touch, arms embrace, fingers entwine, lovers join and break apart, tears fall, hearts race, things die. The moon unfolds and overtakes the sun, and silvered constellations stud the black heavens with ancient implacability.

Our goal must be to create more light than darkness.

Whatever happens to me now, the clocks will march on and the skies will spin and the stars will stay their course. I know my destiny; it is to find the light by finding him. To be with Mateo.

I take the sharp white half, the sunlit half of Hyperion's disc, and bare my left arm from the wrist to the elbow, slowly turning it over.

And as I do so, I raise my unveiled eyes to the spot where I pray the house will stand again, against the changeless amber cliffs, a grand and final repose, as I receive the long-sought answer to my question.

ABOUT THE AUTHOR

BORN IN LONDON, Christopher Fowler has written for film, television, radio, graphic novels, and for newpaper including *The London Times*, for more than thirty years. He is a regular columnist for *The Independent on Sunday*. Fowler is the multi-award-winning author of more than thirty novels, including the lauded *Bryant & May* mystery novels. In the past year he has been nominated for eight national book awards.

For more information visit
www.christopherfowler.co.uk

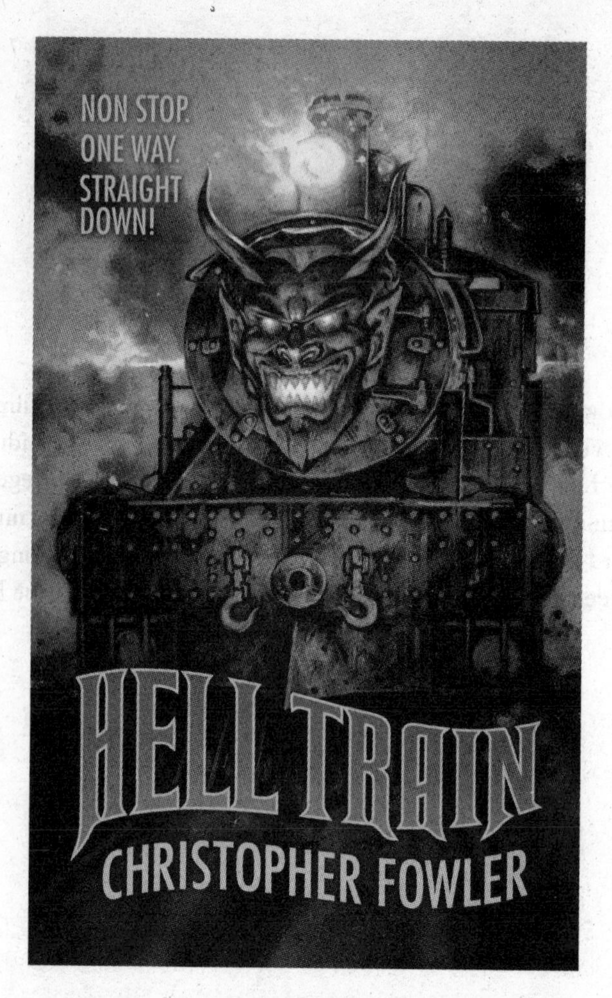
NON STOP.
ONE WAY.
STRAIGHT
DOWN!
HELL TRAIN
CHRISTOPHER FOWLER

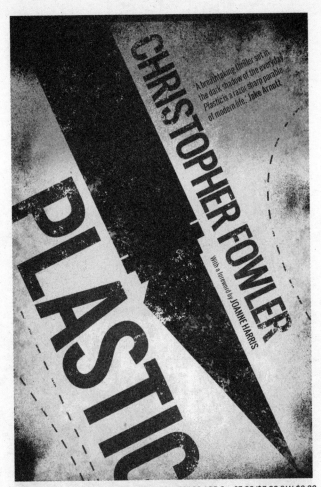

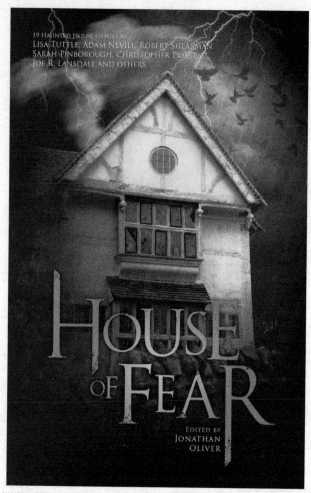